Praise for *Slow Down*

"*Slow Down* is a frenetic first novel...full of unedifying characters scrambling for the elusive, perhaps imaginary, brass ring."
—*Publishers Weekly*

"Lee Matthew Goldberg writes like a young Bret Easton Ellis doing a line of uncut Denis Johnson off the back of a public urinal. Memorable in the best possible way, also mostly illegal, Goldberg's *Slow Down* is a mad man's tour of Manhattan's vices, follies, and ultimate betrayals."
—Urban Waite, author of *The Terror of Living* and *Sometimes the Wolf*

"What would happen if one of Raymond Chandler's 1940's femme fatales were to join forces with one of Jay McInerney's enfant terribles? Lee Matthew Goldberg wrings every delectable trope imaginable out of this mashup while still managing a fresh spin. A writer to watch out for."
—David Kukoff, author of *Children of the Canyon*

"*Slow Down* starts fast and gets faster quick, gunning through yellow streetlights on its way to a full collision with your shattered soul. Lee Matthew Goldberg takes on the American Zeitgeist in this stunning debut."
—Stephen Jay Schwartz, *LA Times* bestselling author of *Boulevard* and *Beat*

"*Slow Down* is a brilliant rush of a work charting the rise and fall of Noah and other pretentious losers. Savor this book."

—*Foreword Reviews*

"Dark and hard-boiled writing that grabs you by the throat. *Slow Down* is one of those rare novels that's so good you want it to go on forever!"

—Nick Pengelley, author of
Ryder: An Ayesha Ryder Novel

"The plot takes off...there's no denying it's fun to watch rich snots destroy themselves."

—*Booklist*

"Goldberg's portrayal of the New York demimonde is one of the book's strengths and brings to mind Bret Easton Ellis' *Less Than Zero*. He also succeeds in marshalling a complicated plot."

—*CrimeFictionLover.com*

SLOW DOWN

BOOKS BY LEE MATTHEW GOLDBERG

Novels
Slow Down
The Mentor
The Desire Card
The Ancestor

Novellas
Satellite of Love
Middle of Nowhere

LEE MATTHEW GOLDBERG

SLOW DOWN

All Due Respect Books
An imprint of Down & Out Books
3959 Van Dyke Road, Suite 265
Lutz, FL 33558
DownAndOutBooks.com

Cover design by Zach McCain

ISBN: 1-64396-102-0
ISBN-13: 978-1-64396-102-6

Home is where I want to be
But I guess I'm already there
I come home—she lifted up her wings
Guess that this must be the place
I can't tell one from another
Did I find you, or you find me?
There was a time, before we were born
If someone asks, this is where I'll be...where I'll be.

—Talking Heads, "This Must Be the Place"

Prologue

NOAH WATCHED THE PRODUCER'S ASSISTANT PLACE HER purse down on the stolen red couch. He'd taken everything in the apartment, all of it part of another man's life that he pretended to lead. The full-wattage smile never left her face, clear evidence she hadn't been in New York long. With her perky personality and strawberry blonde hair, she couldn't have been a native New Yorker like Nevie Wyeth. Nevie, with her panther-black hair and need for Fast—or any other drug someone had to offer. He was only reminded of Nevie because he'd been waiting endlessly for her to call. He was about to give up hope that she ever would.

"Kristy Edson," the woman said, shaking his hand. She gave two quick pumps. "Mr. Bronfeld sent me over from the L.A. office."

Noah knew that a guy like Barry Bronfeld was too much of a power player to ever appear in person, even though Apex Studios was giving Noah a gigantic deal for a novel and for a film based on that novel. The problem was that he hadn't written a word yet.

"Kid, I can't wait much longer," Mr. Bronfeld had yelled over the phone the other night. The sound of honking cars echoed in the background. "Just get it done, whatever it takes. I'm scouting locations already. We're already spending a fuckload of money. Christ, I'm headed into a tunnel. *Ciao.*"

They had decided to say that the book and subsequent film were "based on a true story" to avoid any legal ramifications. They would change all the names, but at the end of the day, Mr. Bronfeld wanted as much of the truth in there as possible. The public craved answers and those answers sold books—*reality* sold books. In this replaceable news-cycle era, people still managed to speculate about him, making Noah just as infamous as he was famous. Now the terrible things he'd done to make

1

it in this business would be revealed in the guise of a story. Sins that nibbled at his soul more and more until all that remained were crumbs.

"So you're here to…facilitate this?" he asked Kristy, nodding for her to take a seat on the red couch. He took out a pack of cigarettes and flipped one between his lips. His habit had ballooned from zero to two packs a day.

"Think of me as your cheerleader," she said, smiling so hard that her back molars showed. He knew she was hungry for this "tell-all" coup, this bad boy bankroll in front of her. She pointed at his T-shirt that said, *Who am I?*

"So who are you?" she asked.

"Why don't you tell me when all this is done?"

Yesterday Mr. Bronfeld had threatened over the phone that Kristy would be Noah's last chance; he'd be sued for breach of contract if the book wasn't finished on time. Noah would dictate his "novel" to her and then they'd clean it up later on.

"She's in love with me," Mr. Bronfeld told him. "She can be trusted. And she stands to move up a bunch of rungs if she can get you to open up. She has no reason to go selling your story to some rag. Like I've told her some dark shit. About rising up at Apex in the '80s, wild parties where I snorted blow off girls' tits, this hobo I once hit with my car on a stretch of the Pacific Coast Highway. You're so damn young, Noah. This is your fucking time to shine. All you gotta do is get me that book."

"I'm ready whenever you are," he heard Kristy say. She removed a digital recorder from her purse and placed it on the glass coffee table between them.

"I'm trying to think of the best way to start," he said, his mind racing.

"How about when you first met Dominick?"

He put on a pair of sunglasses. There was no need for her to keep looking directly into his eyes.

"Listen, there's an expiration date with something like this." She was still smiling, but it seemed strained. "Gossip only lasts for so long and then people stop caring. They forget."

It was hard for him to concentrate on what she was saying. He didn't know if it was because his brain had turned to mush from all the Fast he'd done the year after college ended, or if it was something else.

"I'm just a little on edge," he said, checking his cell. "I'm waiting for a call, an important call."

2

"Forget about that right now," Kristy said, and motioned for him to put the cell in his pocket. "And it's normal to be on edge. So how are we gonna get you to calm down?"

She placed her hand on his knee. She had a tiny gap between her teeth. He pictured her ten years ago: getting off the bus in Hollywood with an overstuffed suitcase, overfed on impossible dreams.

"I have to say that *Slow Down* was robbed at the Oscars," she said. "You totally deserved Best Director."

She hadn't taken her hand off his knee, rubbing it now and casting her spell.

"How can I be sure that you won't screw me over?" he asked.

She stopped rubbing to put a hand over her heart.

"Why would I want to do that?"

"I promise you'll have a different opinion of me after we've finished."

"I have too much to lose if we don't deliver your book. Barry is financing most of your deal himself, and he'll attach me as producer. He'll give me the world."

"You do know he's married."

She pouted her lips and shrugged.

Noah felt his cell ring. He fumbled around in his pocket before picking it up after the first buzz.

"Hello," he said, chewing on his lip.

"Noah!" a gruff voice shouted through the receiver. "Barry Bronfeld here. How's it working out with Kristy so far?"

Noah pictured this bigwig on the other end. Manatee-sized and wearing globular rings filled with cocaine that he'd snort in between meetings. The only bastard in Hollywood that promised double anyone else's offer.

"Tell me we got a fucking masterpiece here, kid."

Noah took another drag and exhaled the smoke through his nose.

"We've got a fucking masterpiece here, kid."

"Noah, you are a hil-a-ri-ous son of a bitch. You hand me a goldmine and I'll give you carte blanche with the entire project, even forget about any of these delays you've been struggling with. Oh fuck, I got Tommy Cruise on the other line. *Ciao.*"

Click.

Noah tossed the cell from one hand to the other, rubbing his tired eyes. He glanced down as if willing it to ring again.

"Sometimes I think about taking a permanent vacation. Away from

3

all the paparazzi..."

He looked out the window toward a crowd of photographers below.

"Is it like this every day?"

"With the film being so big, and of course what happened...."

"So, how true are some of the rumors?" she asked.

He noticed her staring at the giant painting hanging on the wall above him. A blank white canvas with a yellow circle in the center and traces of red splattered across the bottom in the shape of a handprint.

"The painting caught your eye?"

"Yes. I'm trying to understand the significance of the red handprint, obviously the yellow circle represents—"

"Not everything has to have a meaning."

"No, of course not, it's just the yellow circle resembles the tattoos the different girls had in *Slow Down*, so I thought the red handprint symbolized blood or death."

"I'm ready to begin," he said, more forcefully than he intended.

"Right...absolutely. Time is money."

She turned on the digital recorder, her fingers lightly shaking. The apartment remained silent for a long, drawn-out minute.

"I met Dominick Bambach four long years ago." He let out a laugh that sounded like he was gagging. "And I can't help but wonder, what if I never had? Where would I be now? Who would I be? Sometimes I feel like the real me died a long time ago, or at least whatever part of me was worthwhile."

He took a deep breath, one last moment of quiet before the purge. He knew that once he'd begin, he wouldn't allow himself to stop until he reached the brutal end. He sucked in a last hit and crashed the butt into an ashtray filled with a pile of other snuffed casualties.

"So here it goes...."

1

THE STEPS THAT LEAD ME TO MY CATACLYSMIC ENCOUNTER
with Dominick Bambach were put in motion two days earlier when I got
the news about being double-fired from my soul-sucking job. Ah, Classic
Screw-Up Noah. I'd come home a little buzzed from a Yankees game to
hear my parents' cook, Consuela, shouting from room to room trying to
find me. Since my parents' place was big enough to get legitimately lost
in, I had no clue where she was, but I did run into my brother Dex ripping
bong hits on our wraparound terrace.

"That mad Guatemalan woman has been huffing and puffing around
the apartment for over half an hour," Dex said.

"Is she okay?"

"*Importante!*" Dex mimicked, rather poorly, sounding more stereotypically Asian than stereotypically Spanish. "*Más importante, señor*
Noah. *Su jefe llamando!* Your boss called!"

I caught up with Consuela in what my parents dubbed their "conservatory," named with pretension like we all lived inside the game of Clue.
Actually, it was a shoebox of a room that had wedged in a piano, a piano
bench, and a rather spectacular view of Central Park. I found Consuela
perched on the window seat, hands folded in her apron like she was praying,
breaths heavy and sad. She was a whale and I had made her sweat.

"*Señor* Noah. Oh, *señor* Noah," Consuela heaved, the life drained
out of her, ready for her deathbed. "Message for you."

She had written the message in Spanglish on a Post-it stuck to her large
left breast. She displayed it to me like it was a medal of honor. It also had
a blob of her famous *diablo* sauce and basically said that my *jefe* sounded
muy angry and would call my cell at nine tomorrow morning.

My father had adopted Consuela fifteen years ago, a rotund woman who fancied spiced rum and sour looks. My parents had met her during one of their "slumming vacations"—meaning a stay anywhere in the Third World, even if they shelled out for five-star hotels. This time it had been in Guatemala, where she was an overworked cook who made delectable tamales at the breakfast buffet. After one bite of her tasty creations, they whisked her back to the States as their latest charity case. But my father, all red nosed and with a jarring demeanor, had stated the real reason one night at a dinner party:

"You should see some of these people, just ghastly," my father, a swirling glass of port in his hand, spouted to an audience of wondering blinks. I couldn't stop looking at his blinding white teeth, which made him look demented. "That is where Consuela would still be if Janet and I hadn't opened up our home to her. But my God, can that good woman make a tamale!"

I had passed out from a couple of late-night bong hits and woke up the next morning thinking about the note Consuela had given me. The sheets had been pulled up to my neck, the open window letting in cool hums of early spring air. I ran one cold big toe over the other as some morbid indie band played from my iPod alarm, soft and sweet as if they were singing me back to sleep. I had to download some new songs soon.

It was odd that my boss Irene had called, since the company only had a few days left before it shut down completely. So calling me on a Sunday night, a time better spent basking in her wonderful glow, meant that something huge had gone down.

I'd been recently fired. No big deal, most of the company had been "downsized" or "let go," or any other nice way of describing permanent termination. An economy in the toilet meant a whole lot of trouble for an independent media production company with only one client. Recently, all my coworkers had been summoned one by one into her office situated away from the rest of the peons.

The day I got the ax, I'd been ignoring the red light blinking on my office phone, which always meant that the Queen wanted something. *Email this, call so-and-so, walk my dog while I get my hair done for an upcoming interview on CNN* (that would probably never air). I finally picked up the receiver.

"Noah, come into my office."

Click.

I wanted to be "let go." Really I was aching to do nothing but come up with an idea for a novel and then adapt it into a film, my guaranteed tickets to fame. Back in college, a story I wrote for a fellowship won me five hundred bucks and a trip to a writers' colony in Wyoming, so I knew I had chops, but since then I'd written zilch. I had only one year left before I turned twenty-three and became older than F. Scott Fitzgerald when he wrote his timeless classic, *This Side of Paradise*. And, if I wanted to direct an adaptation of this yet-to-be-written novel, I had to hurry up before I turned twenty-five and became older than Orson Welles when he directed *Citizen Kane*. I longed to give an interview that would bring up both these bits of trivia and anoint me into the history books, but time was running out fast.

So this bullshit job where I booked authors for an interview series that aired on a Big Bookselling Chain's website was really just holding me back. I pitched the project to the authors' publicists, set it all up, and sent them an embarrassing questionnaire that my boss created with questions like:

If someone described you as an animal, what animal would you resemble on the outside, and what animal would you identify with on the inside?

Unfortunately, this whole venture was happening right around the time that Big Bookselling Chain was going bankrupt. Anyone who didn't anticipate a downsizing was in serious denial or too stupid to breathe.

When I stepped inside the Queen's office that morning, it felt like walking smack into Calcutta. She had cranked up the heat on a day that didn't require it. Her panting dog greeted me by doing an interpretive dance on the rug. The thing was about a hundred and sixty-five in dog years and begging to be put down.

"Have a seat, Noah."

She gave me a smile devoid of any emotion. I could tell that it had taken so much out of her to produce, and it still managed to only be the smile of a stroke victim, one end being pulled up by a puppeteer's string and the other end long forgotten.

"How are things?" she said, grimacing.

"Super." I nodded.

Her half smile had already vanished.

"I'm sure you know that the Big Bookselling Chain is in dire straits right now."

Yes, I did already know this. I had figured it out one month ago when all of the authors the company filmed were mysteriously pulled from the BBC's website without any explanation, and then *The New York Times* reported that one third of the BBC's staff had been terminated.

"So, Noah, along with that, I don't think that we can keep you on any longer as a talent booker," she said, with a sigh to show how traumatized she was by having to fire me, a sigh to convey her plight. Forget the fact she had just closed on a two-million-dollar property in the Village a couple of weeks ago.

"As of today?"

"No, I am giving you two weeks' notice. Any interviews you want to go on are fine by *me*, but this is the way it has to *be*."

Her little rhyme made her sound like an *Alice and Wonderland* character, the caterpillar atop the mushroom blowing plumes of smoke in my face. I choked on a fake cough to keep from laughing since I'd been waiting for a day like this for the last few months. At least now I wouldn't have to quit and go through the process of telling her off, something I honestly did to people in power too often and was a trait I needed to rectify.

My cell rang at exactly 9:00 a.m. The moody music had lulled me back to sleep for the past hour, but the phone was relentless. I found it under a pair of balled-up khakis and a *Fight Club* poster that had floated down from my wall.

"Hello," I said, out of breath.

"Can I speak with Noah Spaeth?"

The voice was curt and cold. This couldn't be good.

I am Noah's complete lack of surprise, I thought, as I pictured Edward Norton's sad-sack character from *Fight Club*.

"This is Irene, your *boss*. I don't want you coming in today or any of your last days."

"Uh, why?"

"Well, *Noah*, over the weekend I decided to go through some of the *emails* that you wrote on your office account…"

She said it as if it was the most normal thing to do, as if I should be proud of her shadiness.

"Since I was allowing you to use me as a reference, I needed to make sure you had been spending your days here productively, but I *realized* with some of the things you wrote about me and the company itself that you *never* took this job seriously and that you're just some *immature* twenty-two-year-old child. This means that you're *fired*."

"I was already fired."

"No, you were *let go*; now you are *fired*."

"I'm not understanding the difference."

"Meaning you will *not* be able to use me as a reference anymore, so good luck finding other employment."

I blew a raspberry into the receiver.

"*Excuse me?* Is that all you have to say?"

I blew another raspberry.

"You little shit."

Click.

I stayed on the line, the dial tone pulsating in my ear. I had trashed her as a person and a boss, emailing to friends that she was a trust fund baby who got the company as a type of hush money from parents who just wanted to get rid of her, but worst of all (well maybe not *worst* of all because, at least, it was making me laugh at the time), I had emailed to a friend about her big ass, how it was über long and flat in the white miniskirts she'd always wedge herself into and made her look like a pulled tooth when she bent over due to that sizable rear and bowling pin legs. All of this she had now read and dissected; she probably fled to the bathroom afterwards and planted herself in front of a long mirror that only proved those accusations right. Her frequent mentions of a personal trainer weren't fooling anyone.

My cell rang again to the sound of breathing at the other end.

"Hello," I said, ready for her. Her breathing sounded winded, as if she was trying to blow up a balloon from across the room.

"I—" she began, but I was too fast.

"Have a big ass. I know."

I threw my cell to the floor without hanging up and could hear her muffled shouts, but I was cracking up so hard that I couldn't care less. I held my stomach and rocked in a fit, wanting her to hear.

My laughter echoed down the hallway as my teenage sister Cassie passed by, yakking on the phone. She was dressed in the skimpiest amount of clothing that the Baron School for Girls allowed. Just a few years ago she was wearing leotards and tumbling through the house with her hair in pigtails.

"No, Maddy, we're totally gonna make her cry at school tomorrow...I know, I'm so psyched. All the Untouchables deserve to cry."

I stepped out of my room in front of her so she couldn't get past. She twisted a finger around her bra strap and let it snap against her skin. Her expression looked as if someone was using her face to juice a lemon.

"Move out of my way, Noah."

"Why does everything you say need to have its own lingo?" I made a grab for her cell. "What the hell is an Untouchable?"

I could hear cackling coming from her cell. Cassie rolled her eyes as if I wasn't worthy of sharing her air.

"It's someone at Baron that's poor. Just like you'll be one day."

She snapped her gum and continued past me with her middle finger in the air. The finger had become yellow from her new smoking habit, the nail caked with white powder. As if her bloodshot eyes weren't enough evidence that she'd snorted her breakfast.

When she was born, I thought she'd been stolen from another family in the hospital because her hair was so blonde. My parents had let me hold her, and I whispered "my baby" into the tiniest ear I'd ever seen.

That seemed like many lifetimes ago.

Heading to Consuela's kitchen for breakfast was always the best part of my day. I could already smell her Hollandaise sauce, which meant that I'd be eating eggs Benedict soon. A perfect cure for my newly fired self. Good ol' Consuela, with a work ethic like an Alaskan race dog in the Yukon, knew what I needed. The fact it was Monday and her "Noie" (as she sometimes called me) wasn't already at work had indicated that something was up. A wise shaman had once told her during a trip to the jungles of El Petén that "food cured all," so she lived with that mantra and preached it unabashedly.

But as my nose followed the Hollandaise aroma through the hallways, I began to feel unsettled. Five minutes ago the whole boss-reading-my-emails thing had been ridiculously funny, but now reality was starting to sink in. My girlfriend at the time, Margaret, was bound to dump me because she had a firm plan of a career path and life for us both. Being attached to an unemployed *artiste* and wasting her *glory twenties*, as she called them (which always made it sound perverse) was not part of the plan. So if I wanted to keep her around, I knew I'd have to scour the job sites, go on interviews, and pretend to be interested in whatever lame experience some company offered.

I entered the kitchen to find Dex and Consuela whispering to one another.

"Why aren't you at work already?" Dex asked, studying me through his thick glasses without any lenses. His hair was a brown ball of chaos, and he wore a lopsided sweater over pajama bottoms that he'd probably live in for the rest of the day.

"Why aren't you in school?" I shot back, knowing Dex had dropped out of Franklin & Marshall College last spring because he couldn't take the Amish people in the town anymore, obviously an excuse that sounded better than his likely suspension.

"Touché, brother. Consuela, chop-chop with the eggs Bene. I'm about as hungry as an Ethiopian at a smorgasbord, or a newly fired boy desperate for another job."

He gave me a condescending squint while pushing the bangs out of his eyes only to have them fall into place again. I knew that he kept those bangs to give his fingers something to do: at parties, talking to girls, it was his *thing*. He could hide behind his hair if he wasn't interested, or flip it away, show you his eyes, and pretend to care.

"Maybe you wouldn't be so hungry, Dex, if you didn't have two joints for breakfast already."

"Haha, double touché, brother Noah."

For the past year, Cassie, Dex, and I lived in our childhood apartment parent-free with Consuela as the only authoritative figure; primarily there to make sure we ate. Our parents occasionally traipsed back home with stories of the south of France, or the wonders of Vanuatu before clearing out the gin and scotch and slipping under the cracks in the door to board any type of transportation away from us all. Our grandfather, Hubert, my mother's father, had finally choked on his own vomit in his sleep from an overdose of morphine medication that a hired specialist insisted was necessary for his emphysema. Hubert had paid for our pre-war, Classic Eight masterpiece on 79th and Central Park West, but mostly kept his "little princess Janet on a tight leash" (his phlegmy words) with a monthly allowance that included weekly spa indulges and daily lunches at Le

Cirque and the like. He let my dad foster his career as an art dealer and insisted on private schooling and a maid for his three grandchildren whose names he always mixed up.

Since I could remember, my parents had been planning their ultimate kids-free journey once the old geezer stopped breathing, complaining about a "youth idolized" New York. So when Hubert upchucked his last breath, they packed up their suitcases and vowed to live out of them. After air-kissing us, they left some vague numbers in case they needed to be reached (but only for an emergency!), along with some martini-soaked advice about the real world before slamming the front door and returning mostly through postcards.

I always imagined what I'd say to them and the rest of my family if I ever made it big:

"Mom and Dad, I'm a famous author-slash-filmmaker and you two did nothing for that. Cassie, you've become a hideous lost cause, but Dex, you can stick around. You may not be a good friend, but you'll always be my brother. I know you'll keep circling back into my life each time your antics stop being amusing to everyone else, and I will be all you have left."

An overpowering smell of weed pummeled my nostrils as I opened Dex's door to find him inhaling a massive hit and drumming on his knees in a lotus position. Dex held out a smoking bong as an offering.

"So what happened with your job, bitch?"

I shook my head and gazed around Dex's room, a study in dementia. Retro *Playboy* magazines created a nonexistent carpet, a mob of tits and eyes scrutinizing me. Chynna, the mannish wrestler from back in the day, seemed to be the most inquisitive, spreading her legs and giving me a *yeah, why'd you get canned?* glare.

"My boss read some nasty emails I wrote about her."

"Haha, you fucked up big time."

"I was already let go, it just means I can't use her as a reference. It doesn't really matter—"

"Tell that to the judge, or rather, tell it to Margaret and see if she'll ever let your irresponsible ass touch her cooter again."

I'd been dating Margaret for almost a year. We met as seniors at Connecticut College, a tiny enough school where we knew everything about each other before ever really having a conversation. The first time we actually spoke, I was bombed out of my mind and found myself in some ethical debate with her, which sounded life changing at the time. We left some party, the Connecticut sky pure and smelling of the surrounding woods, dizzy with one another. Throughout the rest of the year, she became more of a convenience than anything. The type of girl who joined every amnesty-animal-feminist rights organization to compensate for her bland personality and championed her pre-law studies as being more important than whatever anyone else was doing. I kept her around because a few months before I met her I had tried to kiss Nevie, who then cut me out of her life for good.

"You should come to a party tonight," Dex said.

"I should write tonight."

I thought of Nina, the only character I'd created so far. I pictured her at a bar, twisting away on a stool, smiling wide from all the drugs she'd consumed. People would be naturally crowding around her because she had that magnetic effect. She longed to be in movies, using her skinny but still rocking body to work her way into chic clubs and get close to anyone with connections, but she wound up vomiting a cocktail of pills by dawn. She had peaked too early and knew her biggest accomplishment was bound to be a tragic headline. She'd need the hero of the novel, a guy just like me, to remind her of the Nina that she used to be, someone who'd stop her from rushing toward an early death and let her find solace in his arms. I could be that hero.

"Dude, come to the party. You can even bring Margaret."

"No, I should stay home and get serious about my writing."

"You are such a pretentious loser. You'll lock yourself in your room and write some dumb story with me as this screw-up who's going nowhere and you'll be the protagonist who gets him to go back to school or some shit like that. Oh, wouldn't *that* be lovely?"

"Are you done?"

"I heard your whacko girlfriend going off on me the other day. Evidently, I gave her some look that she misinterpreted when she was here with her nose on the ceiling."

"Yeah, she can't stand you, what's your point?"

"My point is that you can still bring her to this party because I can see you need a night of fucking fun after getting canned. You can always write tomorrow. And the next day. And the day after. In case you didn't realize it, we're basically living a charmed life here without any expenses and can do whatever the hell we want to do."

"You're right, man," I said, shoving Dex and making sure, as always, to play the role of Older Brother. "You are so right. Why should I agonize over getting another job and dealing with another possible Queen? And Margaret can kiss my ass if she has anything to say. I'm about to create something that'll blow people away and no one can stop me."

I imagined my character Nina again, home from college at her country house in Southampton, deliriously stoned after a round of golf at her parents' club. I envisioned myself beside her as we danced around a bonfire on her private beach.

But I knew she wasn't actually a creation, just a substitution. That night on the beach in Southampton was based on one of the last times I saw Nevie. I can remember she was leaning in too close to the fire while high on something, and that I caught her before she burned herself.

"Are you okay?" I had asked.

My hero, I longed for her to say, but she only wriggled out of my arms, staring at the fire as if she wanted to fall in.

"I'm never okay," she said, and stumbled up toward her house where she locked her bedroom door and didn't even come out to wish me goodbye in the morning before I had to board my train.

That weekend had also been one of the last times I was able to write anything.

I told myself not to stress about that now. Tonight I'd be Nevie free. And maybe if I'd be able to keep forgetting about her, a bevy of dazzling ideas would flow once again.

"The Spaeth boys will be out for blood tonight," Dex cheered, taking a final bong hit. "Brother Noah, I think I know how to get you started on the fast track to living."

A cloud of smoke obscured Dex's face as he continued preaching.

"Zoom. Zoom. *Zooooooooom!*"

2

FRESH FROM CLASS AT FORDHAM LAW, MARGARET SHOWED up to my apartment already on the offensive. The perfect budding lawyer, never off the clock. Her blouse had been buttoned all the way up to her neck, which looked suffocating, but she refused to open a button and let herself breathe. She monopolized the conversation with a dissertation about some case she learned that day where one boring person sued another, before complaining about the idea of a party on a Monday night.

"You don't have to come," I mumbled.

"Is Dex going?" she whistled to her watch, checking it for the second time in less than a minute.

"Yeah, he knows the guy who's throwing it."

"I just planned on dinner tonight. I have a *ton* of reading on tort law to do—"

"I ate already."

"Noah, you know I'm hypoglycemic."

"I just told you I was fired again from my job today, you could be a little more sympathetic."

She shook her head. "It's totally legal that your boss read your emails. You wrote them on the company's account."

"I never questioned the legality, but she's still a crazy bitch for doing it."

"Noah, don't stoop to misogyny. If your boss was a man you would not be calling him the B-word."

"Fine, I'd say *asshole* instead, what's your point?"

"Whatever. It happened, move on, find a new job."

She gave a careless yawn, uninterested with my problems in the least. *The feeling is mutual, B-word.*

"I don't want a new job. I'm gonna start my novel and just kill it these

15

next couple of months until some editor gives me a huge deal."

"Right," she said, grinding her teeth, her little barracudas that might as well have been taking tiny bites of my soul.

"I'm gonna make it, and I won't keep you around when I do."

"What a cruel thing to say," she said, playfully slapping me on the cheek as if our whole rapport was just mindless flirtation. "You're such a comedian."

"Daniel Fucking Tosh."

"Who's that? Your trivial obsession with pop culture never fails to amaze me."

"As does your obsession with maintaining that permanent stick up your ass."

"So trite." She yawned again. "Now where is Dex? I want a bowl of New England clam chowder and a Gibson already!"

Some Franklin & Marshall fool who Dex used to buy his drugs from was throwing a party at his boss's loft in the Flatiron area while the guy was on vacation. Stopping for a quick bite before, the three of us sat at Long-shoreman's Oyster Bar and Grill while Dex popped some Vicodin and Margaret slurped up her New England clam chowder.

"I heard this dude's loft is endless, like room upon room. Some even have midget-sized doors and shit," Dex said.

"Good, maybe you'll get lost in one," Margaret chirped, pleased with herself. Dex threw a Vicodin pill at her, and she ordered another Gibson.

Dex and I escaped from her with lies about smoking a cigarette and met at the bar. He started talking to an older woman with a long neck and thinning gray hair.

"I take it back," Dex said, giving the older lady a fake smile and pulling the ends of his sleeves over his hands. He looked like he was fourteen, and suddenly I felt very overprotective. "You can't bring the tampon, bro."

"Give me a cigarette for real, I need one."

"Dude, there will be p-u-s-s-y at this party. Pussy unlike that steel trap over there with her chowder."

He flipped his cigarette box open and licked across the top.

"You are a mental case."

"Anyway, so I had this brilliant idea, you ready for it?"

"I'm on the edge of my seat."

"OK, we make Margaret get really sick, like with ipecac syrup so she can't go," Dex said, brushing it off as nothing. He offered a freshly licked cigarette to the older lady with a wink.

"You want to make her vomit? Do they even sell ipecac syrup anymore?"

"Abracadabra, motherfucker," Dex said, removing a bottle from his front pocket.

"Was this something you planned, or do you always carry around nineteenth-century, vomit-inducing medicines?"

"A little bit of both, and I can tell from that gleam in your eye that you're intrigued."

We looked over at Margaret who was dunking bread into her chowder and giving me a shrug as if I'd ruined our wedding day.

"I bet it'd make for a great story," Dex whispered, baiting the hook, knowing my weakness.

Outside, after we paid the bill, Margaret walked a step ahead of us wobbling a little from the Gibsons. Dex caught up with her, catching her by the arm as a sign of gallantry while moving in for the kill.

I never took Dex seriously before and figured the ipecac syrup was all talk. Instead of worrying about it, I receded into my own world, wishing I had more people in my life whose company I enjoyed. My eyes became a camera's lens documenting all the random passersby, momentarily imagining their lives to avoid my own.

My thoughts became interrupted when Margaret yelped and weaseled out of Dex's grasp. She looked beautiful in that moment, lovely in her defiance. I thought about the sweet smell of her long brown hair and kisses like nibbles that made me feel like a young boy until one day she mutated into a Snide Comment Machine. When I'd first met her back at school, we had eased away from a party with beers in our fists, her breast in my mouth and a population of stars in the sky. That one night was all the two of us ever needed to have. She never should've become my future.

Finally she broke away from Dex, the back of her hand swiping across her mouth as Dex closed the bottle of ipecac syrup and rubbed his hands together waiting for the show. She was two steps ahead now, hips swinging wildly, face beet red, a tear streaming into her mouth as she gagged. I felt a pinch in my stomach and wanted to hold her, to protect her from this night, which she'd never be able to live down. She gagged again, cat-like, tossing her hair out of her face before spewing a river of chowder all over her cardigan and the street below as onlookers pointed. She

17

stayed there, wet and white, as I came up behind her. With quivering lips and drool down her chin, she mumbled one final sentence:

"Please take me back."

At first, I figured that what Margaret had muttered in her moment of shame was a direct request to be taken home, but underlying it all, I realized it was a plea for us not to break up. But I wasn't ready to say that to her face, so I got her in a cab and told her address to the driver.

If she cried for me, I wouldn't have known, since I had already turned down the block toward the party by the time the cab sped away.

"You're welcome," Dex called out, trailing close behind.

The loft where the party was being held looked more like a club than someone's home and had an eerie, ultra-modern vibe of a sterile future, where color was only designated by shades of gray. I sat on some over-priced couch the size of a studio apartment as terrible music blared. Dex sat to my left with two attractive girls bookending us. The one to my right seemed as unimpressed with the party as I was. Because of that, I imagined us falling in love.

"How do you think pukey is doing?" Dex asked. "I'm still waiting for my 'thank you' by the way."

"Dude, c'mon."

"You think I'm an asshole."

"The verdict is still out," I replied, trying to act serious, but soon I was punching fists with Dex, still feeling a little guilty, but honestly glad that Margaret wasn't one of the girls bookending us.

"That was one of the top ten funniest things I've ever seen."

"I should've broken up with her months ago," I said, shaking my head.

"Well, I would say that deserves a joint."

Dex slid one out from behind his ear and lit it up.

"I've been ready to switch my brain off all day," I said.

"Do you know what your problem is?" Dex said, taking a ton of puffs before he even thought about passing it on.

"Enlighten me."

"You can't accept being normal. You've always believed that you're gonna start some revolution."

I swiped the joint and exhaled through my nose, cleansing my senses. Spring and allergies had settled in, seasons changing in my bones. I didn't want to listen to Dex right now.

"*Viva la revolution*!" I shouted.

"Well, what if your lot in life is to be ordinary? I know from the time you were twelve you believed you'd make it big one day, but would it really be the end of the world if you didn't?"

"I scoff at that, dickweed."

"What if I was the one destined for greatness?"

"That would never happen," I said. The pot was chewing at my brain, words and ideas jumbled beyond comprehension. "You were a mistake from the start. I once heard Mom and Dad say that."

I failed to see Dex's reaction because the two girls joined in on the conversation. My girl had a swoop of black hair that covered one eye as if she'd stepped out of an old noir film, while the one next to Dex began an ethical debate about marijuana and reminded me of Margaret.

The rest of the party had filled up even more since we arrived, a smattering of people colonizing the endless rooms, no one I gave a damn about. The fool named Wally who hosted this party, normal only by Betty Ford standards, seemed delighted with himself and his new friends, all of whom were there to trash the place.

"He lets me have the keys to the rooms, all of the *keys*," Wally said, to my Noir Girl. She blew a train of smoke in his face.

Wally tossed a little baggie of yellowish powder in Dex's lap before hopping away and getting lost in the burgeoning clamor.

"What is that?" I asked.

"Sweet! I've been fiending for some Fast. IOU, man," Dex shouted, and shoved the baggie in his pocket.

"Isn't his boss going to be pissed with all these people messing up his place?" I asked my Noir Girl.

"Wally sucks his dick and gets to water the Big Shot's fichus plants while the guy detoxes at a spa in New Mexico."

"Lame," I said, miming a gag reflex that made her laugh.

"Don't pretend like you haven't done the same," Dex said to the Noir Girl, and yanked on a swoop of her hair.

"*You* should have leprosy," she said to him, and then got up in a huff. By the time I looked up, the party's crowd had devoured her whole.

Dex sat back and twisted his legs into a lotus position. I hadn't noticed before that he had worn his pajama bottoms out. This whole disheveled hipster persona thing of his was getting way old.

"So for reals, bro, tell me about this novel you're gonna work on."

"I was hitting on that *fucking* girl," I said, punching him hard in the arm. Dex was a little guy, and I had about twenty-five pounds of pissed-off energy on my side.

"Ow, what the hell?"

"Why would I even talk to you about my book? It's not like I'm titling it *The Titty Invasion*, so what feedback could you really give that would have any value?"

"You don't have any ideas for it, do you?" Dex grinned and gave his girl a look like I was a joke. "I don't know much about writing, but I know you need to start with something. Maybe I could help you brainstorm—"

"You have no clue about me, Dex. You've been in a marijuana cloud since high school."

"Whoa, I'm just busting your balls. You don't gotta take everything *sooooo* seriously all the time."

"You're not going anywhere," I mumbled.

"What's that?"

"Like I said, you were a mistake. Just picture twenty years from now, and yeah you've got Mom and Dad's wealth to coast on if you kiss up to them in postcards and they don't piss their fortune away, but you will always be in my shadow."

Dex lowered his head, bangs covering his eyes, ashamed. He knew it was true, but never needed to hear it out loud. All he could do in defense was pretend not to be demolished.

"I'm getting another beer," he said, standing up even though the bottle he held was half full. The other girl remained to give me the side-eye.

"You've got issues," she said, sadly.

"Sometimes I think I'm a bomb ready to explode."

I jumped up, revitalized, roaming through the rooms. The lights had dimmed and all the people smoking obscured my view. I tried to catch Dex's eye as he talked to that fool Wally in the corner, but if he saw me he didn't acknowledge.

I passed a hallway at the far end of a room. Two girls in matching outfits talked with their hands over the din of music. A kid yammered on his cell about a script he was positive had been picked up. The girls seemed to be gossiping about the kid. I floated past them all.

In the adjoining hall, I found myself staring into the mirror, studying my reflection as if I were a misunderstood painting. Sometimes I said things without thinking; I didn't mean to hurt Dex but often went to great lengths to make him feel bad. I wondered if it was because Dex was the only one who took my abuse.

How messed up is that?

I remembered a time when Dex and I were little kids at Lake George running in the sand and catching hermit crabs getting washed up by the tide. Dex would squeeze their heads until just before their brains popped out and then launch them still alive into the water like skipping stones. To Dex it was all a game, but when I squeezed one of their heads it burst. The brain goo dripped down my hands, and Dex had cried for hours. I'd done it because I wanted to see how my baby brother would react. Even back then, I knew that wasn't normal.

Through the mirror, I noticed a small red door, no bigger than up to my knee. I swiveled around and touched the doorknob cautiously.

"What are you doing?" I heard.

I traveled up a pair of long legs to my Noir Girl from earlier. She bent down with a cigarette dangling from her lips, the smoke dancing in waves between us.

"What's up with this door?" I asked. "It's tiny. You're not curious at all?"

She lifted up the miniature welcome mat in front and procured a miniscule key.

"Look what I found. Maybe it'll lead us far away from this wonderful night," she deadpanned, and then opened it as a stream of red light poured into the hallway.

I couldn't stop staring at Noir Girl's back once we wedged ourselves through the tiny door. The ceiling was low but high enough for us to stand stooped. A red lava lamp cast shadows along the walls. She moved to the window, her shirt rising up and revealing skin. On the small of her back was a solitary tattoo of a yellow circle. Its shape altered when she moved, never perfectly round but always intriguing. I wanted to run my tongue around the edges and taste the salt of her skin. She finally opened the window and turned on a record player in the corner as The Eagles filled the mini room.

I leaned against a bed in the center with feathered sheets.

"I'm Lindsay," she said, sitting on the other end of the bed.

"Noah."

"This is totally this guy's seduction room. I would've invited my boyfriend here instead of you if he was even paying any attention to me tonight."

She walked on her knees across the bed until we were close enough to kiss.

"Your boyfriend's here?" I asked, wanting to see more of that tattoo since it was hidden now.

"He probably left. He's a movie director."

"So am I," I said, without a second thought.

"He makes independent movies, *very* successful."

"What's his name?"

"I can't say, he's married. What movies have you done?"

"I can't say either, I'm married too," I smirked.

"That's convenient, Mr. No Wedding Ring."

She kept probing me about being a director, not necessarily to prove I was lying, but because she was a hungry actress seizing all opportunities.

"Yeah, the movie I'm doing now is going to be really big," she said. "My role is pretty substantial, ya know the key to the whole plot, but I earned it. Since my boyfriend is the director, I didn't want nepotism."

I kissed her just so she'd shut up, and we collapsed onto the feathered sheets. Her shirt had bunched up again as the tattoo came into view. A bead of sweat hung on the small stage that the yellow circle provided, rolling around in an exotic dance to "Hotel California." My fingers touched that bead of sweat as I smeared it around the tattoo—it seemed to awaken a demon that she'd been hiding. She kissed me harder, full of fire. I pressed the tattoo harder and she roared. So I kept on, fingers exploring her yellow enigma, never letting it out of my sight. I flipped her over on her stomach, whispering "Nina" into that tattoo, pretending that I was seducing someone magical instead. Lindsay prowled beneath me before mumbling under her breath and swiveling away. Standing up, her shirt covered the tattoo once again and my boner softened.

She lit a cigarette, gazing out of the mini window.

"Where did you get that tattoo?" I asked, in awe.

She kept smoking and didn't answer.

"The yellow circle on your back?"

"My boyfriend wouldn't like this," she said, with a nervous twitch in her eye.

"No, I can't see that he would."

"Is that supposed to be funny?"

"No, not funny, just, I don't know what to say right now."

"He wouldn't like it at all!"

"I didn't know you two were that serious."

"I told you about him!"

"You don't need to yell at me."

"I'm *not*!"

"You're like a big exclamation point right now. We made out, no big deal, no one's gotta know."

"You are a little boy," she said.

I wanted to probe more about the tattoo, but it was easier to slip out of the tiny door when she paused from yelling at me to sneeze. When I finally wedged myself back into the hallway, I couldn't remember her face. She was just that yellow circle, glowing. I licked my lips and still tasted the way that tattoo made me feel alive.

As I left the hallway, the light from the party was an eyesore. The same girls still talked with their hands while the dude on his cell boasted about his script. I thought of Nevie again and my steps felt weighted, but her face had become less of a clear shape; fragmented in my wasted haze and a struggle to put it all back together.

I swiped a Corona as I headed for the door. Maybe I'd walk home with the city since it seemed like better company than anyone else right now; but then, like in some perfect film, I saw Nevie by the front door.

I was shocked by how different she looked from what I remembered. Some prick was putting on her coat, her shoulders whittled to the bone and egg-shaped. The guy fondled her breasts, aware that the party watched their foreplay. She turned toward me, black pupils dilated like giant marbles, but she didn't register my existence.

My Corona crashed to the floor as it slid out of my perspiring hands, but by the time I looked up, she had vanished. I bolted out of the door to find her, but she was gone. I flew out onto the street but she was still gone.

Back at home I was blazing with an outpouring of ideas flowing from my brain. That was when I saw the green light blinking on my cell. I hadn't even heard it ring. I threw my laptop aside, my heart beating in the hopes that it could be Nevie. She could've seen me at the party. I dialed my voicemail, and sure enough, her voice snaked through the air.

"Hey, Noah, what's up…it's Nevie. Hope you're all good, definitely good. I know it's been a while and we don't have to get into why for the moment, but I thought of my little frog for whatever reason. So, I don't know, make my night I guess and give me a buzz. My number hasn't changed. Bye."

I listened to the message two extra times to make sure it had been real. I'd been trying not to think about her for so long. We'd grown up together, close as can be without ever becoming lovers, never dipping in because she chose for it to be that way. She knew how I felt and kept me around to idolize her while I forced my body to be platonic.

And then at a party thrown by some agent she met—Nevie in a strapless dress the color of soap. Stars of beauty marks dotting down her pale legs. She swished through the party as if she owned it, but she didn't own this crowd yet, not like she owned me. Spending hours sweeping her black hair across her face, slightly covering just one eye. Sleek. Sitting on a stool, she threw one bony leg over the other in a fit of giggles from the tab of Molly we each took an hour before. The rest of the party was all a cartoon to me except for her. Because of the Ecstasy, the fuzz along her arms gracefully flapped, the outlines of her body vibrating to a pulsing beat. She had a warm, pressed smile that looked stapled shut. She called me over, my name never sounding so good. She drew it out, making it two long syllables, No-Ahhhhhhh, refreshing like a good sip of bubbling cola.

More tabs in the bedroom between us, a mirror-reflecting bedroom creating endless Nevies. I'd become a different version of myself with hands I couldn't control. Those hands with a mind of their own fumbled with her breasts until she pulled away, and then they fumbled some more trying to tear off her dress until she slapped me across the face, the sound like a truck backfiring, the sting like the worst hangover ever. I crammed my tongue inside her mouth, her lipstick smearing across my cheek, but there wasn't another slap, just the sound of an exit, heels clomping away until all I wanted was to feel that slap again, her addictive touch the only thing I craved, finding ways to hurt myself later on so I'd be reminded of her.

Now a phone call after a year of nothing. I had tried to forget her by turning her into an enemy while creating Nina, an apparition. I knew that after hearing her message, Nina would no longer be enough.

I took a deep breath and dialed.

She picked up the phone in the midst of a sentence spoken to someone else. She'd been laughing, I could never forget her high-pitched giggle, but that laughter had already slowed down. When she finally spoke, my heart broke because it sounded like she was drowning.

"...Hello," she said, her voice wobbling.

"Nevie?"

"Yeah? Who's this?"

"Your frog," I croaked, and then waited endless hours to hear if she'd respond, or if her message from before had just been a dream.

3

AS I LEFT MY APARTMENT THE NEXT NIGHT TO MEET NEVIE at a lounge down on Avenue B, I smelled an aroma in the air that reminded me of her perfume. Like a psycho, I once even bought a bottle of her favorite scent just to keep in my drawer. I still had it, and sometimes took a whiff. Shaking away that embarrassing truth, I got on the B train, which contained a multicultural mix of people from the Bronx with Upper Westsiders headed downtown. Usually, I was able to keep my shit together, but not that night. I was sweating and knew I needed to lose those jitters since Nevie was good at exposing someone.

A light drizzle welcomed me once I got off at Union Square before transferring to the L. We were meeting at The Penny, a tucked away lounge in Alphabet City that supposedly didn't even have a door, just a wall that slid open if you knew the right spot, something the untrained eye or tragically unhip would walk right past. I'd heard of it in passing, but it wasn't my style to jump on trends.

Nevie said she'd wait outside for me, an admission of my status, needing her to show me the way. That summed up our relationship—I was always the one following while Nevie manned the whip.

When I turned the corner I saw her. She didn't see me yet, rotating on the tips of her toes and playing with her cell. A cool yellow coat was cinched tightly around her waist. Her black hair damp and dripping down her face. She was high, her little rotating dance too overzealous for sobriety. I longed to be reckless like that, realizing that I used to be more impulsive. She had taken that away when she stopped speaking to me.

She looked over and smiled right away.

"Hey," I said, gathering myself as I gave her a hug and held on for a while.

"Noah," she hummed, resting against my shoulder. "Let's get out of the rain."

She touched a stone on the wall behind her and a part of the wall slid open. We showed our IDs to a giant bouncer. Inside thousands of pennies covered the walls.

"Drinks, drinks," she said, patting my back. "Drinks then conversation. Drinks make for better conversation."

Her fingers felt shrunken to the bone, a skeleton futilely tapping against my back.

"I'll have a Pennytini," she said, to the bartender. "And this stud will have a beer."

"A Harp is cool," I added.

"Harp's cool, Harp's cool," Nevie laughed. "It's on me."

"Thanks."

She moved her body to the electronic beats glittering over the speakers. We took our drinks and found a couch. Her bruised knee grazed my leg as we sat. She sucked down half of her rust-colored martini.

"So good," she said, with a chill.

Her body seemed stringy and undefined once she removed her coat; even her breasts had deflated since I'd seen her last. I fought the urge to put her coat back on to cover her up.

"So, what's up?" I asked, licking the foam off my lips, no idea how to begin again with her.

"God, I've missed you, No—" she said, her hand on my leg.

"I've missed you, too."

She gave me a lopsided grin.

"Really?" she asked, as if she was unsure.

"Of course."

"Sometimes," she began, her eyes spinning wildly as she collected her thoughts.

"Sometimes people need a break from each other for a while. I'm healthier now. I wasn't before."

"It's cool," I said, holding back what I really wanted to say.

"Noah, you are my best friend in the world. When I think of us, I imagine us in the long run. Relationships always fucking end, but we won't. Like your kids'll know my kids, and your wife and I will have our shopping Sundays and shit. That's totally what I want."

"I love you, Nevie. C'mere."

I wrapped an arm around her, and she rubbed her neck against my touch like an animal in heat. It caught me off guard at first, but I decided to just go with it.

"I was so happy when you called me back," she cooed. "I needed my frog."

She relaxed against me, limp in my arms.

"I'm so glad we got any awkwardness out of the way," she said, reaching for her Pennytini. "I had a crude premonition that you'd be harboring resentment. But you fell away, too."

"No, I called you. After what happened at that agent's party. I apologized to your voicemail for everything. I was so fucked up that night."

Nevie batted her eyes and fiddled with a stone earring while shaking her head.

"It's not about who called who last, it's what we both wanted. If it didn't happen, things would've gotten bad between us. We're here now, so it's fine. And now we've put the awkwardness in a little box and shipped it off to China. I'm in awe of seeing you, my little frog. Tell me everything that you've been up to."

And like that she had won me over again. Nevie the actress, manipulating others' emotions. Even watching her in a crappy high school rendition of *The Crucible*, I could remember believing every one of her Goody Proctor's desperate pleas.

"You mean like *all* I've been up to this past year?"

"Don't make a novel out of it," she said, jabbing me in the stomach.

"I was working as a talent booker at a media production company."

"Cool, since you graduated?"

"Yeah, after the summer, but I kind of got let go, well…fired."

"Which one is it?"

"Fired. My boss, this psychotic middle-aged trust fund baby went into my computer the other day and read all my emails."

"How scandalous."

She knocked back the rest of her Pennytini and then removed a shiny penny from her tongue. Sucking on the penny seemed to wake her up a little more. "What did your emails say?"

She hadn't taken her hand off of my arm yet.

"You're gonna die," I said. "I said she had a big ass and looked like a pulled tooth when she bent over."

Nevie laughed so loud that heads turned, like she was deranged. I was startled at first, but eventually I joined in until we became locked in an embrace of happy tears. I hadn't laughed like that with someone else in a while.

"You come up with the best things," she said, and finally let go of me. "Remember that annoying-ass girl Courtney from high school who you called Vagina Punch because everyone wanted to punch her in the vagina each time she spoke?"

"You know she works for the UN now?"

"Ugh, the world is doomed. So what are you going to do now?"

"I'm gonna write a novel that'll make me famous and then it'll be adapted into a film, like that's what I want to do."

"Then you should. Everybody should do whatever it is they want to do all the time. That's the recipe for world peace. Wars would end. Kumbaya."

She shrugged and left her little shoulders hanging up by her ears.

"I feel yummy," she said, her eyes drifting, a million miles away.

"You all right?" I said. She was gazing at the penny she'd left in her empty glass.

"So yummy."

"You look beautiful. As always."

"Thank you." She reached into her purse, raising one eyebrow. "Noah, if I give you something will you eat it?"

"Right here?"

She didn't respond, just handed me a yellow pill.

"What's this?"

"Fast," she said, as if I was dumb.

I nodded, pretending to know what she was talking about. I could take this pill and pull her into the bathroom, take a chance by seeing if she'd be down for whatever. But I knew a thought like that was no more than a fantasy.

"So what have you been up to this last year?" I asked, rolling the pill between my forefinger and thumb and closing it in my fist.

"Fucking my boyfriend," she said, with an evil smile, as if the entire conversation before had been a game leading up to that reveal. "He's over at the bar on his cell; you should join us."

She stood up, unsteadily.

"I've told him all about you. How the last time you saw me you tried to put my *tit* in your mouth."

Another Nevie had entered the room now. The one who could be cruel and liked to remain in optimal control by turning Sweet Nevie's switch off.

"I remember telling you what our boundaries were that time back in ninth grade when we were forced into Billy Meyer's closet for a game of Seven Minutes in Heaven and you told me you loved me."

My stomach got tight from the memory of this. Back then her cruel words had made me want to kiss her even more. No girl had ever sounded so adult before.

"And I said I loved you too, but I always needed to have you wanting me so you'd never go away. Because everyone always goes away."

"You're real screwed up, Nevie."

"Well, you're real screwed up too. Neither of us had a chance. I'm thirsty."

Fuck you. You don't even know what you do to me.

I slipped the yellow pill in my unfinished pint and handed it to her.

"Take my beer," I said, wishing her the worst, switching off Sweet Noah just like she had done to herself. "I need something stronger."

She gulped down the entire pint, eyeing me as if she knew exactly what I had done.

"Grab your jacket and come and meet Dominick," she said, licking the last taste off her lips. "I'll see you by the bar."

As I headed to the bar, I had no idea that my life was about to change. This would be the moment I'd always go back to because if I had been pissed enough at Nevie to walk out of the door...well if that happened, then there'd be no story to tell. I can remember feeling annoyed as I watched Nevie paw her so-called boyfriend. I'd been trying to convince myself how much she'd decayed since I saw her last, but she had always been teetering, and that only made me want her more than ever.

This boyfriend of hers looked vaguely familiar. At first I figured I knew the guy, met him at a party or something. But then I realized the dude was a *somebody*, not overly famous but famous enough. Passersby did double takes on the street, people requested autographs once in a while. This pseudo-famous guy looked at me as if I was nothing more than a common fan coming his way, but when I placed my hand on Nevie's shoulder, the guy's gaze turned predatory.

By giving her shoulder a playful squeeze, I was marking my territory, staking claim. No guy ever had held Nevie's fancy for too long, but I managed to stick around, despite our year apart. Because of that, I expected Nevie to introduce me right away, but her wasted eyes seemed to be sad to have me there, as if I wasn't needed for her survival anymore.

"I'm ready for another drink," I said to Nevie and her new paramour.

The prick sipped from a glass of neat scotch and tapped his diamond-studded watch against the bar, drawing attention to its glint.

"Noah, this is Dominick Bambach."

Dominick Bambach. The name sharp and intense, a spew of hard consonants. She said his name with an air of respect. She did not say, "Dominick, this is Noah Spaeth." My name was the less important of the two.

On cue, Dominick shook my hand, giving a powerful squeeze to show he was the alpha. Once he let go, he put his arm around Nevie and started massaging her throat like it was an arousal point.

"Noah and I went to high school together." Nevie giggled, about to have an orgasm in the bar as Dominick traced circles along her throat. "High school, like eons ago. When did we become old enough to use the term eons?"

"I'm not about to divulge when I was in high school," Dominick said.

Dominick was an easy thirty, clean shaven with slick curls of gelled black hair and well-cared-for skin. He introduced himself as a filmmaker. His tan may have been fake, but he paid good money for it and it looked as close to real as one could hope. He knew he was good looking, an actor's face instead of a director's. Nice Roman nose, carefully observant eyes, probably high on something with the way he bobbed his foot, but someone whose presence ate up the room and regulated everyone else to second billing.

"This girl is wild," Dominick grinned, tickling her neck like a puppy's. He kissed her tastefully with no tongue, but it was enough for me to turn away, especially once Nevie unbuttoned the top button of his shirt and played with a tuft of chest hair.

"Girl, you are on tonight," he whispered. He turned to me. "I love it when she's like this."

"Noah, don't you recognize Dominick?"

"Stop it, Nevie," he said, but then glanced at me as if I should.

"Your name sounds really familiar. God, I'm embarrassed," I added, even though I really wasn't.

"Don't be embarrassed…Noah? Am I right? Nevie is a media whore, but is fame that fascinating? Just comes along with the territory."

He said this all rolling a cigarette, sprinkling in tobacco that smelled like caramel. He planted it in between his lips. Nevie waited with a match.

"Thanks, doll," he said, taking a giant puff. "I've got a lot of shit on The Penny's owner, so I can get away with murder here, even a stealth cig at the bar."

Dominick never really looked at me when speaking; his words were thrown all over the place so I had to bob and weave to catch what was being said.

"Chris," he said, snapping his fingers at the bartender and indicating for two more glasses of scotch.

"Have you seen *Detached*?" he then asked.

"Oh, shit, sure," I replied. "You directed that?"

"That's what they tell me."

"I thought it was great. I mean really great."

Dominick took a drag and nodded modestly.

"The writing was kick ass," I continued. "You wrote it as well, didn't you?"

Only then did Dominick fully look at me.

"Yes, I did. Are you a writer?"

"Not published or anything," I said.

The bartender poured two drinks for us. I grabbed one, the glass feeling cool in my sweaty hands.

"Noah has always been a writer," Nevie chimed in.

"Why didn't you tell me this?" he asked, scolding her. "What are you writing now?"

"A novel."

"Full time?"

"Yeah, I guess, since I lost my job."

"Jobs are bullshit," Dominick barked, each one of his sentences a continuous threat. "Creativity is real, and mindlessness is a quick way to the grave. Is money an issue?"

"No, I live at home still."

"Ah yes, the post-college standstill. Where is home?"

"Central Park West."

"Ah, silver spoon?"

"Yeah, well, I guess."

"Look, if your fortunate upbringing allows you to fuck that idea of a job, fuck it as hard you can. When I was your age, I worked in the goddamn mail room at a big talent agency in L.A. with these killer fluorescent lights that made me feel like I was dying, but I said to myself, 'Salty fucking balls, I am talented and will rise like a phoenix.' So this novel, you any good?"

Nevie still rubbed at his chest, but he grabbed her arm and moved it away.

"Nevie, he has chops?"

She nodded dutifully.

"I'd bet you'd be interested in getting a taste of what I'm working on now, Noah?"

"Seriously?" I squawked, and then dialed it down a notch.

"Seriously, I do not shit around. New York City has become a toilet with people dumping out their bullshit on one another. I have at least twenty industry fuckers wanting to take a peek, but fuck them, they have no soul. You have a soul, Noah?"

"Yeah, I do," I said, my brain firing in all directions, thinking of how I could use Dominick's status for my own gain. That was the kind of soul I had.

"Lean closer," Dominick whispered to us both. He had the whitest teeth, bleached to perfection.

"I'm making a new film. Very radical. Nevie, you of course know all of this."

She gave me a sly look.

"I won't go into details now. Trust needs time to build, but I applaud other writers. We are all thieves, stealing bits of conversations, others' cherished memories, manipulating our own lives into page-turning tales. The better the writer, the greater the thief."

"Yeah, man, I know what you mean," I said, having thought all of this before, but never hearing it spoken out loud.

Dominick clapped me on the back. "Noah, we are the great minds. Doctors, businessmen, the hell with them; they finish work and get to shut their thoughts off. Well, my mind spins twenty-four seven. Even when I'm sleeping, I'm creating."

"Dominick's new movie is going to change the world," Nevie said, soaring, the drugs in her body reaching a full tilt.

"*Detached* was well done," Dominick admitted, and then raised his

33

eyebrows at me until I chimed in that "it was, it definitely was."

"But this next one is my *Kane*, my *Raging Bull*, my *Chinatown*, my *Godfather*. I put my spirit into *Detached*, and when I rewatch it tears drip down my face like a little girl who lost her bike, but it doesn't revolutionize, and you only are remembered if you start an uprising, if you make people feel like their world has tilted once those credits roll. That is my true salvation. But not here!"

"Not here...what do you mean?" I said, trying to follow.

"These walls have ears, and in this day and age, spoilers are massacres. We'll go back to my place in SoHo. I'll give you a tease, and you can tell me what you think. Also we can discuss your...novel, right?"

Dominick glanced over at Nevie.

"This one's already high enough to occupy her time with the feel of, I don't know, wallpaper or something. So knock back your fucking drink fast, Noah. Time's already ticking down."

4

I HAD NEVER SEEN ANYONE AS MESSED UP AS NEVIE WHEN we all got back to Dominick's loft. Every part of her was in motion. Her thoughts were all over the place but she actually made sense, or maybe I just thought she did because I wanted a taste of what she was on and then a taste of her as well.

Dominick unlocked the front door and opened it quietly. He then slid a gold ring out of his pocket and put it on his ring finger in one fluid movement, as if it was something he did each night. He disappeared into the darkness of the loft until I couldn't hear his footsteps anymore.

Nevie turned on a lamp and sat on a big red couch. She took off her high heels and gyrated against the cushions. The loft had a minimalist vibe: a few paintings on the wall, giant windows, and a home theater in the living room. It smelled like money to me.

"Where did Dominick go?" I whispered.

"You don't have to be quiet," she yelled.

"He seemed to want it that way."

"Don't you love him?" she asked, begging me to agree. "I do."

"I think he's married."

She heard me but pretended like she didn't.

"I'm gonna be in his movie, Noah."

"That's great." I eyed a magnificent bar off in one corner. "Can I make a drink?"

"I don't have a specific role yet. This movie is going to be different."

"Yeah, you guys said that."

I opened up a bottle of Johnnie Walker Blue and took a sniff. Even my parents only kept Gold in the house. I poured a glass and decided it tasted like all the rest. Maybe I wasn't refined enough yet.

"So you're like his mistress or what?"

She was staring out of the giant windows. SoHo was quiet on a Tuesday night, definitely a different animal than during the weekends. I hadn't been downtown in a while.

"Noah, I'm twenty-two. You don't have to be my bodyguard."

"I'm not."

"I know he's married, but he looks at me differently than he looks at her. We live by passion. He told me that."

I made a motion like I was jerking off.

"Have you ever lived by passion?" she shot back.

"Sure."

"No, you haven't, and you've never been in love."

"Last time I checked, Nevie, you haven't been in my life for the last year so you don't know shit."

She rolled over on the couch and gave it a light hump before lying down completely.

"You can lie to yourself if you want, but we both know the truth. It's why you use your writing as a crutch, as if it could take the place of what you really want."

I took a strong sip of the Johnnie Blue, summoning all the will I had to not throw the glass at her.

"I doubt you're his only mistress."

She sat up, looking old all of a sudden.

"I knew you stuck the Fast in my drink," she said, not angry with me but disappointed in herself.

I knocked back the rest of the scotch. "I knew you knew."

"It's not like it mattered anyway. What do you think they coat those pennies with?"

"You mean the Pennytinis are laced?"

"Dominick can do a lot for your career," she said, ignoring me like always and steering the conversation. "He knows a lot of insider people. Don't fuck it up with him like you do with everything else."

"Man, you are *really* something."

She clenched her fists, seeming desperate.

"I'm sorry." She shook her head wildly. "The Fast sometimes comes on so strong, makes me mean, but that first rush is the purest thing I've ever known."

A mascara tear ran down her cheek. She left its stain as a mark.

"What is Fast?"

She gave a laugh that amounted to no more than a peep. It sounded like it was the last laugh she'd ever have.

"I really wanted to introduce you to Dominick. I want to see you succeed in doing the thing you love to do."

I sat next her on the couch, the red leather slippery. I took her hand and stared at a large painting of a yellow circle on an entirely white background.

"I'm sorry for trying to kiss you at that party."

"I'm sorry for giving you such a hard time."

We remained silent like an old married couple. We had years on our side that outweighed anything else. Fights always disintegrated into smiles. I wiped away her blackened tears.

"I knew how you felt, and I took it too far that night. I wouldn't take no for an answer."

"Noah, we don't have to get into it."

"I know that sometimes I can get out of control."

"We all slip," she said, puckering her lips.

I almost dove in and kissed those lips, but I held back, would always hold back now.

The lights in the loft were turned on before I had the chance to slip again. Dominick stood at the other end of the living room, watching us as he bounced on his feet. I let go of Nevie's hand.

"Were we being too loud?" I asked, not knowing what else to say.

"Not at all." He shifted over to the bar and picked up the opened bottle I had left.

"I see you've found the Johnnie Walker Blue. A man who knows his liquor."

Dominick walked toward the fireplace and grabbed a pipe with intricate carvings from off the mantle. He pushed a button on a tiny silver stereo system and jazz music filled up the room. Nevie had something to move to now and blew him a kiss that he ate.

"I'm going to let you boys talk and take a shower. Nothing better than a shower on Fast."

She glided over to Dominick and wrapped her thin arms around his neck, swinging like a child. I envied them as they rocked to the beats with one another.

"I'll be in the guest bedroom a little later," she whispered into

Dominick's ear. He nodded with a grin.

"Good night, Noah. I'll see you again, soon perhaps, no bars or drinks, just you and me: coffee, conversation, and catching up. Is it a date?"

"Definitely." I kissed her on the cheek. She stayed awhile and closed her eyes before dancing her way out of the room.

Dominick poured himself a glass of Blue and then topped off mine. He sat down on one of the red couches. I leaned back against the other one and thought of how it would feel to be bookended by a wife and a girlfriend, the pleasure of choice between the two each night.

"It's late," Dominick said.

"Oh," I replied, catching Dominick's hint that he wanted to be alone with Nevie.

"I love the late night; it's usually the only time of day I can get any work done."

Dominick played the air like a piano, eyes half closed, one leg crossed over the other, his pipe dangling low as a weird odor filled the room. He seemed more refined at that moment than I ever thought I could be. The song ended and the room got quiet.

"Thelonious Monk is great. Imagine if he was doing what he did today? Would anyone care? We only want fast products now, carbon copy pop and fizz."

I finished my drink, crunching down on the ice methodically.

"What about with film?"

"I like how you call it film," Dominick said. "It adds an element of class. I'm not here solely to entertain, I'm not in vaudeville."

"You think that's all people want?"

"People work hard. Life is hard. Movies are a form of escapism, but the right film can transcend. It can change your entire view."

"Sometimes I feel like I'm alive in the wrong time," I said. "Even things that are worshipped now get discarded a moment later."

He knocked back the rest of his drink and pointed the glass at me.

"I couldn't help overhear you and Nevie. The end of what you were saying, bits and pieces."

A wave of nausea flooded over me as I yammered, "Oh, shit, man. I was drunk, I didn't mean anything—"

"No, you are not drunk. We were just having a perfectly intelligent conversation, but I'm not accusing you of anything. I do have a wife. She is sleeping right now, and she and Nevie know about one another."

"Yeah, it's not my business, Dominick."

"I don't know what Nevie means to me as of yet. I see she means a lot to you."

"We go way back."

"I'm sure you do. What she and I have doesn't need to be defined right now. Do you find the need to define everything in your life?"

"Sometimes too much."

"That's just naivety. With age you learn that things do not always go as planned."

A silence filled the room again. Dominick seemed fine with letting it simmer.

"So I'm curious to hear about your new film," I said, skewing the conversation over to something that mattered, not wanting to talk about Nevie anymore. Here was a rare opportunity that I needed to seize. Dominick was someone who could green light a movie while taking a dump. I could even chuck the idea of writing a novel and finish a screenplay instead while I got close enough to Dominick to wow him with my talent.

"Why should I tell you anything about my film, Noah?"

He squinted his eyes, scrutinizing. I shifted in his place.

"Maybe 'cause I'm just a kid with a good ear and an empty glass of Blue."

Dominick flexed a smile. He rose from the couch and dropped some more scotch in my glass.

"There is no script."

"What do you mean?"

He pointed to his head. "It's all in here. That's where I'm keeping it. To create a complete idea is to fill it with bullshit. I want my actors to be surprised each day they show up. I want to be surprised as well."

"Like improvisational?" I asked, reeling back on the couch as Dominick hovered.

"No," he laughed, in a mocking tone. "Reality."

"I'm not following."

"Reality," he said again, taking a long drag from his pipe and letting the word hang in the air.

"You mean like reality television but as a film?"

Dominick shook his head, disappointed.

"I will create circumstances for my actors. They will have roles to play. But their emotions will not be make-believe. They will live and breathe and die as their characters because it's time for art to be dangerous. I will put the fear in them and therefore the audience will feel their fear as well. We've played it safe as artists for way too long."

Maybe I was too drunk to think clearly at that point, but I was intrigued beyond belief. I had an overwhelming desire for Dominick to be my big brother, someone to guide me, someone to bring me into this world I longed to enter.

"That sounds so cool," I said.

"Yes, it's very *cool*, Noah. I am a *cool* guy looking to do *cool* things."

"No, I mean, it's like guerrilla filmmaking, anything can happen, right?" I began, getting a surge of inspiration. "That's how I write. I want anyone reading my work to be uncomfortable; I want to say what people are thinking but would never say out loud. We're all capable of the worst things imaginable, but we maintain, we try to live productive, moral lives, but our characters don't need to be that way, our films don't need to be that way. You talked about a revolution before..."

"I did."

"I know what you mean."

Dominick nodded, a drop more impressed than before, but I could tell that he wasn't sold yet. He poured himself some more scotch and twirled the amber liquid around his glass, pretending to be more interested in that.

"You might think you know what I mean in theory, but you have no idea what I have planned."

"You want to stir shit up," I said, louder than before, feeling like I was losing control of the conversation after I had just taken it back.

"To sum it up crudely, yes I want to 'stir shit up,' but so much more."

In the distance, the shower cut off violently, the knob screeching as drip-droplets of water plinked against the bathtub and naked skin. I had forgotten about Nevie, too wrapped up in Dominick's magnetism.

Dominick placed his glass down and gazed toward the bathroom, his eyes clearly saying that his film played second fiddle to a good wet screw.

"Another time?" I asked, knowing it wouldn't do any good to push. The appeal of a naked Nevie trumped all else.

"You remind me of me a decade ago," Dominick said, sneering. "You're hungry. You want what I have so bad it burns."

"Yeah," I nodded, inching to the end of the couch.

"What would you do to make it, Noah? Would you do anything?"

I could feel my heart beating so fast it stung. "Yeah, I'd do anything. I'd get your coffee, anything to learn from you."

Dominick showed his blinding white teeth and let out a bark of a laugh.

"Well, I don't drink coffee."

He patted me on the cheek as a swirl of his cologne clogged the room. "Good night, Noah, you know where the door is."

I hung my head, dejected.

"We should do this again," he called out on his way to the bathroom. "Maybe I'll even let you in on some of the plot." My head perked up. "Although, next time the Blue is on you, Silver Spoon."

He turned off the lights and disappeared down the hallway, leaving me on the couch with the solitary lamp beaming the only stream of light in my face.

I rose from the couch with the intent to leave, but I could hear them going at it in the bathroom. Soft moans leaked through the crack at the bottom of the door. So I placed my ear up against it and listened. I closed my eyes and imagined myself entering the bathroom instead of Dominick. Yanking open that shower curtain and taking Nevie by surprise. Slipping my wet fingers inside of her and getting her ready until I'd slip the rest of me inside of her too.

When their moans finally ended a half an hour later, I removed my ear from the door. A shadow of a person hung at the other end of the hallway. We stared at one another, neither speaking, until the shadow finally darted away. I caught the glimpse of a nightgown before the figure disappeared into the darkness. Maybe the shadow had been listening as well; maybe it had wanted to be in that bathroom as well for different reasons.

I had a hangover the next morning, nothing I couldn't handle, but as I headed down the hallway I heard Cassie's yells echoing from the kitchen. She was throwing a fit and ruining the oozing smell of Consuela the Saint's chocolate pancakes. Apparently Consuela had run Cassie's iPod through the washer and dryer because she left it in one of her jeans' pockets. Arms crossed and spit flying, Cassie was intent to ream Consuela, but Consuela didn't even blink. She was making her renowned *panqueques de chocolate*, and even an atom bomb couldn't stop her now.

"Do they not have music in Guatemala? Consuela, what the fuck am I supposed to do now?"

"Cassie, no language like that in this house."

"Fuck you, you're not my *madre*, and chocolate pancakes, what are we, three-year-olds? I have braces, hello, I cannot eat chocolate for breakfast. I'm telling Mom and Dad."

"Fine, you go do that," Consuela said, plopping the pancake mix onto a sizzling grill. "See if Consuela care."

"Cassie," I began, not wanting to get involved but simply wanting peace to ease my hangover. "She didn't do it on purpose or anything."

"Noah, lick me. Don't stick up for the *foreign*. And Mom and Dad are gonna hear about your grand theft auto fiasco."

"What are you talking about?"

"Hello, my car smells like pot and Doritos. Did you think you could get away with taking it?"

"That was Dex and his crackhead friend Endo. They took it to Boston last weekend."

Consuela looked up from her chocolate pancakes and stuck her tongue out at Cassie.

"Well what if I told the 'rents about you getting fired from your job instead?" she asked, this little girl who in two short years had gone from hanging on my every word into a spiteful teenager.

"Why would you do that?"

"Why the fuck not? What will you do to keep me quiet?"

She licked her lips, thinking she had me. I wondered how Dominick would handle the situation; he wasn't the type of guy to get had.

"Fine, do that, Cassie, I'll just tell them I caught you giving a blowie to your boyfriend last week in the conservatory."

Consuela cackled, which just made Cassie boil more. Cassie put her hands on her hips and stomped off. As she pouted away, something caught my eye. She was wearing a short pajama top, the small of her back bare. I could've sworn I saw a yellow circle just like that girl Lindsay had from the party the other night, but then Consuela waved the chocolate pancakes under my nose, and nothing else mattered but sinking my teeth into their sugary bliss.

After two massive servings of pancakes, I rubbed my belly as I passed by

Dex playing the piano in the conservatory. He was sipping from a martini glass full of orange juice while puffing on his morning breakfast and bopping to each note.

"Yo, Noah, our awful sister woke me up by yelling about her precious iPod on the phone to her friend Maddy," Dex said, sweeping down the keys from the lowest note to the highest and then closing the piano.

"She was so rude to Consuela," I said, stepping inside. Through the windows, Central Park seemed to have blossomed overnight. *One day bare, the next day there.* Something Nevie had always said.

"I saw Nevie last night," I said nonchalantly, as if I hadn't come home and dreamed a month's worth of dreams about her.

"Oh yeah, how is she?"

"Well, it's been a while, you know?"

"Yeah, bro, I know, you haven't shut up about her for the past year."

"I mean it was fine seeing her I guess. But she's kind of with this married guy now. He's the director of *Detached*."

"What's *Detached*?" Dex asked, taking a large toke and running a ring on his finger across his teeth.

"That movie about the married couple. The guy's a filmmaker and he obsessively films her all the time, like when she's cooking pasta and when they're having sex."

"Right, and he can't get it up. I saw that with this girl Elise at the Angelika, and she wanted to make out the whole time and these two elderly ladies kept shushing us."

"Well this guy is directing another film, and he wanted to bounce some plot ideas off of me."

"Dude, he said this to you?"

"Yeah, is that so crazy to believe?"

Dex played with his sock, pulling it up and down until it limply hung. He shrugged and took another gulp of juice.

"Why do you have to make a face?" I asked, getting pissed.

"What face? I'm not starting nothing."

"Like you think it's bullshit, like you don't believe Dominick would say something like that to me."

"Who the hell is Dominick?"

"The director!"

"Noah, for a guy who claims to be so intelligent, you can be so naïve. People talk out of their ass. I do it all the time. Just don't get your hopes up. That's all I meant. Okay? Peace?"

He held out a fist to punch. I was too tired to argue anymore and lamely punched back.

"You got a call. On the main line."

"From who?"

Dex gave a full smile full of orange teeth. He wiped them with the back of his hand before continuing.

"It was Margaret."

Margaret. I pictured her after she showered off the clams, milk and bile, deciding not to call my cell because she knew I might delete the message so she called my parents' landline instead. When Consuela or whoever else would hand me the phone, I'd have to listen. She had wanted a role in my life so badly that she'd sacrificed her dignity, but unfortunately, her plan backfired because I had more important things to deal with now.

Instead, I went over to Best Buy to buy a copy of *Detached*. It had been about three years since I'd seen the film. I'd spend the rest of the day pouring over its shots in an attempt to impress Dominick. On the way over, I had a zinger of an idea. Better than just studying the film, I could adapt it into a short story, keep the gist of it the same but truly explore the characters' inner thoughts and even add a little of my own pizzazz to the plot. That way I could display my talent since everything else I wrote already seemed too juvenile to show to a guy like Dominick.

When I got back home, I stared at my room. It all seemed childish now as well, memories of high school that I hadn't bothered to take down since I'd been at college. Things had already become so much more complicated than those years. Easy problems like where to drink, who to hook-up with, and how to bullshit through some English essay—these felt like someone else's worries. Now I was dealing with real life.

I tore down a bunch of posters of bands I no longer cared about and classic '80s movies like *Gremlins* and *The Goonies* that I loved as kid but weren't part of the essential oeuvre I wanted to have as an adult. I only kept my *Fight Club* poster and re-hung it in a nice frame over my bed.

Fight Club was, by far, my favorite film. I could relate to someone like Tyler Durden. Mild-mannered, ordinary Jack on the outside, but a whole different story underneath. With a fuck-it-all attitude, Tyler Durden wanted to start a revolution just like Dominick; maybe that was why I had acted so strongly to hearing about Dominick's own Project Mayhem.

I am Noah's smirking revenge. I vowed destruction against anyone who scoffed at my wild dreams because I hadn't done anything to bring them to fruition. I popped *Detached* into my Blu-Ray player, leaned back in bed with a laptop in my arms, and began a transformation, writing straight into the night without a break, my fingers furiously typing away, speed being of the essence, not wanting to pause for a breath that might let in that evil creature called writer's block—the wily beast who had plagued me for too long.

Slowing down only meant giving it satisfaction.

Fast-as-I-can might as well be written on my shiny new nametag.

5

DETATCHED

(Adapted by Noah Spaeth)

THE CAMERA WATCHED THEM EAT DINNER LIKE IT DID EVERY NIGHT. Sadiora made a steak au poivre for Nick and a salad for herself. Another camera in the kitchen had filmed every detail of her leaving the steak on the grill for too long instead of cooking it rare like Nick preferred. They sat facing each other, each at the end of a long table in their large dining room that echoed every sound. She was blindly stabbing at the lettuce on her plate when she lost her grip on the fork and it clanged against the floor. Only then did Nick look up.

"I'm going to get a new one," she said, picking up the spinning fork while watching her reflection in the camera's lens. She could see her frizzy hair that always seemed out of sorts, an untamed animal atop her head. Her long painter's fingers covered up the strawberry birthmark above her collarbone that looked as if she'd been beaten there. But it was her mouth that saddened her the most: tiny lips that made her smile barely there and not worth the attempt.

The camera's red light continued to beam a bull's-eye on her forehead. She swept by its scrutiny and escaped to the kitchen.

Nick rose from his chair, dabbed his mouth with a silk napkin, and turned on some Thelonious Monk. He often played jazz after dinner. The dining room had tall ceilings made for acoustics, and only the finest speakers had been inserted in the walls. He closed his eyes, imagining he was somewhere else, the music making his head bob, the notes reaching his soul. When Sadiora came out of the kitchen, she seemed unhappy with his choice of music. He could tell this from the way her high heels clomped against the floor, so he lowered the volume with a remote.

Sadiora noticed that half of his steak still sat charred and untouched under his nose. A lilting sigh escaped from his nostrils to indicate that he dreaded eating anymore of its leathery consistency. She clutched her new fork, her knuckles straining.

"Joel and Olivia are coming in two days," she said, sitting back down and stabbing at her plate again.

"For dinner?"

"I was going to make pasta. I know Joel likes..."

She stopped herself because Nick was giving her an exaggerated frown.

"Joel is too strong minded sometimes," he said. "The universe does not entirely orbit around him."

"He was your friend from college."

Nick chose not to answer, a common game he played, always keeping her on edge. He poured himself another glass of red wine, his third. His eyes began to hang low, his head starting to sway. After three glasses he appeared older but less dignified, his shorn beard more derelict than artsy, his slumped shoulders making him appear slight rather than imposing. He stuffed the last few bites of steak in his mouth with a giant gulp of wine and slid his plate away, its sharp screech causing Sadiora to cringe.

"I'm done, but I could use a cigarette."

She rose with her full plate of salad in one hand and scooped up his plate, the leftover sauce swimming around as she struggled to balance one on top of the other while clearing the wine glass as well. She imagined dropping everything and the camera documenting it all: the china, the expensive wine glass he bought in Copenhagen with his dead former girlfriend Astrid, probably irreplaceable. She'd have to see this over and over once he burned it onto a DVD for them to watch, possibly even in slow motion. She managed to keep her balance for long enough to reach the kitchen, then grabbed a box of cigarettes and returned to the dining room.

"Thank you, Sadiora."

He kissed her on the cheek and lit himself a cigarette.

"Did you like dinner?" she asked.

"Steak was a little tough. You cooked it for too long."

She ran her fingers through her hair as the lens caught her eye again. She focused on its red beaming light until she felt his lips on her earlobe.

"I think I'll be horny tonight."

"Okay, Nick."

He groped her breast, careful not to burn her with the cherry.

"I love red wine...with steak...after a long day of work. Good red wine, though, a Brunello di Montalcino, something that improves over time," he said, speaking right through her into the camera. "My father knew his wine. This bottle was from his collection. I was never allowed even close to his 'children'; that's what he called them."

He laughed at that, a small chuckle that he had developed recently when mentioning his father. This had been a man he hated but now revered in a way that bordered on obsession, especially right after the car accident that seemed to erase away any bad memories of his father and Astrid becoming lovers, like they existed on some far-fetched soap opera.

She imagined he was thinking about them as he finished his cigarette and stubbed it out in a green porcelain ashtray shaped like a woman with the words *La Fée Verte* written on the bottom.

"I got that in the South of France. Did I ever tell you that story?" he asked, and then began before she could say that he had.

"I was there filming a documentary on absinthe. Astrid had come along."

He peered over Sadiora's shoulder so he could still speak into the camera.

"I was filming one day at an absinthe distillery, and I stole it for her. I saw it in the manufacturer's office; I knew I had to take it. The words mean 'the green fairy'; I used to call her that."

"Do you wanna take a shower?" Sadiora asked, wrapping her arms around him and attempting to bring his mind back from Astrid, his other borderline obsession.

"Want to, darling," he said, with a wagging finger. "'Wanna' is for people who are uneducated. Your father was an English professor at Cornell."

"I know."

The camera had seen all this with its little red light that refused to wipe its mark from her forehead.

"Give me a kiss and then I'm going to do some reading. We'll meet up later."

Their lips locked for a moment. She could taste the gritty steak and knew he was drunk from the way he messily kissed her. His tongue jammed down her throat, bumpy taste buds rubbing against her uvula. She would've choked had this not been something he'd done before and she knew how to handle.

"Sometimes I want to consume you," he said, once he had finished licking her insides, barely above a whisper as if he was reminding himself. "So I could have all of you at once."

Her cheeks flushed as she rose to her feet and slid toward the kitchen.

"Sadiora," he said, in a voice that suddenly made her want to follow everything he did. It sounded like the time he asked her to marry him, his baritone bass sturdy enough to make her feel safe; but that had been a while ago. "Take the wine and cap it."

"Sure."

He went over to the other side of the table and looked into the lens before shutting it off.

"We'll watch this later."

She turned on the overhead fan to spread the smoke and cut the silence. As it spun wildly, she felt cold; maybe she even had a fever, because she felt as drunk as he looked.

Sadiora waited on their bed in a nightie, splashing perfume up and down her freshly shaved legs. One strap of the nightie kept slipping off her shoulder and hanging on the groove of her arm. She could hear Nick's slippers shuffling up the stairs.

"Sexy," he said, reaching the doorway in his bathrobe. "I want to fuck you."

"I know," she replied, licking her lips and still tasting traces of steak that made her nauseous.

The air conditioner gasped. Nick liked things chilly, even though it was fall and already bitter outside. Sadiora couldn't remember the last time she didn't feel cold in her own home.

"You haven't seen my camera have you?" he asked, leaning on the windowsill and looking out into the night as New York City rushed beneath them.

"I haven't...since dinner."

"I wanted to watch...dinner."

"I know."

Her words were slow and spaced out. She knew he didn't believe her because she always clammed up when she was lying. He figured she had seen it but wouldn't tell him where it was. Their SoHo loft was very big and things tended to get lost. Her hand ran up and down her long neck that was starting to get red.

"I want to kiss your neck."

He took off his bathrobe and slippers and slid on top of her, resting his lips against her throbbing neck. He threw off the sheets between them and watched her.

"Las Vegas showgirl," he said. "It's Thursday."

"Oh, I forgot."

"I don't think it will work if...you forget."

"All right."

Her bare feet sunk into their carpet as she walked to the closet. She slipped her nightie off and could see him in the darkness staring at her. She put on a glitter red top and black stockings with a matching red miniskirt.

"The light is too dim."

"I know," she sang, turning on a lamp beside their bed.

With her red glitter showgirl outfit and black stockings she felt like a deck of cards. Her teeth chattered, mimicking the sounds of shuffling. She was hoping that he wouldn't ask her to dance for him, but he didn't have time for that; he ripped off her outfit and pounced.

Her eyes roamed from the ceiling where she would normally count every little bump over to the bookshelf. A red light beamed from across the bed and she had to struggle to see it. Every book was closely stacked together except for a gap about two book lengths long where a lens stuck out. She could hear its moaning buzz.

"Come on...come on...come on," he muttered, as his glasses slipped from the perspiration dripping down his forehead. "Fuck," he said, in a voice that resembled a sob.

She let her lips break apart into a smile, imagining that camera zooming in until she became unrecognizable.

A knock on the door broke my concentration. I was sweating, shut inside with the windows and blinds closed. The hours had obliviously gone by, documented only in keystrokes. I was starving, having forgotten to eat lunch. My stomach was pissed off and growling at me, but I was writing. It would have to wait.

Knock. KNOCK.

The knocks had to wait too. Spaced out and hollow with a muffled voice as well. Sadiora's lips were in full view on the television, kissing my sublime mind that was finally free from writer's block.

"Go away," I yelled, my fingers pulsing with blissful energy as they danced over the keys on my laptop.

"No," a voice murmured, and the knocks continued.

I opened the door to see Dex leaning against the wall in a wifebeater.

"What'cha doing?" he asked, jumping inside and playing some song on an air guitar he made out of his stomach. His tongue was red from a lollipop that he sucked down to the core and tossed over his shoulder.

"I'm busy," I said.

"Do you know what happened to Endo?"

"I really don't care," I said, cradling my laptop and feeling my inspiration slipping away.

"So the douche nozzle stayed in Boston after I left last weekend, and he ran into this waitress he was flirting with at a Charley's restaurant. They wound up going to a Red Sox game and became smitten with one another, but here's the capper: he's all excited and shit because he's found this girl, but then after the Red Sox game, she says she has to do something, so he goes with her and it's to pick up her *kid*! She has a goddamn *kid*! So Endo freaks out, tells her he's going to the bathroom, jumps out of the window, and runs down to U Mass to stay with a buddy. Isn't that crazy?"

"Insane. Now get out."

"What's your problem, dude? Lighten up..."

"Dex, shut up. I'm really busy."

"Doing what?"

"I'm making a story out of *Detached*."

On the television, Sadiora's lips still smiled seductively for the camera.

"You watching a porno?"

"No."

"'Cause I got better ones in my room. Tasteful. I'm only into softcore, booby caressing and stuff, no penetration."

"It's not a porno. I'm seriously...I can get on this director's good side. I can show him I can write, and he could introduce me to people. I don't know people, I don't have connections, and I don't want to take another shitty job where I waste my life away. I don't want to do that."

"Why don't you show him your own stuff?"

To Dex it was all so simple, but I knew this adaptation would be my only shot. I pushed him out of the room and must've looked desperate because for once Dex chose not to provoke me. He patted me on the shoulder with an empathy he usually only reserved for himself and backed away. The door shut as I dashed back to my laptop, my fingertips once again blazing.

The next day Nick was filming Sadiora cooking pasta, inching closer until the camera almost touched her face. Her eyes kept catching the lens by accident while trying hard to concentrate on the pasta as she added in dashes of olive oil.

"I'm filming your birthmark. You know, the one that you think makes you look ugly."

"I never said that."

"I left the camera in the living room, right by the television. I don't know how I could have missed it."

"Sometimes you can miss what's right there...."

"Last night," he interrupted, but his voice trailed off and the camera swiveled away from a close-up of her face.

"What about it?"

52

"It was because...I couldn't watch dinner. That was it."

"It doesn't matter, I was tired anyway."

The doorbell chimed halfway through her sentence as she wiped her hands off on her apron. When she looked up he was gone. She could see him filming his way through the swinging kitchen door, just as she noticed she had added too much olive oil to the pasta that now floated on top.

Through the lens, Nick meandered around the pieces of scattered furniture in their expansive living room toward the doorbell that chimed, chimed away.

No one was there when he opened the door.

He stared through his camera at the hallway. A police siren called out in the distance. Their neighbor, a young NYU student all of twenty in boxers and no shirt, reached down to pick up his newspaper and gave the camera a lingering, penetrating look before disappearing back into his apartment.

Nick bent his knees, dropped down, and picked up the mail. He backed up into his house and closed the door, feeling a package. He threw all of the other mail onto the coffee table.

"Got a package," he yelled across the room as Sadiora stepped inside, wiping her hands on a dishtowel.

"What is it?"

She studied the package from a distance, blowing the loose strands of chaotic hair away from her eyes.

"Feels like a DVD. There's no return address or anything."

"Weird."

He carefully opened it, making sure to keep the box that it came in intact. Inside was a burned DVD that said *WATCH ME*.

"Should I do what it tells me?" he asked Sadiora, and rested the camera on the couch.

"I'm curious."

He slid the DVD into their player. An image of endless snow came up on the television. Nick was about to dismiss it as nothing when Sadiora appeared on the screen. Her lips had pursed into a tense frown that she was duplicating in person as well. She was sitting on their bed with one strap of her nightie hanging from the groove of her arm, wildly looking into the lens.

"What is this?"

"Me."

Nick saw himself enter the bedroom in slippers and a bathrobe and felt his stomach drop. He dashed in front of the television, blocking it from Sadiora as if she didn't know how the rest of the scene would play out.

"This was from last night."

His voice rose to a level she didn't like. Even though he never hit her, she thought he would pull his hand back and smack her across the face so hard it would leave a permanent mark. She almost wanted him to. But he only rested it on her shoulder.

"Can you explain this?" he asked, eerily calm in a way that gave her a terrible chill.

"No."

"Someone was watching us last night," he said.

"You said the camera was in the living room."

"I said I found the camera in the living room when I woke up."

"Maybe you were drunk and didn't realize you had brought it into the bedroom?"

"And then sent a DVD copy to myself?"

"I don't know. Maybe you did it and forgot? You film so much that I bet you don't even realize when the camera's not in your hand."

He looked down at his hand as if it had all the answers, then he closed it into a fist and left the room without saying anything more.

She turned back to the television and watched him squirming unsuccessfully on top of her. "Fuck," he said, rolling off of her and attempting to finish himself off: determined, malicious in the extent of his stroking, and then, defeated. He curled up into a fetal position, whimpering, and cried into her wild hair.

She picked up the remote and shut the TV off.

Sadiora left Nick alone for the rest of the day. She bided her time with painting the people passing on the street until she began watching a crazy woman watching her. The woman had removed her top, bare breasts swinging in the wind, and yet she wouldn't break concentration. Sadiora was her world, and everything else had fallen away. So Sadiora accepted the challenge, observing even more closely with a pair of binoculars at how every person walking past slowed down for a moment of superiority, but Sadiora was still this woman's only muse, calling out to her with moonbeam eyes that seemed to see every thought she ever had in her warped mind. It became too much, her insides rumbling like a blender crushing ice, and she had to break their dueling stare. She felt a cold tear slide down her cheek once she had turned away. She took out her camera to snap pictures of it all in case she wanted to paint the scene once it turned dark, but later that night, she no longer had the desire to swirl her emotions on a canvas. She found Nick in the den nursing some expensive wine that was already half empty. She thoughtfully brought him a snack.

"I made popovers," she smiled, showing him the lipstick stain on her front tooth. She placed a silver tray of food in front of him.

"You have lipstick on your teeth."

Her face turned its signature red, as a nervous finger swiped across her teeth. She looked for approval, but he had already forgotten. She made room on the couch and sat next to him, lightly stroking his leg hair.

"A game is being started, and I am going to figure it out."

She nodded.

"Who has access to this apartment when we are gone? The cleaning lady? The super? A sneaky doorman looking to blackmail us?"

"It's puzzling," she said, covering her neck that was beating red again.

"I can't imagine that this is the last we'll hear from our elusive filmmaker."

He lost interest in the popovers and focused on the television.

"What are you watching?" she asked, stepping closer and seeing the two of them picking away at their food.

"Thursday's dinner. You are going to drop your fork soon."

"I know," she said, exhausted.

"Watch how I am fighting to chew my steak. I told you it was tough…"

"I'm going to bed," she said, cutting him off, but her tone was polite. Once she had gotten up and already left the room, she wished she had said it nastier.

***

A new package came the next day, fueling Nick. He filmed it all: the action of opening the door, seeing the package, feeling the outline of a fresh DVD. When he brought it inside, Sadiora was already waiting by the television.

"You were right," she said, turning it on. "Whoever it was sent another one."

"I told you it was a game."

He was more excited than he had been in a long time.

"Who plays games like this?"

"I'm going to show this to Joel. Since he's a lawyer, maybe he could give us some advice. Besides if this Peeping Tom was looking to jerk off to whatever sexual act we would have gotten into last night...we fooled them. You went to bed and I passed out on the couch."

"I guess we outsmarted them...you outsmarted them," she said, correcting herself as one of his eyebrows rose.

Nick didn't know what to do with himself for the rest of the day. Endless thoughts of who could be filming them ran through his mind. He was so preoccupied that he didn't have time to follow Sadiora around the house with his camera. They only spoke when she asked him if he wanted lunch and that he could have some of tonight's pasta if he wanted. He was staring out of the window, lost in the yellow show of cabs zooming down East Broadway, and he didn't respond until she asked him again. He often chose not to hear her the first time she said something.

The doorbell confused him when it rang at six. He had been concentrating on what he was going to do tomorrow when the next DVD appeared. He didn't even notice Joel and Olivia walking in until he smelled their cigarette smoke wafting through the air and saw them hugging Sadiora. Joel and Sadiora held their embrace for a long moment, much longer than when Sadiora and Olivia exchanged their brief hellos.

They made small talk while standing in a semicircle until it began to be unbearable for Nick. Joel boasting about a client whose case he won and the day they had on the guy's yacht, which ended at a seersucker party out on Fisher's Island. Joel had become fatter since they last saw each other, but a healthy fat, a thousand dinners at five-star restaurants kind of fat. Conversely, Olivia seemed to shrink, all protruding collarbones and toothpick legs. An expensive black dress hung from her shoulders as if she was nothing more than a coat rack. She was still beautiful in a way that made Sadiora plain, diamonds to Sadiora's jade, more like Astrid, lovely Astrid with her chic nonchalance as opposed to the morose intensity that seemed to follow Sadiora around.

"I have something to show you both," Nick snapped, relegating thoughts of Astrid until another time and picking up the DVD from the marble coffee table. "Sadiora, what if we have a bottle of wine first?"

Sadiora looked as if she was about to object but then sauntered out of the room.

"Is this one of your movies?" Olivia asked, sitting next to him on the couch and playing with her loose, jangling necklace.

"No, but you won't believe this. There is someone filming me…and Sadiora in our bedroom. They've sent a copy to us two days in a row with no return address or anything. I'm going to show you what they sent today. We haven't even seen it yet."

"That is strange," Joel and Olivia said at slightly different times.

"Isn't it? But intriguing, too. I mean at first it bothered the fuck out of me, but whoever it is, is talented."

Sadiora stomped back into the room and placed a bottle of wine and a corkscrew on the coffee table.

"Talented," Olivia blurted out. "I would say they were sick. Joel, what would you do if someone was taping our private moments and what not?"

She turned to Sadiora, shaking her head in disbelief and picking up a slight British accent.

"You haven't called the police? I would certainly involve the police."

"I didn't even think of that," Sadiora mumbled to the bottle of wine.

"Can we just see it for today?" Nick pestered. "Before police, before anything. Just as what it is?"

He let himself take a breath before popping in the new DVD. Snow flooded the screen like before, and they all covered their ears from the surround sound until Nick lowered the volume to a normal level. Sadiora appeared on the screen. Like before, she was sitting on her bed smoking a cigarette and looked at the camera situated in the bookshelf. The only sound was from the buzz of the air conditioner in their bedroom. The camera poured over her lips as she took a drag and let out a large exhale until something blocked her from being seen, and then the screen faded to snow.

"That was a person!" Olivia shouted.

Everyone turned to Sadiora who was standing so far behind all of them that she might as well have been in a different room.

"Sadie, what...?" Nick tried to say.

"That didn't happen," she said, not sounding like she was defending herself but more like she was questioning whether she saw it or not.

"That did happen," Nick said. "We just saw it."

Sadiora shook her head.

"I don't remember that."

"Do you sleepwalk?" Joel asked. "Maybe you were asleep when...?"

"She sleepwalks and smokes a cigarette at the same time?" Olivia snapped.

"Or on medication?"

"No," Sadiora said. "None of that. I mean, I remember having a cigarette in my bed last night. Nick was asleep on the couch, and I didn't want to smoke in the living room and wake him up."

"I saw a person!" Olivia shouted again. "Joel, did you see a person?"

"I don't know if I saw a person, but I saw something blocking us from seeing her."

"I wonder what tomorrow will bring?" Nick asked, as he ejected the disc, fascinated. He held this new treasure in his quivering hands. "Everything has to have a logical explanation. Something is being glossed over."

The three of them remained arguing about what had happened, but Nick blocked them all out. In his mind, he fast-forwarded and rewound the image of Sadiora sucking at her cigarette, her lips pouting as if she was giving it a kiss. He became aroused, leaning back and not caring who might see, proud to be a man. He poured himself a glass of wine, puckering his lips as he imagined Sadiora doing the same, and then downed his glass in one delicious gulp.

***

My cell phone rang. Answering it was easier than ignoring it. I learned that from the first time it rang repeatedly and blocked my inspiration. So I answered, quick and forceful, almost wishing that it were someone like Margaret so I could give a good yell, but it wasn't. The caller was far from who I expected it would be.

"Hey, Noah? Is this Noah?'

"What's up?" I replied, still having no idea who it was.

"It's Dominick. Nevie gave me your number. What are you up to, man?"

I looked at the television. Nick's mouth had turned dark red from gulping down the wine. I felt foolish watching this film with its creator's voice on the other line. My stomach churned from embarrassment, and I had vertigo like I was heading down a speeding roller coaster.

"Just…hanging out. I had like errands and shit to do today."

I didn't know why I lied, but it came out naturally.

"I'm having this party tonight. I know you and Nevie said you wanted to hang out so you should come to this party. I know a lot of people, from just good people for you to meet to really hot girls who won't be wearing much."

"Yeah. That sounds cool."

"Good, man, good. It'll be at my loft on Greene Street. You remember where it was?"

"Yeah, thanks a lot, Dominick."

I was about to call him Mr. Bambach; it almost slipped. I was glad I didn't.

"Show up whenever you want, but not too early. Everything always starts late, so judge by that."

"Thanks for thinking of me."

I could hear him sucking on his pipe through the phone.

"Yeah, yeah. I'll see you later."

I hung up, giddy. *Detached* only had a few minutes left. I could finish my adaptation and bring it to the party. Maybe I would show Dominick, or maybe it would just sit in my back pocket waiting, but at least it would be something FINALLY completed.

So I pushed play to wrap it all up….

***

Nick woke up clutching an empty bottle. He wished he had brushed his teeth the night before because a fermented wine taste clung to his gums. He heard one chime of the doorbell and the sound of mail being dropped to the floor.

"Another one." He smiled, standing up too fast and forgetting about his hangover.

He turned on his camera to film the hallway. His next-door neighbor was passing by with a cocky swagger. The kid threw a pair of deuces up at the lens. On the street below, someone cursed at a car that wouldn't start.

"I heard about your little *voyeur*," the kid said, with a wink that Nick found unsettling. "Sadiora told me."

"Did she," Nick replied, already half inside the loft and closing the door before the kid could respond. Nick hated the cockiness of youth, mostly because he never felt like that when he was younger. His father had stripped him of any swagger he aspired to have, belittling him at every chance: his amateur documentaries, girlfriends who were never beautiful enough, even down to the way he chewed. Every moment between them was an opportunity to attack.

Sadiora waltzed into the living room fully dressed at such an early hour on a Sunday morning with a pocketbook slung over her shoulder. If he cared to notice, he would've seen that her hair had been slicked back to avoid her standard electric frizz, rather Olivia-like, and she had painted her face just the right amount for a woman who normally showed the world her crow's feet and frown lines as if it were signs of achievement.

But the new DVD was his only concern. He slid it out of the package and slipped it in the player, fingers trembling, heart triumphantly palpitating. Snow came up on the screen.

"Another one?" Sadiora asked, as she saw herself again, this mysterious doppelganger that they had begun to get to know over these last few days.

He nodded without looking at her, only interested with that doppelganger on the screen. Her alter ego stood in front of their bed completely naked except for a nightie, its same strap hanging on the groove of her arm, so pale. Her hair zigzagged down her face and covered up any expression.

Finally, she tossed the mane of hair out of her eyes and let out a huge smile that made her almost unrecognizable to Nick.

"Come here," she said, as the young next-door neighbor in boxers with little hearts hopped over. The two of them fondled each other before he pulled the nightie over her head and wrestled her onto the bed.

"Is it necessary for me to see anymore?" Nick asked, refusing to turn and face her, in awe at this new creature twisting beneath their neighbor's muscular body. The Sadiora on the screen let out a luscious yelp, destroyed by his frat boy's thrusts, a yelp that Nick had never produced or even attempted to eke out of her with his flaccid love.

"You can see as much as you want."

"I don't want any of it," he said, but they both knew that was a lie because he still watched, even stepped closer to the screen, his camera gliding over their digitized lust.

The car on the street finally started its motor that roared through the silence, a relief to both of them until it petered out.

"I knew it was you filming, Sadiora," he said, finally swiveling his camera away.

"No, you didn't. You thought it was something a whole lot more than it was. Some crazy person. Someone after us. It was just me. You called me talented."

"I can think of a lot of things to call you now, but I am going to restrain myself."

"I want you to get angry. I want you to care."

"Do you love him?"

"No. Well, what is love? I loved two years ago...when I could still smell the beach from our honeymoon in St. Croix. When things mattered. When I mattered."

"You do," he said, but he practically had to cough those words out.

"Astrid mattered," she hissed.

His hand holding the camera started to shake uncontrollably. This rabid trembling had become a part of him now; she had gotten used to his spastic flutters. He hadn't been the same since Astrid and his father began seeing each other. Sadiora didn't know which one of them pursued the other to be cruel. They both seemed to be winking when they broke the news. He had always spoken about Astrid as if Sadiora could never match up, his fleeting moment of coming close to a goddess. The sculptress who traveled around the world and left him because things had gotten too intense and her brilliant art had suffered. Nick had never seemed to look at Sadiora's paintings as anything more than objects in the way.

But at least Astrid stayed on the periphery when he and Sadiora first married. Astrid had broken up with him, and he kept silent about her for the most part, even though sometimes he'd call her name out in his sleep, desperate. Sadiora was the present, and she'd do anything to remain there, taking on his occasional moodiness as if it could bring them closer together. But then Astrid and his father began their own twisted relationship. At his father's house during a dinner party they pawed at each other like cats, rubbed their sex in Nick's face, and Nick took it, which surprised her. He had vilified his father for as long as she knew him, the abandoner who left him with a Prozac-devouring mother, but now Nick stayed mute and pretended not to be bothered, to be actually happy for the bastard. She was sure this had to do with the fact that Nick's father had funded his production company, and she couldn't help but lose all respect because of Nick's disappointing reaction. Sadiora wanted blood, wanted heads to roll, and for her and Nick to get swept up by the passion of it all, the united hatred; but his father's hold was too strong. Nick's only response was to recede into his work, to spend more time looking through a lens rather than at her.

And then, a year ago, a car crash fueled by whiskey and cocaine. His father behind the wheel, foot locked on the gas with the speedometer pushing unreal numbers, Astrid bobbing down on his cock as they swerved along an extra twisty Connecticut road and rammed into a looming tree. Astrid and his father's heads decapitating from the impact, as the phrase *heads will roll* ran through Sadiora's skull, even though she tried not to think it. The villains had finally been defeated and Nick could be hers again, but it only got worse. The look on his face when he stepped out of the morgue made the hairs on her arm stand on end; there was nothing there, vacancy, no lights in the windows, a ghost's gaze. And that look never left.

When they returned home from the morgue he immediately began setting up all his cameras around their loft. Over the next few weeks, he became a shut-in and she became the mad scientist's muse, as if by filming her around the clock he'd be able to keep watch over her, keep the control he lost, keep her head permanently attached. Reality had abandoned him, and it slowly seeped out of her own life as well.

"Nothing matters," he said, bringing her back from the past to the simmering present.

"I know," she said, slowly. "You have documentation of every lull, every boring minute."

"I don't think that."

"That's because you don't exist behind that lens. To you our life is some perverse work of art."

He had nothing to say to that, angering her even more.

"Where did you learn how to use a camera?" he asked instead.

She stared at their front door as if she was telepathically hoping it would open and whisk her far away.

"Was it the kid? The one you were fucking?"

"It was me. He was there. He could have been anyone. I planned it all out."

"Are you going to leave me?"

He pointed the camera in her face. She didn't shy away, knowing he'd only understand her that way.

"Are you?"

"Yes. I'm already packed."

The camera lost its focus on her as it slipped to the floor, bouncing around a little, but he picked it up and found her again.

"Where are you going?"

"I don't know."

"Am I going to see you soon...ever?"

"I don't know. Not soon at least."

He moved closer to her, the lens practically caressing her cheek.

"Can you put down the camera so I can give you a goodbye kiss?" she asked.

He didn't even know how to do that. The camera felt like a long attachment of his body. He didn't want the actual kiss, he only wanted to watch that kiss again and again; only then it'd be able to make his toes curl in delight.

"I don't think so," he said, ashamed. She could hear the regret in the tone of his voice.

Her bags were packed. He hadn't noticed them before, but they were at the foot of the couch. Through the lens, he watched as she picked them up and headed to the front door before swinging it open and standing in the frame. She seemed to stay there for hours. He almost wanted to give her a push to help her along, but he remained steadily catching it all on film, as if she was depending on him.

The camera jittered in his hand, but he made sure not to lose focus until a piece of dust swirled into his eye, and in a blink of no more than a second, she had disappeared. He let the camera linger on the doorframe for a minute longer before pressing stop and rewinding it until she came up on the viewfinder, watching him: today, tomorrow, the next day, the day after, and for as long as he wanted.

He finally kissed her through the screen and shut the camera off, the taste of her drunk on his lips, his hand calmer than ever.

When I finished, I held the pages in my shaking hands. The wily beast called writer's block had been defeated, and a microscopic tear hung from the corner of my eye. The sun had already set and Dominick's party waited. Without even checking myself in the mirror like I usually did, I bolted out of the room into the night, my heart swelling at the thought of Dominick fawning over my work. This party would be the beginning of a brilliant career. Years from now, I'd look back at this day, at this achievement, at these pages that would allow me access into an exclusive world I couldn't wait to enter.

I pictured this brand new life as my cab slugged toward SoHo through a haze of traffic. I yelled at the driver to speed through the yellow lights that slowed us down. I even tossed an extra ten to the front seat to make it happen.

Before I knew it, the cab was going so fast that I'd reached Dominick's loft without even realizing it.

6

DOMINICK'S PARTY HAD ALREADY STARTED WHEN I GOT there. Clusters of people swirled around one another. Funky music vibrated through my soles. Lots of models and actresses, more of an adult vibe than the party I'd hit up with Dex the night before. The goal here was not just a social night out. Everyone spouted credits in lieu of actual conversations, always angling. Eyes passed over me as if I was nothing. I kept my leather jacket on and bopped my head to the music, slightly drunk from the forty-ounce I brown-bagged in the taxi.

No Dominick and no Nevie yet. I eavesdropped on a girl in a camouflage print dress bemoaning the perils of fashion trends replacing one another at more of an alarming rate than usual. She was a model, is still a model, I couldn't remember how she introduced herself. This wasn't why I came, but I always acted polite to pretty girls, even though she barely glanced my way during her entire diatribe.

And then I finally saw Nevie sitting on the counter in the kitchen. One beautiful leg of hers rubbing up against the other. She wore a green dress that awkwardly hung from her body, as if it were once made for the old Nevie, the full Nevie, not the percentage of a girl who barely filled it out now. She wore green eye shadow that matched her dress and caused her eyes to look heavy and sad, even though she was laughing with some dude who was fawning all over her.

"Noah," she said, jumping off of the counter. She gave me a big hug. "I'll catch up to you later," she said to the guy who slunk away.

"Who was that?"

"Take your jacket off, aren't you burning up?"

She wrestled off my jacket and draped it over a chair.

"He was some actor that filmed a new Clint Eastwood film; we were

65

just talking about this new app that's big in L.A. and alerts you when you're ten feet from a casting director."

She was sweating heavily and wiped her brow.

"Are you all right?" I asked. "You look really hot."

"Thank you, I've been dieting," she said, and then something caught her interest as she barreled past me. When she came back, she was holding two orange drinks.

"Dom always makes these frozen mango margaritas, they're exceptional."

"Where is he?"

"Around, he's always around."

I took a sip, as an ice-cold jolt shot up into my brain. They tasted amazing. I went in for another sip, and the drink seemed to flow through my veins. The party appeared now as if it was in high definition, and I felt like everyone suddenly loved me. I looked over at Nevie who ravenously sucked at her drink and then held the bridge of her nose. At that moment, I believed she loved me best of all.

"You're looking at me weird," she said.

"How so?"

My heart slammed into my chest, as if it was dying to break free.

"I don't know. Like you're trying to locate me in a crowd, but you can't seem to find me."

A sea of people collected around us. They all began to move at a rapid pace, as if the party was controlled by some large remote control with a giant finger on the fast-forward button.

"There's Dominick," Nevie said, and pointed into the distance.

Through the blurs whizzing by, I was able to make out Dominick watching the party from across the room. Over his head hung a painting of a red-haired woman with a glass of absinthe in her hand. Her eyes drooped, and she looked bombed out of her mind. Her dress had a trail of voluptuous snakes slithering from the ends. On her arm was a coil of jewelry that had morphed into snakes as well. The words *La Fée Verte* had been painted in an elegant script across the bottom part of the frame. I could've sworn I recognized those words from somewhere, but my brain was too waterlogged to recall.

"Go to him," Nevie said, giving me a light push through the sea of people until I came face-to-face with Dominick and we shook hands. When I looked back across the party, Nevie seemed a million miles away.

I turned to Dominick, amazed at how wasted I'd gotten from one mango margarita; but it all felt wonderful, so wonderful.

"Glad you could come," Dominick said, from seemingly far away.

"It's a cool party," I mumbled, my eyes half closed, my body jerking around to the music.

"Eh, it's fair. People flock to trash a place. I don't know half of them. That girl," he said, motioning to a confused waif on a couch who was staring into space with a colorful drink between her legs, "she wormed her way into my last party and wound up in my bed, but my rule with those kind of girls is they only get me one time."

"I watched your film again," I said, too eager, too excited, my face screaming to be noticed.

"Oh yeah?" Dominick asked, paying minimal attention. His eyes were on his loft. "I don't know that fucker either," he said about a guy dressed entirely in black with facial hair sculpted into paisley shapes. The guy was boasting about the movies he'd been in to an older woman who was only interested in her cell phone. "I hate that shit, like who did you come with?" he yelled, as a piece of spit flew from his lips.

"You invited me…"

"Not you, Noah. I meant that guy. Mr. Fucktwat. Who the hell are you and why are you in my house?"

"Maybe your wife knows him?"

Dominick got in my face. I could smell his breath: strong, oozing with great scotch.

"My wife? Isadora?"

Her name hung in the air, echoed off the walls. I didn't know what made me question Dominick about her, but I imagined she was beautiful. Tall and slender with a rocking body. A solid ass like two giant cantaloupes stuck together.

"Why would you bring *her* up?" Dominick asked, as if he was the only one in the world that could speak of her, his sole pleasure kept captive in a locked room at the end of the loft.

"I dunno…" I shrugged, aware that my brain was no longer working like I wanted it to.

"Let me tell you, Noah, you are so young. You think you aren't because there are kids in high school and college that seem like babies, but you are still fucking young and you know nothing."

Screw him. What did he know? A rage burned through me like I'd never experienced before. The party slowed back down to a regular speed, and everything became bathed in a harsh red hue. I blinked until it finally switched back to normal.

"That's not an insult, Noah. I was fucking young too; you'll grow out of it. You may think 'the one' waits for you out there, but a love like that will only die eventually, just like mine did."

He rubbed his chin, his eyes off in another world.

"My wife is someone I've learned to accept," he continued. "If you crave a life like mine with all of its dazzling fame and importance, someone is bound to get their greedy and conniving hooks into you along the way. It's par for the course."

As he spoke, he still kept watch over his party, growing bigger now than before. People melded together like some all-consuming organism that just wanted to feed itself sick. There was an evil energy stalking around the room that I could sense inside of myself as well, as if I could see my near future and all of its reeking glory.

"You do want this life, don't you?" Dominick asked.

"I've always lived on the edge of it."

"On the edge?" Dominick mocked. "What the fuck does that mean?"

"I grew up in the Beresford on Central Park West," I said, feeling like I had to fish for those words from an endless pond. "My parents...uh...*smoked* parties like this in their time." I swayed back and forth, my head a deflated balloon. "I've lived."

Dominick jabbed me in the chest.

"You're so serious, man. I know where you came from. You think Nevie would've ever hung out with you if you weren't on her level?"

"What level is that?" I asked, as the world slanted and then righted itself again.

"You two are exactly the same."

My stomach dropped. The back of my neck got all prickly, too.

"I'm nothing like her," I said, pissed at the thought, but deep down I was scared because I might be, tragic and peaked before I really had a chance to peak at all—a rich brat with a trust fund and an aimless future, a New York City sob story of decadence and banality like so many others.

Dominick could smell all of that on me.

"No, man, you are her," he said. "I didn't come from parents with endless money. My dad had it and lost it up his nose so we grew up in Pennsylvania in a fucking split-level, Noah, like every other average waste of breath, but that gave me a motivation that both of you lack."

He brought out his pipe and puffed. It smelled rancid and left the air around us sick with the scent of painful truths. Dominick was the type to work his damndest to make me feel small.

"Nevie dances through life," he said, and both of our eyes found her. She twisted seductively to a song in her green dress, but she was fading, riding on another pill that would dissolve once the sun found the sky again. "She's certainly a fun girl, but only because she's never had to work for anything and her life is one big party."

I was finally able to tug on the receptors of my brain again and form a semblance of words.

"I might've had a silver spoon, but I don't want that on my grave." I was sweating profusely like Nevie had been, the sweat like hot coffee dripping from my forehead. "My brother Dex will coast with his silver spoon, my little sister Cassie too, squeezing whatever they can from my parents, but I'd rather have nothing."

"Doubtful," Dominick said, dismissing my declaration with a flick of his wrist.

I reached into my back pocket, my hands sweating as much as my forehead. The story I created from *Detached* was all crumpled when I pulled it out. I smoothed out the pages lovingly and handed them to Dominick.

"What's that?" he asked, as the party grew louder and started to consume us even more: the noise, the energy, the bodies. The crowd bulged and forced us into a corner.

"It's...*Detached*."

My words traveled for what seemed like forever until they reached Dominick's ears. I waited for a response, fidgeting in place. Dominick took the pages and flipped through them, puffed on his pipe, and caught a glance from an adoring young girl on the couch, as he rocked back and forth on his heels. When he looked back at me, he seemed more together and centered than ever before.

"You did this?"

I nodded.

"Would you mind if I read this when I wasn't so fucked up?"

"Yeah. Sure."

"First thing in the morning. That's a locked promise. You can keep the key."

He dropped an imaginary key into my hand.

"I remembered something I have to do now, but color me impressed, man."

He floated away toward the swirls of people until he became lost in the burgeoning clamor. I swayed and swayed and worked to keep up my heavy head. I longed for a pillow to marry and settle down with.

Out of the corner of my eye, I saw Nevie slink over.

"What did you give him?" she asked, through a cloud of putrid smoke.

"Something," I said, trying to find her, but she was all over the place: movements and words but nothing solid. I was drifting. She giggled. "What's so funny?"

"Nothing."

She giggled some more.

"What? Tell me."

The laughs were in my face now.

"I slipped two Fast pills in your drink."

"Huh?" I said, tripping into a table.

"I wanted to get back at you for putting the Fast pill in the beer you handed me last night. I don't forget."

"I just wanna lie down."

"Go find a bedroom down the hall."

I followed where she pointed and stomped down what looked like a tunnel. People scattered to my left and right. I finally fumbled with a doorknob, opened a door, saw a bed, a glorious bed, but a bed with company. Many voices talked over each other, one of them Dominick's, and the others coming from a harem of girls: tosses of blonde hair, big breasts that jiggled and bounced, and tan bodies writhing. Something familiar had been etched into one of the girl's backs, a tattoo of a yellow circle. But then an alarm clock was launched at my face sending me out the room, away from all the bouncing fun. I was back in the hallway among the scattered people, the dim lights, the smoky conversations.

Nevie ran behind me and held me up.

"Jesus, Noah, maybe I shouldn't have given you two Fast pills. Shit, I'm sorry. Go back in that room and sleep it off."

"NO!"

Even in my inebriated state, I knew I couldn't let her see those girls with Dominick. I needed to keep him perfect in her mind. I'd just handed over an intense day of work and still required Nevie's link between

Dominick and me to last just a little longer.

"Why can't you go lie down in that room?" she asked.

"Someone...puked there."

"Oh shit, Dominick will flip. Okay, I'll take you to his and Isadora's room. No one will bother you there, and she's gone for the night."

"Thank you, Nevie," I said, falling into her arms as she dragged me down the hall. People watched and stared, whispered biting remarks, but once we reached the bedroom she tucked me in nice and tight and kissed my forehead, mumbling something about her "little frog" through it all as a dead sleep soon took over.

7

I WOKE UP ATTACHED TO A PILLOW BY A STRING OF DROOL.
A drum major had played an all-night salute in my head. The world looked
foggy—*where am I?*—but a superhuman charge coursed throughout my
body as well, a warming and consoling presence rocking me tight. From
behind me, a chair scraped against the floor. I rolled over, gave the bed
a good hump, and reached around in my boxers. Lying on my back, I
saw a woman.

She sat in front of a huge antique mirror fixing her face. Copper-hued
angels and roses fornicated together along the trim. She hadn't noticed
me yet as she swiped on lipstick with a determined glare, only settling for
the precise amount on her lips. She had wild and curly hair, seemingly the
product of an intense electrocution, something she poked and primped at
in an effort to achieve the perfect styling. A prominent strawberry shaped
birthmark splattered across her collarbone like a grape juice stain. She
finally saw me through the mirror with her piercing blue eyes. I immediately removed my hand from out of my boxers.

"I didn't mean to wake you, but you are sleeping in my bedroom,"
she said.

I couldn't tell if she was being apologetic or sarcastic.

"Oh, I'm sorry. I don't even remember getting into this bed last night."
She brushed away my apology.

"It's all right. When Dominick throws these, well, I don't even have
words for them, these soirees from hell. No, that's harsh. He likes to have
a good time. This room is usually closed, though."

"Someone slipped pills in my drink. I was put here by…"

I almost said Nevie's name. That the girl who this woman's husband
was screwing had been in her room, and afterwards maybe that same girl

had joined her husband for a romp, once he finished with his harem, of course, while this woman listened outside.

"Fucking idiots," the woman said. "Eighty percent of the people he knows are certified morons."

She sprayed perfume on her ankles, light and honey-like. I stared at her legs; she'd crossed them and I had to look. I had a morning stiffy that had been stifled by her sudden presence and was rearing to go again. Her legs were thin without looking emaciated, freshly shaved and smooth. I imagined them wrapping around my body, squeezing the circulation out of me.

"What does he call you?"

"What do you mean?"

"Dominick always gives people these collegiate nicknames."

"I don't have one yet. I just met him two days ago."

"And you're already in his wife's bed? You move fast."

She pawed at her hair, breaking up the curls, and eyed me with a predator's gaze.

"My name is Isadora. You still haven't told me yours."

"Noah Spaeth."

The corners of her mouth turned upwards, but it was not quite a smile. Later I would learn that she never smiled fully, except of course when she was stirring up trouble.

I wound up at breakfast after being invited by Isadora. She made Eggo waffles and hunted for syrup, but there was none. We sat at a table strewn with bottles of alcohol and crunched on her burnt waffles. Isadora ate hers delicately, nibbling on the edges like a mouse. I delved in, chewing through three and ready for more.

I was wearing the same clothes as last night. Isadora had offered Dominick's closet, but I refused. I pictured Dominick walking out of his harem and finding me in his clothes while I ate waffles with his wife. It all seemed too out of place.

She had turned on the small kitchen television and we watched New York 1. A newscaster who looked all of twelve reported on today's top story.

"Britta Myles here on a sad morning. The body of Katrina Wixler was found by her roommate after an apparent overdose."

A picture of Katrina Wixler at her college graduation appeared on the screen. I looked closer thinking I knew this girl, but my mind felt too clogged to really try to figure out if I did.

"According to her roommate, twenty-one-year-old Katrina, an aspiring actress who recently moved from Ohio, had been at a party downtown all night. This is the third young girl in Manhattan to overdose in a similar way this year, and if autopsy results match the other two, the drug ingested is one that doctors have not encountered until a few months ago but has picked up the street name—"

Isadora shut off the TV with the remote.

"It shouldn't be called 'the news' anymore," she said. "They should just call it 'tragedies' and be honest with us."

I tried to keep picturing the girl's face, but I was already starting to forget.

"How old are you, Noah?" she asked, tossing aside the morning paper. Thick glasses hung from the tip of her nose, a teacher ready to give a quiz. Once she removed the glasses, she became bangable again.

"I'm twenty-two," I said, waffle crumbs dribbling down my chin.

"College?"

"I graduated last year."

She seemed impressed, as if the array of artist types who usually filled up her loft had skipped out on a higher education. A twinge of jealousy reflected in her eye.

"Do you have a girlfriend?"

"Sometimes."

"And what do you want to be?"

"I want to write novels and make films. I want to be famous."

She sat back and folded her arms with a smile. "My husband is certainly a good person to know then."

"Dominick has been really cool to me."

"Has he?" she said, a little colder than before. I didn't know how to respond so I just asked the first thing that came to my mind.

"What do you do for a living?"

She sipped her coffee with a frown. Clearly I had asked the wrong question.

"I've put my own career on hold to help Dominick with his movies."

"What was the career?"

Her eyes darted around the room, seeing if anyone else was listening.

The house played with the silence by magnifying every slight sound.

"I was a writer," she said, as if it was a secret.

A creaking sound could be heard from down the hallway and then Dominick stepped into the dining area. Isadora immediately became flustered, the coffee practically spilling from her hands as she placed it down. She spread out her arms for a cold hug, and he pecked her on the cheek without ever looking in her eyes. Once he had unraveled from her embrace, she still held out her arms as if she longed for more.

"Noah?" Dominick said, surprised. He hadn't noticed me sitting on a stool by the counter. "Couldn't get enough of the party?"

All of us made a sound at that remark, something in between a laugh and a sigh. Dominick patted me on the back, but the joke was over and he waited for an answer.

"I had to crash here after someone put a pill in my drink."

"How do you know they did?"

"They told me so."

Dominick pounded the table in a fit of laughter that made him seem like a giant in a fairy tale laughing at the misfortune of all the little elves around him. The remnants of booze and sex oozed from his mouth. I remembered flashes of girls, bouncing and blonde, and an alarm clock tossed at my head. I wondered if they were still in the room waiting for his return.

"My friends are fucks, Noah. I apologize for them." He swiveled around as if he was being filmed and pulled a grapefruit from out of the refrigerator. He slit it in half and grabbed a spoon.

"Noah tells me he's interested in making films," Isadora said.

"Yes, I know. He's a writer as well."

I couldn't help but beam.

"Noah gave me a short story adaptation of *Detached*."

"And how was it?" she asked, enjoying putting him on the spot. She gave him a slick smile, which licked at the edge of her face. It turned her into a different person, a radiant woman as opposed to a brooding one.

"Well, *honey*," Dominick said, chewing on that term of endearment, "I wasn't in the right frame of mind last night to give any feedback."

"How surprising," she said, losing the smile all too quickly.

"But I can already tell that Noah has gumption. You wanted to impress me, didn't you?"

He got in my face again, something he did often, always making sure to appear a little threatening.

"Yeah, your feedback would mean a lot."

"And why is that?" he asked, unsatisfied with the amount of adulation I was giving. The guy wanted minions, followers, a trail of trumpets at the foot of his parade.

"I value your opinion," I said, practically having to cough those words out. Sucking up had never been one of my strong suits. I wanted the trumpets already tooting down the street and to fast-forward life until I reached that kind of status.

"And what about my opinion do you value?" Dominick asked, clearly stepping over into asshole territory at this point.

"*Detached* inspired me to write again," I mumbled, hating to admit my recent bout of creative blockage. "When I'm your age, I want to be exactly where you're at in life."

"Well, it's a lot of hard work."

"I'm a hard worker."

He stared into my eyes, making sure I wasn't bullshitting. I didn't even blink, the consummate poker player. Finally he stepped back, satisfied with the amount of praise.

"I'll read your writing today, and if it's got some bite to it, maybe you can help me with some storyboarding on my new film."

"That'd be awesome, I'd be willing to do anything," I said, thinking over and over that I must *appear eager, appear thankful.*

Isadora slammed her chair into the table as she got up with another groan. Her interruption didn't even faze Dominick's showboating.

"I've also been thinking of hiring a non-industry person as an assistant, just someone outside of Hollywood who hasn't fallen over to the dark side yet."

Isadora banged her plate into the sink so loud that I thought it might've broken.

"I'm getting some air," she said to no one in particular. As she left the dining area, she brushed past me and placed her hand on my arm. "You should take up Dominick's offer; I'd love to see you again."

She gazed at me as if there'd been some secret shared between us that morning. I gave a goofy nod and could've sworn I saw Dominick gritting his teeth.

Once she had left, he attacked his grapefruit.

"Did I ever tell you how I got started in this crazy business?" he asked.

I'd been watching Isadora as she disappeared down the hallway; I turned back toward Dominick at just the right time before it seemed suspicious.

"You said you were in the mail room, right?"

"You really fucking listen, don't you?"

Dominick finished the grapefruit, chucked it into the sink with a hook shot, brought out a pipe from his bathrobe pocket, and puffed a few hazy clouds. The smell was akin to the burnt waffles I'd just ingested, but I found myself licking my lips, wanting a puff as well, needing a taste. The clouds finally dissipated and my yearning subsided.

"Yeah, I started in the mail room, but it's more complicated than that," he began, ready to tell the story of his origin that he'd probably boasted about a thousand times. "I always knew I was talented, you just *know* if you got that 'it' factor. But to really make it, you have to repeat the mantra that you are the goddamn best and everyone else is just that redheaded stepchild in the way."

I had to laugh at that analogy. I imagined a redheaded stepchild blocking Dominick's path and him knocking the ginger kid to the side.

"You're laughing, but I'm serious."

"I'm serious, too, it was just the last thing you said."

"I am fucking serious, you have to be ruthless. You've probably never really been ruthless before because you're so young."

"I've been ruthless."

"Oh yeah, how? Give me a scenario."

I took a beat to get the story right.

"I wanted to break up with my girlfriend Margaret the other day. She was a stuck-up bitch, but she's in law school so I figured she'd just argue her case forever if I tried to break up with her normally. So I took her out for New England clam chowder and then made her drink ipecac syrup so she'd throw up all over herself. I made her cry big clam tears, and I knew she'd be too embarrassed to ever want to see me again."

Dominick let the pipe hang between his lips as he clapped his hands in approval, even though my example was only half true since the ipecac had been Dex's idea and when it happened, I'd felt bad, not victorious. Looking back, my initial reaction seemed weak, a trait Dominick never would've exhibited.

"Haha, Noah, I've done some similar shit with exes in my youth." His face glazed over with faraway memories of yesterdays.

"I'm sure you have."

"Fuck yeah I have."

"So how'd you get to where you are now?"

He geared up for the tale by holding up his finger as he continued his smoke, its smell now like garbage on fire. My nose twitched delightfully as pools of saliva collected around my molars.

"I don't tell this story to just anyone."

"How come?"

"It's good material, book-worthy someday, so get ready to listen."

I leaned in and told myself to act astounded at whatever the tale would be, because I knew then, even at such at early point, that I was slowly gaining access to this man's life: first with his mistress Nevie, soon with his wife Isadora, and finally weaseling my way into this guy's film until I'd find a way to wring as much as I could out of our burgeoning relationship, to use Dominick and then discard him because this man had no idea how ruthless I could be: this slightly funny, moderately genial, good-enough-looking kid who was always plotting. Soon they would all know Noah Spaeth, permanently embedded into the pop-culture dictionary.

"Here it goes," Dominick said, with his hand on my shoulder, as if we were long-time buddies.

Little did this man know who we really were to one another.

"So I was getting a twitch in my eye," Dominick began, rubbing his hands together. "Have you ever seen the movie *Joe Versus the Volcano*? It's a Tom Hanks movie with Meg Ryan playing three different characters, as if anyone ever needed three Meg Ryans. Anyway, the mail room I worked in had these killer fluorescent lights like the ones Tom Hanks had to deal with in *Joe*. They would flicker and bugs would latch onto them. My skin, look at my skin now. Tan, right? Well back then I looked like I had dysentery.

"When you work in the mail room at CAA or any of the big ones, you fucking work. You get paid sure, but it's peanuts. It's all about 'the experience' they tell you, and you hope that someday the brilliant script made from your blood, sweat, and tears winds up in the hands of someone who actually matters, even though in all likelihood you can barely cover your rent and your savings are dwindling, dwindling away.

"What you develop in this mail hell is a camaraderie because we're all fucking drained working from eight in the morning to ten at night, and we all look like we spent the last four months of our lives in a nailed-shut coffin.

"So there was this girl, this agent's assistant. She had thighs like ham hocks and a face that wasn't much better, but she was fucking good at her job. At least it allowed her to let the mail boys lick her pussy on the off chance that she'd put in a good word with her big deal boss. In L.A., a girl like her is invisible. She came out there after a fiancé had left her at the altar, and she'd turned into a forlorn, jilted mess.

"Now my biggest problem at the time was that I had no brilliant screenplay. I knew I had one in me, but I never had the time to bring it to life. My roommate at the time, Eddie Deavers, did. He stayed up every night till dawn working on his screenplay after his day job and constantly bounced the ideas off of me. Some stupid psychological drama about a husband and wife and the disintegration of their marriage. Hey, it was better than anything I had back then. So sure, I could have eaten out this ham hock like everyone else, but what would've been the point if I had nothing to show to her?

"So one day this Tara, the ham hock, she comes down in a little professional skirt that she's completely wedged into and starts flirting with me in the best way she knows how by offering up the custodial closet with the promise that 'this was my lucky day.' She says she'd been eyeing me for a while and would show her big deal boss anything I was working on if I 'made her day.' I'd honestly rather do anything than stick my tongue in that big old tuna fish, but then she starts saying that her boss was looking for a psychological drama, something that focused on a troubled marriage but with a disturbing edge, something that could garner buzz at an indie festival and possibly even wrack up a bunch of Oscars. Instantly, I think of Eddie Deavers's supposed masterpiece and yank her into the custodial closet.

"So I'm eating her out, and even back then I was a master of ceremonies at it. I can make a woman go from zero to sixty in no time flat. Anyway, once she starts getting real into it, I change tactics and finger her while talking about the entire plot Eddie Deavers had babbled to me over the last few months. She's eating up *everything*, having an orgasm because of my new hot screenplay and my jabbing middle finger.

"Weeks pass and I start wining and dining this Tara, reading Eddie Deavers's screenplay during any off time I had and realizing it was actually fucking good. One night I blow two hundred bucks on her at this trendy

L.A. restaurant, and as we're walking out, I kiss her delicately without any tongue and lie that I'm falling for her, which is something the other mail boys never did. They'd do her while talking about their scripts the entire time, each new thrust ending with a pitch, and when they'd finally be able to come, they'd toss her out of their bed with their screenplay shoved in her hands—but not me. I kissed her and pretended to love her and refused to sleep with her, saying I wanted to get to know her soul and not just her body, and she ate that shit up since no one had ever treated her like a human before.

"Finally, once I saw she was smitten, I stole Eddie Deavers's computer and his backup hard drive and took her to San Diego. She read Eddie Deavers's words on the beach, and when she was done, tears dripped down her eyes and she promised to show it to her boss after the weekend. I told her I didn't even care, that she was the only thing I needed to be happy. That night, I made a sacrifice by finally sleeping with her, fucking her every which way and knowing that I was fucking my way into a successful career. Let me tell you I came harder that night than I ever had before, spraying my come all over her, drenching her with what she thought was her brand new life.

"Sure enough, her boss fucking loved the screenplay and optioned it for an insane amount of money. The film never got made, which happens all the time, but that was even better since Eddie Deavers never found out about my theft. But the minute I got the deal I dropped her cold, didn't return her calls. Nothing. She tried to drag my name through the mud with her boss, but he was a bigger dick than me and couldn't care less. In fact, he loved it when I told him what I did to get my foot in the door because he'd done the same thing. All the big shots did, except most had to suck a lot of old dick while I just had to lick one bad puss, and even though Eddie Deavers's script never got made, her boss got me my deal for *Detached* a few years later, and the rest, as you know, is all history.

"I never really saw Tara again, but I've named my place after her like I'm Scarlett O'Fucking Hara or something, my 'Tara,' because without her none of this would've ever happened. And let me tell you, Noah, despite whatever kind of morals I lost long ago, I shit happy every single day."

"That's a really good story," I said.

"It's all truth. The best stories are usually that. Life makes for wonderful fiction."

I was staring at Dominick's apartment that looked like an art gallery: the girl with the red hair giving a never-ending absinthe toast, the lone yellow circle on a blank white canvas. This man bought class but reeked crass. He'd been a basic prostitute, but he had worked hard to get where he was, even if his first success had been something he stole, and now he went home to a bangable-as-hell wife in a magnificent SoHo loft with a truckload of girls waiting in every room and people at his disposal. He had stolen this life, and I could steal just as well as he could, probably even better, and stealthily take everything he had.

"What are you thinking about, Noah?" he asked, taking a puff from his pipe as the rank smell filtered through the room.

"I was thinking of how ham hocks could look like thighs," I said, making sure not to reveal an inkling of my true thoughts.

And then us two men, differing a little in age, laughed obnoxiously at our new friendship based on who could be the bigger asshole. At the time, neither of us realized what the other one had planned, both thinking we had the upper hand, while in reality a war was about to begin. It was Dominick who ended his laugh abruptly. He scared me when he looked my way.

"Come tomorrow to Gramercy Park. I'll be shooting on the west side of the park at nine in the morning. Be there or be a fucking square."

And with that, he tossed his chair into the table just like his wife had done before and left a trail of dense smoke flowing behind him as he shuffled out of the room. Maybe he sought Isadora down the hall, or maybe one of his harem still lingered, maybe even Nevie.

But I wouldn't stay to find out. I'd gotten what I needed out of last night's party and finished the last piece of my Eggo waffle in one savoring bite.

8

I DECIDED TO WALK ALL THE WAY HOME TO THE UPPER
West Side. I began in SoHo with the massive amounts of people along East
Broadway, and then headed over to West Broadway past art galleries and
lunching ladies yapping on cell phones at overpriced outdoor cafes. Soon
I hit the Meatpacking District and relished in its quiet, knowing how
different an animal it was during Friday and Saturday nights with everyone rushing to get into hot clubs. When eventually I hit Herald Square, I
felt oppressed by the mob of people pushing each other out of the way
as they navigated toward Macy's and the schlocky stores up 34th street.
Times Square was even worse with rubbernecking tourists snapping
pictures at the circus around them while businessmen and women were
stuck walking behind large fanny-packed fools whose kids shrieked "Oh
my God" at nothing in particular. Rockefeller Center wasn't any better.
I wanted solitude, but a treasure like that barely existed in this city. I only
found silence in Central Park, still littered with people of course, but the
only place that held moments of calm. I breathed in that wonderful
silence as my pace finally slowed, and nature delighted my senses.

When I turned out of the park, New York City's madness waited for
me again, but at least the Upper West Side seemed like suburbia compared
to the rest. I'd been rejuvenated by the park after blocks and blocks of
feeling like I was on speed, and that was why I wasn't as upset as I
normally would have been when I saw Margaret by my beautiful, castle-
like apartment building. She sat like a catcher with her ass rising an inch
above the sidewalk, wearing jeans, Puritan-style boots, a flowery blouse,
and dark sunglasses that hid her face. Her hair had been pulled so tightly
into a ponytail that I imagined she'd lost some strands to get it that taut.

At first she didn't see me, and I thought to even turn around to the paradise that Central Park offered, but it was the way she looked at the street ahead of her, hoping to finally see *me*, the importance of *me* in her life at that moment, which made me go to her.

"Hey," I said, holding out a hand to help her up.

"Your jerk-off brother wouldn't let me in. He told the doorman he didn't know who I was."

"He does that sometimes."

She took off her sunglasses and I pulled her up. We walked into the lobby as she sneered at the doorman, good old Charlie, with teeth that looked wooden but who had watched me grow up and was the kind of nice that only existed in small towns. Charlie even smiled right back at Margaret's sneer, as if he didn't know what a nasty glance was.

Inside the elevator, we rode to the top without speaking. I wanted to ride in silence forever with her, not looking forward to when the doors would open. She squinted as each floor beeped, looking as if she was about to cry, not because she really felt sad, but probably as a tactic to make me feel optimally lousy.

We finally reached the penthouse and the doors opened. I led her inside my apartment.

"Aren't you going to say anything?" she asked, after a few dull seconds. We wandered toward the kitchen. I swiped a grapefruit from the refrigerator and slit it in half as a response.

"I don't want an apology, Noah. I'm not looking for that."

"Did you get home okay?" I bit into the grapefruit to avoid focusing on her, devouring the juice until it was just a pulpy mess.

"Of course I got home. I was in a cab. What am I, inept?"

"No."

"What pisses me off, what really hurt, was that it was so easy for you to let me go," she said, much more calmly than I expected. "If you didn't want to be with me, I could have handled that. We had a year together, my life would have been fine, but what you did was so cruel. You could have acted like a man instead of a little boy."

"It's not like I planned it out. Dex brought the ipecac syrup and it just happened."

"I don't think you ever tried to get to know who I am," she said, so softly, as if she'd just realized she'd been nothing more to me than a way to pass the time.

"Margaret, we're nothing alike—"

"Screw you, get down off your high horse for two seconds. I'm not trying to get back together with you; I would rather be dragged naked through nails and mud. I don't want you and sadly I never really liked you very much at all."

"You were into me," I said, tossing the grapefruit into the sink with a hook shot.

"Did you know I was seeing other people?"

I swallowed the last chunk of grapefruit, its taste filmy and sour as it slid down my throat.

"Who were these people?"

"Just some guys since we graduated from Conn. Just once in a while to wake myself up."

"So you went to clubs and brought home guys?"

"No, I knew them. There were two. You can put down the 'whore' sign. They were both at Fordham and were both very nice and concerned."

"Concerned about what?"

"That I looked sad. I've been going through a lot. I don't want to be a lawyer, or maybe I do, but I really don't want to be in school again right now, and I was never able to talk to you about that. Your problems always took center stage, and I didn't know a lot of other people in the city so I was sad."

"I'm sorry."

"I never would've embarrassed you like you did to me. I never hated you like that."

She found something in the distance to focus on. Whatever it was, it made her pleased. Maybe she was thinking about one of those nice guys from Fordham, the way he kissed her earlobe and then whispered how the two of them would be nice together. How they could have a future of a modest house filled with two-point-five children, and that she could feel safe with him in their moderately happy existence.

"I'm ruthless," I replied.

"What?" she asked, floating away from her dreamy, average fantasy.

"I'm ruthless. That's how I need to be to get ahead."

"That's why you made me puke?" she said, crossing her arms. "Because you're ruthless?"

"If you really want to make *something* out of your life, you can't get there by being nice."

"What are you talking about?"

"I'm gonna be big one day, Margaret, and I'm gonna have to step on a lot of people to get to where I want to be. You were just that first step."

"Who are you? I look at you right now and don't recognize anything."

She swiped back on her sunglasses, clearly so I wouldn't see her cry, and stomped toward the door. She took a breath before she turned around.

"I hope you only find sadness in the end, Noah. I really, truly do."

I closed my eyes to make her go away. Sure enough, when I opened them, she was gone. I had more important things to think about anyway. Tomorrow would be my first foray into Dominick's film, and for now, I needed a nap.

It was already dark, god knows what time. The Fast pills from the night before had knocked the shit out of me in a weird, primordial way, globs of gunk attaching to my brain that refused to let go. A sharp aftertaste sat on the back of my tongue, something like melted metal and candy corn. Momentarily, I wasn't sure if Margaret had come by earlier or if it was just a dream, but then I realized that she had and I'd been able to get her out of my life for good.

I was half asleep lying on top of the sheets, still wearing my clothes as New York City swooshed outside. Light rain tapped against the windows, lulling me back to dreamland. Tomorrow I'd be on a film set. I grinned to the ceiling. Things were finally being put in motion.

Dex barreled in without knocking like he always did, fully waking me up now, adding obnoxious light to the room. He kicked my sneakers out of the way and sat on the bed.

"Dude, it's like six at night, you have to get up."

I rolled over, cursing under my breath.

"Your friend Nevie is in the other room."

I shot up, almost knocking him off the bed.

"How long has she been here?"

"Two seconds, spaz, she just got here."

"Tell her I have to shower," I said, shoving Dex out of the room and closing the door.

I did a little exuberant dance once I was alone again, and then freaked out while I decided what I was going to wear.

**

Fresh from a shower and ten minutes of grooming after finding the perfect ensemble of worn jeans and a brown collared shirt that exposed my chest hairs, I found myself spying on Nevie and Dex from down the hallway. They faced each other on the two-seat couch in the living room. Dex had a flirtatious grin tucked up by his right cheekbone and wore a shirt just like mine with his chest hairs peeking through. When he had walked into my room before, the sneaky bastard's shirt had been closed to his neck. Now he kept flipping his hair out of his eyes and laughing at every inane thing she said.

Nevie was high out of her mind, her eyes doing a little jig. She was barefoot and sipping on a drink; Dex was drinking something, too. They sipped together and laughed some more. I knew I had to break it up.

"Hey," I said, storming into the room like an army general. I wedged between the two of them on the couch so no one had any room.

"Noah," Nevie purred, placing her drink down.

"Tell him what you told me," Dex said, touching her shoulder like they were lovers.

"This deaf woman signing about the apocalypse in Union Square told me I was going to die today."

"I hate Union Square," Dex added. "When did it become the battleground for every warring religion out there?"

"She wanted money, and when I wouldn't give her any, she showed me this horrible picture of all these dead rotting bodies writhing around in some type of hell. She pointed to me, actually touched my boob with her crooked finger, to indicate that hell was my future. Well, I wasn't going to stand for that. I pointed right back at the picture of rotting bodies and then poked her in her old boob to indicate that she was the one who'd be banished to the underworld because of the apocalypse. She was so pissed, her hands were flailing around, and I know she was cursing me good."

Nevie held her rib cage and smiled at her slickness.

"Isn't that funny, Noah?"

"Yeah, it is," I said, still eyeing Dex who was staring at her legs.

"Are you still mad about the Fast?" she said, frowning.

"What? No."

"No shit, you guys have some Fast?" Dex clapped. "Gimme, gimme."

Nevie stirred her drink and sipped it casually. She patted me condescendingly on the knee. "I slipped two pills into Noah's margarita last night as a joke and ol' sourpuss obviously can't let it go. Let sleeping dogs lie, my little frog."

If I could've I would've rammed my fist into her face. It was ludicrous what this girl got away with.

"What are you doing tonight?" she asked, flinging her legs into my lap without giving me a chance to respond.

"Dominick asked me to meet him at the shoot tomorrow."

"I asked what you were doing tonight. I want to go out."

"Dude, it's not like you can sleep anymore," Dex said, speaking only to her smooth legs as he licked his lips.

"I am so into doing something," she said. "This band called The Speeds is playing downtown."

"What kind of music?" Dex asked, already inviting himself along. I gave him a *YOU ARE NOT COMING* glare.

"Hard to explain; they've got a new sound. Like each song keeps speeding up more and more until it's just relentless at the end," she beamed, fidgeting in place and suddenly becoming unsatisfied with her legs in my lap. She swiveled away as if I'd done something wrong. "The Speeds are supposed to be amazing on Fast."

"Hell yeah," Dex cheered, rubbing his hands together. "Girl, you got some Fast on you?"

"You know it," she said, tracing a circle into his back until she became lost in the motion.

"All right, I'm in," I said, and pinched Nevie on her knee, hitting her arousal point as she yelped and forgot about Dex. She looked at me with glassy eyes and tucked her head into my chest, feeling my chest hairs through her fingers.

I got my eye on you, I mouthed to Dex.

Good luck with monitoring me the whole night, Dex mouthed back, and went right for her knee as well.

The Speeds were playing at The Hall, a place I hadn't been to since high school. Back then it was awesome. Me and my friends smoking pot out of one-hitters and no one caring; using my solid fake ID to score some beers and be a hero for the night. The first time I'd been drunk and high at the same time had been at The Hall. A bunch of my buddies seeing some jam band, weaving between mazes of hippie kids pushing toward the stage, their hands in the air like a sea of benedictions, tambourines and drums skatta-kaing in an endless looped beat. I remembered thinking about how many kids had been crammed inside, how big the place felt, legs and arms twisting from the balcony as I wandered to a couch upstairs with some hippie girl, kissing the glitter off of her sweaty cheeks. I used to be so young.

Inside, the whole place immediately felt smaller. Some DJ pumped up the crowd with an annoying beat that made the place sound like a construction site. Nevie danced as Dex and I stood still, slightly bopping our heads with Amstel Lights in our fists. She moved through the crowd as dudes gawked at the way her dress hugged her thin body. She procured joints that I figured had been laced with Fast, but I didn't want to be a buzz kill so I puffed, puffed away and watched her raise her hands to the ceiling in praise, as if we were sixteen and innocent again.

The Speeds came on without warning, the sound exploding in my eardrums, making my heart shake. Normally I stood pretty still at a concert, a little too self-conscious to move like I'd really want to, but now I twisted and turned as if a wild entity rocked inside of me. Dex was trying to catch up to the beats as well, as the sound became otherworldly. His body was no longer human but a medley of elastic movements. As I danced in sync, I decided to forget about the way he'd been coming on to Nevie before. I also decided right then that I'd keep Dex close even after I became famous because that was my baby brother, and I couldn't stay mad at someone so foolish.

Nevie was steps away from us, red and green lights emanating from her body. Her body stayed in motion, but her eyes were dead. I thought of her body rotting like in the deaf preacher's prediction. The song lasted for what seemed like hours, and when it ended abruptly, she collapsed to the ground in a sweaty mess of tears. I cried as well, endlessly, until I was all dried out and she reached for my hand.

Our fingers laced together. I helped her up and she fell into my arms.

"Will you come upstairs with me? I just need...I only want to leave all of this. My head is broken."

"Yeah," I said, supporting her heavy, broken head. I tapped Dex on the shoulder. "We're going upstairs for a second."

He didn't seem to care.

She shook in my arms as I guided her up a winding staircase. She was telling me something, but it wasn't in an intelligible language. The music grew louder, faster, as we saw an empty couch on the balcony and ran to get it, pushed aside another couple darting for the same thing, but it was ours, and we smiled wide, laughing at our fortune, our couch. But her laughs died down early, way before mine were finished. She curled into a ball and rocked with her legs up to her chin. Her shoes had been thrown to the floor, lost among the dozens of teenagers jumping around us. I put my arm around her carefully, got close enough to smell her lip gloss. I had to yell in her ear to be heard.

"Are you all right?"

She shook her head. The beats became loud and pounding, the lights hot. I couldn't shake away the image of her rotting body.

"What's wrong?"

"I'm a mess," she said, as tears dripped into her lips. Her face was so pale; she resembled an upright cadaver. I hugged her immediately.

"Why?" I whispered.

"I just am. Can you hold me even tighter, so tight I can barely breathe?"

I asked if she was sure she wanted to be close to me like that. She nodded desperately, and so I pressed her damp head into my chest, hugging her in my arms. She looked up vacantly, and I imagined tasting her lips, longing for a kiss deeply, my taste buds burning. Those pouty lips were closer than they'd been in a long time, but I wouldn't go any further. I had her for now and was too afraid to lose her again. I'd remain holding her at a safe distance, love her from afar. But then her warm breath curled up from her nostrils, and she kissed my neck: a slow, indefinite kiss until a tongue slipped through that felt like a crawling slug. She shifted so she was sitting in my lap now, guiding my hands over her body, our show becoming PG-13, as she placed my hand under her dress.

"Nevie," I warned, wanting her to tell me to shut up so I could continue exploring. She guided my hands even more until she had forced me to hike up her dress. She showed her underwear to a bunch of kids who were too wrapped up in The Speeds to care.

"Touch me there, please touch me there," she moaned.

"Where?" I asked, with my tongue in her ear.

She moved my hands down to the small of her back where I saw a tattoo of a yellow circle beaming from the casting spotlights overhead. I pressed it like it was a button, and she started shaking uncontrollably, showing her fang teeth as she screamed, her cries a mixture of pleasure and pain that left me stunned. She turned into a monstrosity, writhing on top of me now, rabid, her soul floating out of her body and leaving a demonic spirit in its place. She spoke in tongues, got out her claws and left a fresh scar under my left eye, licked up the blood and let it dribble from her lips. I shrunk away and watched as her soul slid back into her body and exorcised the triggered beast that finally vanished.

She coolly lit a cigarette, unfazed by what had just occurred while I was spooked enough to get out a stake.

"What the fuck was that?" I asked.

She pulled her dress back down and covered the tattoo of a yellow circle, refusing to look at me.

"Nevie...?"

"Fuck you," she hissed, spitting out a stream of smoke.

Before I could respond, Dex clomped up the stairs and stood between us. We were sitting far apart from each other now, two strangers sharing the couch.

"What happened to you guys?" Dex asked.

"I have to use the bathroom," she said, jumping up and putting out her cigarette on a support beam before wobbling away.

"Shit," I said, with my head in my hands.

"What happened, dude? Did I say something?"

I watched her disappear down the darkness of the stairs.

"We started hooking up and then she just...I've never seen anything like that before."

"Well, go finish hooking up with her then."

"That tattoo of a yellow circle," I muttered. "When I touched it, it was like she was possessed."

I flew past Dex down the stairs after her, my eyes scanning, trained to only see Nevie, but she was gone. An ocean of smiles danced around me; I was the only one not smiling. I stood outside of the women's bathroom and waited long, empty minutes without her return, refusing to truly breathe again until I knew she was all right. A scowling girl with dyed black hair, black eye makeup, and ripped clothing nervously wandered out.

"Hey," I said, as the tortured girl looked up confused. "Is there a girl in there? She's wearing a short blue dress, no shoes on?"

"Yeah, in the stall." The girl scowled, as I pushed past her into the bathroom, covering my ears from the shrieks of teenage girls staring at me like I was a murderer. I stopped in front of a stall where two bare feet stuck out. I pushed the door open and wedged in, finally breathing again once I saw her hunched over the toilet, her long fingernail down her throat as bile came up. She knew I was there but chose not to acknowledge me yet, pushing the ends of her hair away from her face so it wouldn't get in the way of her intense vomit.

"Here," I said kindly, and held her hair in my fist. She vomited some more and nodded for me to let go. I flushed the toilet, put the lid down and sat her on it, this mess of a human. I wiped the clinging tears from her eyes and cheeks and sighed.

"Let me cool you down, Nevie."

I left the stall and brought back a moist paper towel, smearing it all over her face, wiping away her makeup and her sadness as much as I could.

"C'mon, let's go outside."

I didn't wait for an answer. I picked her up and threw her over my shoulder, walking out of the bathroom and The Hall into the crisp air. Once outside, I took off my shirt and slipped it around her.

"Thank you," she murmured, to the pavement below.

I had to ask her, the curiosity swelling inside of me like terrible heart-burn.

"What's up with that tattoo of a yellow circle on your back?"

She looked at me viciously and shook her head slowly as a warning.

"When I touched it—"

"Please leave it alone, Noah," she said, closing her eyes until they were shut tight, blocking out the world around her. She started shivering again like an epileptic; I knew I couldn't press her about the tattoo anymore. I took her in my arms and hugged her tightly until her shakes died down.

Finally she broke away and launched a finger into the air. A cab pulled up close to the curb. She mumbled her Sutton Place address into the window and slid inside with a lifeless kiss in my direction before the cab rolled away.

I watched the cab trickle down the street until it was just a yellow blur. I could've been replaying what it was like to kiss her again, or even the excitement of being on Dominick's set tomorrow, but the image of that tattooed yellow circle had been seared into my brain, and I started shivering as bad as Nevie had been, shivered all the way home.

Once I got into bed, I wrapped myself up in the comforter until I was finally able to rock myself to sleep.

9

GRAMERCY PARK ALWAYS LOOKED LIKE IT EXISTED IN A different era. Magnificent buildings surrounded the only private park in the city, with silver knight statues as guards of the apartments, or rusted brick exteriors with lone candles in each window. I pictured horse-drawn carriages clomping through its recessed streets, and women passing each other wearing corsets while clinging onto umbrellas as fashion accessories. Even the sirens on Third Avenue and down Irving Place had become muted, and I finally found the moment of peace I'd been searching for since I'd left Dominick's place last morning.

Between the two Fast pills at Dominick's party and then Nevie's Fast joint at The Hall last night, I was still a little messed up, but not hungover like I had too much to drink or in a stupid cloud like I'd smoked too much weed. Fast seemed to tickle my insides, keep me squirrely and on edge, but everything still seemed to be sharper, as if now I was seeing the world in high definition.

As I turned onto the west side, which was punctuated by five perfect brownstones, a man and a woman were squatting by the park's fence in the midst of a puddle of cigarettes. Since I was early, I leaned against the fence a few feet away from them while last night came rushing back. I'd awoken something inside of Nevie when I touched her tattoo. A part of me hoped I'd never have to witness it again, but I also wondered what caused that insane change in behavior and knew I'd try to make it happen the next time I had the chance. The whole thing was even stranger because that girl Lindsay I had hooked up with a few days back also had a similar tattoo and flipped out when I touched it. Those two instances had to be more than just a coincidence.

"It's not," the woman sitting by the fence said to the man, as she blinked suspiciously at me. She seemed to have a movie-star aura, an air of wanting to be acknowledged by strangers. Everything was said with impact, a chewing of scenery.

"Go find out," the guy said, looking up at the sky and smoking his cigarettes to the filter.

"Are you Noah?" she asked, with a slight accent, hard to place but sounding somewhat Eastern European. I nodded as she tugged the guy up to his feet and they both cat-walked over.

"I'm Estella and this is Palmer. Dominick is going to be a little late."

I couldn't tell if her accent was something she was trying to lose or trying to gain; either way it was only half working.

Palmer grabbed my hand and gave it a firm shake. He wore a sleeveless shirt and what looked like leather pants in an attempt to stall the aging process, but it made him look older. He moved with an attitude, a defiance of rules, of manners; his hands were all over Estella's ass that was plump but tight in her skinny jeans.

"We're in the scene today," Palmer said, with a blasé yawn and a fresh cig.

"I knew you were Noah," Estella said, as a trio of one pigeon and two squirrels walked around us. She made a sucking sound with her teeth as the squirrels pranced over.

"No, you don't want to do that, babe," Palmer said, chasing them away. The pigeon lingered. "They have rabies," he continued, looking over to me for support.

"Rabies? They are harmless little pets," she said, rubbing Palmer's knee. "Anyway, Dominick has been saying nice things about you, Noah. No one else has been allowed on any of the shoots."

I couldn't imagine Dominick being the type to say "nice things," but I'd never been one to ignore a compliment so I nodded as if I'd heard it all before.

"What's the scene that's being filmed today?" I asked.

"We don't know," Palmer gushed. "That's the genius of *Da Bomb*."

"Da Bomb?"

"Dominick," Palmer whined, as if everyone on God's green Earth should know his nickname. "The Bambach is a cinematic revolutionist."

Estella kept quiet while she brushed away the strands of Palmer's hair that the wind kept knocking into his eyes. She nodded on cue every five seconds and kept posing for an imaginary camera.

"None of us actors know anything," Palmer continued.

"You mean in general?" I quipped.

Palmer let out a huge guffaw and punched me in the arm.

"Funny. You're a funny kid. I mean none of us know anything about the plot; it's part of the realism that Da Bomb is searching for."

"Yeah, that still seems strange to me."

"But that's how life happens, right, baby?"

Estella pursed her lips and leaned in closer.

"Each time we shoot we are given little slips of paper," she began, and then cleared her throat and resumed speaking without any accent. "Usually it's only what a character is feeling when they wake up in the morning, or a tidbit from their past. I am supposed be from the Czech Republic. Palmer is a rock star from the city, and we've been dating for a few months. If it's a green slip of paper, we can share it with our scene partner; however, if it's a red slip, we are not to show anyone else."

"How many actors are there?"

"Who knows," Estella said. "And Dom solely films them all himself. He wants just one, pure vision."

"I think that's visionary," Palmer said, as if on cue.

After a dissertation about their respective careers, Palmer turned out to be the veteran of the two. He had gotten his start on the original *Beverly Hills 90210* and wound up focusing his energy on the theater since, which really meant that no other TV gigs had come through. Dominick had spotted him while watching an early *90210* episode where a character's mothers was on coke during a fashion show. Palmer couldn't believe when he got that call from his equally disbelieving agent.

"It was very bizarre," Palmer said, as another cigarette burned its way down. "I barely even had a full line and then all of a sudden I'm offered a lead role in a hot film, but you gotta go with your gut, and my gut told me that I was about to be catapulted into stardom."

He puffed out his gut, another defining characteristic of his creeping middle age. Estella seemed to notice and scrunched up her nose like she was changing a dirty diaper.

"I was eating at the bar at Sushi Yasuda," she boasted. "Dom was across from me. He said it was the way I dipped my raw fish into the soy sauce. It was a moment. He pictured my character right there: runway model from Czech Republic, former gymnast, hot."

They looked at me, waiting for my story of discovery. Estella extended her sharp chin, her arched eyebrows rising up on her forehead.

"Well…" she said, lapsing back again into her implacable accent.

"I just met Dominick a few days ago. He's dating my…friend."

I almost didn't know what to call Nevie. My friend? It sounded so fifth grade. How many *friends* did you think about screwing on a continual basis?

"Dominick is dating your friend?" Estella asked, a shred of jealousy visible in each word.

"Yeah, Nevie Wyeth. You know Nevie?"

"*That* girl." Her voice lowered, wallowing as if it was being dragged through puddles. "We should start some acting exercises," she said, rising up and supporting her tall frame on high-heeled sandals, her pink toes wiggling as she regained her balance. Her mouth widened and then closed with escaping ooooooohhhhhs and aaaaaahhhhhs.

I had touched a nerve. Once again Nevie was the center of attention, even without being present. Estella obviously wanted to fuck Dominick to accelerate her career like all his other girls. Even Palmer seemed pissed at the mention of Nevie, flicking the butt of his cigarette into the street like he was annoyed with the habit. Maybe he wanted to fuck Dominick to further his own career as well.

"Here's comes Da Bomb," Palmer cheered, his eyes lighting up.

Dominick appeared: smug, slicked-back hair, a bop to his walk like he owned the street. He was holding a rather large black case. He clapped Palmer on the back and kissed Estella on both cheeks.

"Noah, you've met Estella and Palmer?" he asked. "They bore the shit out of you yet?" He grinned at the brownstones. The two of them grinned wider, like they were in on the joke. As usual with Dominick, I had no clue how to respond.

"More like the other way around," I replied, knowing it'd look best to be self-deprecating.

"Take a walk around the park to get into character," Dominick barked to both Estella and Palmer. They nodded dutifully and set off.

"You don't have to cater to them, Noah," he said, once they were gone. "They are actors. They get all the glory, right, while we, the writers, the true souls of film, are left by the wayside. Let me tell you, those twats would eat my shit if I told them it tasted good. And it doesn't. And they know it. But they would eat it anyway just because I asked them to. Fucking puppets."

He put down his case and took out a camera the size of small dog.

"This baby is what makes magic, not them," he said, petting its lens.

"You don't have any other crew?"

"Why, so someone else can fuck up my ideas? I know exactly how to make this film an experience that audiences won't forget. Hollywood is bogged down right now by sequels, by the uninspired. Well, my MO is a two-hour feast for your senses. That means starting the concept of filmmaking from scratch, making it your own."

Palmer and Estella returned from their loop around the park. She got in Dominick's face, her whines echoing.

"Dominick, how much of ourselves should exist in our characters? Palmer believes that there needs to be some, but I think that's stupid and stupid. Our roles are not always extensions of ourselves."

"Is asking me that question really getting you into character right now?" Dominick asked, softly and tenderly, speaking to her as if she was a young child. I would learn later on that he only spoke like that when he was about to get really mad.

Estella chirped instead of responding, already wary of how Dominick showed his displeasure.

"In short, Estella—and I will be very short since your question bares little poignancy to what I want to accomplish today—the idea of who you truly are is all relative. You show different personalities to the different people in your life. A stranger and a lover are not treated in the same way. So in essence you are always acting, always adding a new role to your repertoire, the many faces of you." He stamped his foot as the pigeon became spooked enough to attempt flight. "Now I want you to walk slowly from one end of the street to the other as the camera glides along this lovely black wrought iron fence. You will speak without directly looking at one another like you are telling each other secrets."

"Slips?" Palmer called out, twisting around from side to side and making a lame attempt to touch his toes.

Dominick handed them both pieces of paper. Since the slips were green, Dominick allowed me to see what had been written: *She has woken up funny. Something is different. She is withdrawn. He is wondering why. He is pressing her, but not too hard because he is afraid. He knows he might not get the answer he wants to hear.*

This seemed like the start of a character's motivation, but nothing to base a whole scene on. That was the first instance that I thought

Dominick's precious film might be a scam, but I only let myself think that for a second. I had to believe that Dominick knew what he was doing, otherwise being here was just a waste of time.

Palmer and Estella perused their slips and placed themselves on the corner. Dominick gave me a passing wink as he hoisted the camera up on his shoulder.

"This is history, Noah," Dominick cooed into the lens. "Someday you'll tell your grandchildren that you were here to witness its birth."

The pigeon finally flew overhead and left a splat of green shit at our feet.

I didn't know if I should take its excrement as a symbol for the history that was being birthed that day.

10

AFTER THE SHOOT ENDED, DOMINICK INVITED ME BACK TO his loft for dinner, although I knew that dinner was just a front since Dominick probably just expected a night of being praised for his directorial efforts of the day. When we walked in, Isadora was waiting on the red couch in the living room. She looked significantly older than I remembered, but maybe it was because when you're twenty-two everyone older just seems old.

Without the clamor of a party, the loft felt empty. Dominick and I maneuvered around a few pieces of scattered furniture before settling across from Isadora who had clearly spent the night enjoying a bottle of red wine. She tilted it toward us, not entirely wanting to part with it, but acting polite because a guest was present.

"I made steak and parmesan potatoes, Noah. I hope you like that."

"Sure. Carnivore here."

She smiled at that and then faced Dominick without the smile.

"How did Noah enjoy his first day on a movie set?"

"It wasn't what I expected," I said, but she wasn't listening.

"It all went fine today," Dominick said, cringing in an odd way, which made me think more about the day. I wondered what Dominick had really accomplished. Sure the guy had filmed some things. He screamed in both actors' faces when they weren't giving him what he wanted and babied them at other times to achieve his "magic," By the end of the day, a semblance of a scene had been shot, an improvisational minute at the most, which involved a depressed Estella having relationship issues with Palmer for some reason never explained. It all seemed amateurish, but maybe I was just the amateur for thinking that.

"Were you surprised by Dominick's style?" Isadora asked. She played with her mane of hair while stealing a glance my way that made me squirm.

"I think I just expected more of a crew," I mumbled.

"Yeah, you would expect that."

I didn't know if she meant I was a moron for expecting a crew, or if Dominick was the moron for not having one. Dominick seemed to believe that she meant the latter since he squeezed his wine glass like he wanted it to shatter.

"This wine has sure hit me," she said, rising with a grin. "I'll meet you two in the dining room with the food, my excellent, wonderful dinner."

"Thank you, Is."

He groped her ass and sent her into the kitchen with a light push. She continued along, chewing on a nail and looking like she either wanted to kill him or fuck him on the spot.

The Bambachs had a long, medieval-style table built of a heavy brown wood. They sat on separate ends with me placed in between like a kid stuck in the middle of a drawn-out divorce where the parents had separated but still lived together. Few words passed between us, but the decadent ambiance of the room was enough to capture my interest: a dripping chandelier belonging in an eighteenth-century chateau, a mural on the walls with various depictions of the redheaded girl from the painting I had seen at the party the other night. In each pose, she clutched a goblet of absinthe, her teeth stained nuclear green.

I chewed on my steak, bloody raw in the center, just as I liked. The room's dim glow cast Isadora in a golden and healthy light, no longer pale like the last time I saw her. Her eyes darted from Dominick to me while an instrumental chime pumped moody music from the speakers and made her appear even sexier.

"Thank you for this meal," I said to her.

"You're welcome," Dominick responded instead, as he struggled with his piece of tough steak that looked like an old tire.

"How is your steak, darling?" she asked him, barely able to contain her laughter.

"It's fine," he grumbled. His knife scraped against the plate as the steak kept slipping out from under it.

"Is it too tough?"

"No," he said, his voice soothing like it had been when Estella asked him a dumb question during the shoot. He went to spear the steak again, but it shot right off his plate down the table.

I wanted to laugh as well and tried to imagine anything unfunny to calm me down. Unfortunately, I wound up picturing Consuela as a *Playboy* centerfold blowing a big Guatemalan kiss to the world. A small laugh slipped out. Dominick gave me a dirty look.

"There's no more steak," Isadora said, sitting back with her hands behind her head, loving every minute. "How is yours, Noah?"

I cut into my steak like I was slicing through butter, perfectly tender, greasy and great. I nodded while finishing up a mouthful and gave her a thumbs-up as she poured me another glass of red.

"Goodnight, boys," Isadora said, her hand on my shoulder. Dominick had selected some Thelonious Monk and was off in the corner by the stereo system choosing the song. He was watching both Isadora and me through the reflection in the window. From my point of view, I could see a stoplight blinking yellow and a lone car zooming through its warning light down Broadway.

Isadora let her lips linger on my forehead with a slow, deadly kiss, pressing hard against my flesh as a tooth slid through. Dominick responded by punching the buttons of his stereo system as if he was trying to tell it something urgent. Isadora ignored his behavior. Her wild hair brushed up against my face while Dominick and the yellow stoplight became completely blocked from my view. Her fingers then fondled my chest, *so brazen*, until I realized she had slipped something into my front pocket, possibly a note.

"Till later," she said to both of us, but I knew she really said it to me. A coy smile dripped across her face after leaving her mystery in my pocket. She then backed away, barely making a sound. When she had gone, I got nervous that I'd have to face Dominick alone.

"Noah, a drink?" Dominick finally asked.

I nodded, still afraid to face him. I felt him hovering behind me, as the hairs on the back of my neck rose.

"Hold on," he said, disappearing into the darkness of the adjoining kitchen. I paid attention to Thelonious Monk glittering throughout the loft, the sound clear enough to believe the guy rose from the dead to play a set right there.

On the coffee table sat a copy of today's *Post*, the headline reading: *The Fast Downfall of an Actress*. I picked it up and studied the girl on the cover, the same one who I saw on the news the other day. I remembered a similar-looking girl from Dominick's party. She'd been sitting on his couch. Dominick had remarked that she shouldn't have showed up, since he bedded her at his last party and believed that a girl like her was only worthy of having him once.

"This girl on the cover of the *Post*," I said, feeling more comfortable talking than sitting quietly. "She was at your party."

"Noah, all young girls in this city look the same," Dominick called back from the kitchen.

I thought back to the party. Suddenly the girl on the couch looked different in my memory: a larger nose, shorter hair, thinner lips. I threw the *Post* back on the coffee table with a shrug.

Dominick emerged from the darkness and moved to the music with something in his hand as an offering. I wouldn't have been surprised if it was an axe due to the way Isadora had flirted with me all night, but once he got closer, I saw a green bottle.

"Have you ever tried absinthe, Noah?"

"Can't say I have."

I studied the bottle: an archangel toasting a gargoyle with their glasses filled to the brim. Both seemed excited to enjoy the neon-green liquid.

"Absinthe is a mind-opener. 'For me my glory is a/Humble ephemeral absinthe/Drunk on the sly, with fear of treason/And if I drink it no longer/It is for good reason.' Some famous poet, right? Whoever, whoever, whoever."

He opened the bottle with a gasp. An uncharacteristic tear collected in the corner of his eye that I figured was from the dust in the air.

I was certainly curious about absinthe. I told myself that this was how real adult men spent their time. They listened to classy jazz music and opened up hundred-dollar bottles of absinthe. Even if I hadn't learned much about filmmaking that day, this would be the start of nights beyond apple bongs and dorm room kegs. I was ready for my life to become a story someone would want to hear, not only one I found enjoyable.

Dominick grabbed a slotted spoon from his bar along with some sugar cubes. He placed all the equipment on the coffee table. He put some sugar cubes on the slotted spoon and then covered a glass with the spoon. He poured the absinthe over the cubes and then did the same with the other glass.

"What you saw today was shit," he said, handing me a glass once he finished the ritual. "Hold it up for a toast, and I'll truly tell you the genius I'm planning."

I raised a shaky glass as the green liquid sloshed around.

"To drama, and action, and romance, and comedy, and sex, and death, and thrills, and mystery, to a mix of every possible evoked emotion. To limits pushed and a frontier before us with a film in the can and an irreversible friendship I'm certain will be around for a while."

Surprised by this unfounded warm toast, I clinked Dominick's glass and figured the guy didn't care about his wife's obvious flirtation. I knocked back the drink, which tasted like poison. The liquid swirled through the gaps in my teeth, dirty and criminal, but once I swallowed it I wanted more.

"Ever hear of lucid dreaming, Noah?"

I shrugged.

"What do you think of my wife?"

The abrupt question made me almost puke up what I drank. The foul absinthe hung from my uvula, swinging along like on a vine, yanking and yanking till I'd vomit. I wouldn't be foiled so early in the night and made myself swallow the bile back down.

"Never mind, Noah, fuck the wife. Lucid dreaming is the key to the ideas for my film, a way of locating the influential parts of my past that I tend to chase and chase when my head hits the pillow. It can make you alive in your dreams."

He took another sip of absinthe.

"Ah, my green fairy," he said, swirling his drink around and taking a slow sniff. "Lucid dreaming on absinthe really makes magic happen. I learned that from her."

"Who's *her*?" I asked, but Dominick had already headed down a trail toward his past. I knew he wasn't talking about Isadora or Nevie or any other girl presently in his life, but someone else, some magician he often imagined. I could've sworn I saw pools of green spilling from his eyes, but it was probably due to the glass of absinthe I'd finished. Dominick shook away those green tears and appeared again as his normal, stoic self.

"We've had a hundred years of filmmaking, and the public isn't fooled anymore by every twist and turn, but my actors will be feeling emotions they can't even control, and that is when an audience will be surprised. That is what will wake the public up because they will be seeing the reality of someone in true ecstasy or true pain on that silver screen. Wake the fuck up!" he yelled, knocking on my head with his fist.

"I am, I am," I said, not releasing how sleepy I was getting.

"You will see fear in my actors' eyes: that ice princess, Estella, and that walking basket case, Palmer. I will be the puppeteer, and when they give their Oscar speech, I will be the only one they can truly thank."

Dominick's cell beeped and he picked it up, angrily shouting a barrage of obscenities. I sat back and enjoyed a second glass of absinthe: the slow disconnect from reality. Tingles crept up my skin like tiny slugs, building houses and erecting societies, before they settled into my pores. I thought of Nevie's kiss at The Hall, which had felt like a slug too, but I didn't want to think about her now. She always seemed to emerge when I wanted my mind to be at peace.

Dominick still talked like a madman on the phone, scolding with gestures now, miming that he was going to throw the phone out of the window. I realized that he was talking to Nevie. She was yelling on the other end, and I could hear every word.

"Are those excuses?" Nevie asked.

"I never should've given you the power of my private cell number," he said.

"You don't love her. You tell me she's nothing and yet you'll never leave her."

"What I tell you is nothing."

"Do you speak of me that way to her?"

"I don't speak of you," he replied, coolly now.

He tossed his cell at me, then stood and turned up the volume of the stereo and sunk back into the couch. He kicked his bare feet up in my face and then parted them as he spoke again, a face between feet.

"You talk to her. I'm done, my friend. I was in a good mood and she destroyed it like she always does: the needy, insulting, little scared girl."

I lifted the phone to my ear, pressing it hard so Nevie wouldn't hear Dominick's slanders. She was already in hysterical tears.

"I just want to hold you tonight," she whimpered. "That's all. I just want to be able to feel something, anything."

Her voice died down as her sobs crackled through the static, hushed and longing, begging for any kind of reply from the other end, still thinking it was Dominick the whole time as she loved him with her uneasy soul. That was why I had to hang up. With one push of the button, I erased her from the room. It surprised me how easy it was to be so nasty. Dominick raised one cocky eyebrow and clapped like a fool.

"That was cruel and unusual punishment, Noah, and I loved every second of it. What do you think of me, honestly?"

"Honestly?"

"Brutally."

"I think you're an asshole," I said, the first words that came to mind. I then wished I had a rewind button in life for situations like this.

"But that is why you like me."

"Yes," I said, knowing that was what Dominick wanted to hear. "It is."

"I'll give you a warning," Dominick said, soft as ever, his teeth already stained green. "You are drinking a poison."

I licked the edge of the glass, soaking up every last bit of absinthe on my tongue.

"And when you drink poison, you can only dabble, just a small taste, nothing more."

Dominick yanked the unfinished glass out of my hand, knocked it all back, and launched it into the wall. I jumped in place. He let out a cheerful howl as the floor became littered with a thousand green-tinted reflections. He stopped cheering abruptly as he leaned in close to me, his voice more soothing than ever, his palm over my mouth.

"My wife is poison," he whispered. "Don't give her any attention. If you do more than dabble, if you fall in like I did, you'll never be able to climb back out."

He pressed harder, causing my front teeth to cut into my lip.

"Do you understand?" he asked.

I nodded as he finally let go. He then picked up his signature pipe from the side table and started puffing away. The putrid smoke clogged the room, as I tasted metal and candy corn on the back of my tongue. Despite the steak dinner, I felt hungrier than ever and clenched my teeth in anguish.

"You can look at me any way you want, Noah, but fuck you," he said. I hadn't even realized I was scowling. "I'm helping you in a lot of ways. So don't fuck it up."

I pictured Isadora alone in their king-sized bed with a candle flickering by an open window. The wind chilled her body as her fingers traveled downwards until she was moaning. Who would she be thinking of? It certainly wouldn't be Dominick.

"I'm having another shoot tomorrow," Dominick said. "I'll let you in on more of my concept then. No one else in the world knows."

"Really?"

"Yes, but I want only you to know. You take my abuse so well."

He stood up and patted me on the cheek.

"I see so much of myself in you. Look at this face before you because you'll be seeing the same one in the mirror in just ten years. You fucking cocky piece of shit."

Dominick didn't smile at his remark, and I got squirmy, thinking the pats on the cheek would soon evolve into stinging right hooks. But I took his abuse for now, even if his star had somewhat dulled over the course of the day. I'd still find a way to steal whatever I could from this man, even if it was only his wife. I had already invested too much time to come away from it all with nothing.

So I offered a hand for him to shake, and the two of us engaged in brotherly affections, a ceased fight with nods and smiles. Dominick accepted the gesture and then did a yoga stretch as he walked away. He lowered the stereo's volume until it sounded only like whispers.

"I'm going to do some lucid dreaming. Meet me tomorrow on the west side of Gramercy Park again exactly at sunset."

He grabbed the absinthe off the coffee table, cradling it like a baby. He shut off the light and danced down the dark hallway. I could barely make out any images in front of me anymore as I closed my eyes and fell into a deep and weighted sleep.

11

I AWOKE WITH A START, MY SKIN STICKING TO THE RED leather couch. Yesterday's clothes felt like a soiled armor from the amount I had sweat through the night. The absinthe had knocked me out good and was still doing its job. As I sat up, a yellow piece of paper floated from my front pocket to the floor. A vivid memory of Isadora popped into my mind, the scar from her tooth-filled kiss still burning. The note simply said: *My private phone. Do call. 917-555-9202.* I placed it back in my front pocket and promised to follow its instructions later.

From down the hallway came a strange buzzing noise, the sound growing louder as I followed its source. In a room at the end, Dominick lay in a reclining chair with two wires hooked up to his temples and large sunglasses covering his eyes. In his lap he caressed a picture of the same redheaded girl from his paintings. She had a come-hither smile that drew you in. It made me want to know who she was and why she had this hold over him.

The buzzing came from a machine Dominick was attached to, the sound static and spooky. The whole scene gave me chills. A dim light bulb swung from ceiling, the room's only light. I backed out and closed the door.

Back at home I indulged in a nap that was cut short by Cassie screaming with a gaggle of her girlfriends. I stomped into her room, which smelled like ammonia and bleach mixed together. The smell wasn't due to Consuela's fastidious cleaning, but whatever lame drug these girls had ingested that morning.

"Do you all have to scream so loud? It's so early in the morning."

"It's almost evening, slacker," Cassie said, giving me the finger.

I sniffed again at the rotten scent in the room.

"Aren't whip-its more of a junior high thing?"

"Whip-its? God, Noah, we're not white trash. All of us have the kind of money to get our hands on whatever designer drug we want."

Her four friends laughed evilly. I shut the door on them as quickly as I could.

In the kitchen, Dex was preparing a ham and Gouda sandwich over the counter. He doused it with oil and vinegar, crushed pepper, and basil before mashing it all together.

"Want some, shit brain?"

"No, I gotta get going. That film, I'm helping out again."

"Sweet, I'm gonna wait till Cassie's idiotic friends get high and horny enough. I heard one of them tell Cassie she thought I was cute. I just gotta figure out which one it was."

"Jailbait," I said, slapping my brother on the back and shuffling off.

As I crouched against the fence by Gramercy Park, I wondered if Dex had gotten with the girl who said he was cute, and thought of my own struggling libido. I toyed with my cell phone, knowing I had Isadora's number in my pocket, but it'd be taking too much of a chance to call now. Dominick was about to show up any minute and then I might as well be wearing a sticker that said: *Hello, My Name is Guilty of Something.*

Besides the kiss from Nevie, that nutbar Lindsay had been the last girl I'd done anything with. My last year with Margaret had been a waste, a series of dull missionary positions with zero exploration and maybe two blow jobs at the beginning of our relationship, something she hated to do, which she said demeaned her. So why should I have ever given her oral? She never seemed to enjoy it much anyway, always looking like she was flipping through one of her law textbooks during the whole shebang, moaning on cue every thirty or so seconds. She might as well have made a tape of her moans so she could save her breath for all the talking she insisted on doing afterwards.

I chuckled at the thought of her drenched in clams. I was finally able to be amused by the image rather than feeling bad. The sound of my laughter caught some girl's eye down the street. The girl was smoking a cigarette, regarding me with a look of pure disgust, a *why the fuck is this loser sharing the same block as me* kind of glare.

She tossed away the cigarette and swished over to me on bird legs. I pretended that I didn't even notice her by occupying myself with a blade of grass that I began slicing with my fingernail. Those bird legs knocked into one another until they were only a foot away. Then I realized this girl was that psycho Lindsay, and only then did her stares make sense.

"I know you," she said, taking off her sunglasses.

"Yeah, I'm Noah."

"I was about to say that. What are you doing here?"

"I'm waiting for something."

"Like what?"

"Like what I'm waiting for. What are you doing here?"

"I'm in a movie."

She said each word like I was nothing more than a piece of shit on the street. This girl always seemed to be pissed off at something.

"I'm here for the film, too."

"Bullshit, you just said that because I did."

"It's for Dominick Bambach. I'm sort of helping him with the creative aspect of the project. He was your boyfriend, right, the guy you got all flustered about back at that party?"

She turned away with a snarl. "I didn't get all flustered. I don't even know what you're talking about."

"When we hooked up last week–"

"We didn't hook up!"

"Listen, nutso–"

"Look, I do remember you from the party in the Flatiron area, but I love my boyfriend very much and I wouldn't cheat on him."

"That's funny because he's probably screwed about four different girls this past week."

"Gross, you are so crude."

She swiveled around, tapping her foot in a frenzy and whipping her sunglasses on so I wouldn't see the poor baby cry. And there on the small of her back was the circular yellow tattoo in all its glory. It twisted on her moist skin, not a complete circle at the moment, but more like an ellipse due to the way she was standing. I reached out to touch its mystery, as it floated between her tank top and her low rising jeans. I pushed it like it was an elevator button.

"Are you fucking crazy?" she snapped, and clocked me across the face with her fist. Then she went after me with her pocketbook. The abundance of makeup in her bag made it seem like it was filled with rocks.

"You are borderline," I said, holding out my hands in defense.

"Dominick loves me very much. He told me so, so there."

She rubbed the tattoo I had just touched. I noticed the sun began to set behind her, a yellow fireball past Park Avenue, playing hide and seek with the tall buildings. She was still yapping away, but I only focused on that setting sun and how much it resembled her tattoo.

"I've seen your tattoo before," I said.

"On who?" she asked, getting in my face. "This is *my* role, understand?"

I was about to speak of Nevie and expected a reaction similar to Estella's. It seemed as if all of Dominick's actresses were at war, each one angling to be his number one. Maybe he had marked them all with these tattoos, a symbol of his territory; maybe even Isadora had one.

"Who else had a tattoo?" she asked, sweating and struggling to light another cancer stick, a term Consuela always used when she'd catch Dex and me smoking on the terrace during high school. "Who else?" she demanded, grabbing me by the collar like a cop nabbing a crook in some old film.

I heard a clapping sound.

"I see you two have met," Dominick said, from down the street.

Lindsay let go of my collar to extend a limp palm. She plastered on the fakest smile ever.

"Wake up that hangover, Noah," Dominick ordered, once he got closer. He looked less put together than usual. His hair was loose and messy, very abnormal for him since he often used an overabundance of product. He was also wearing sweatpants and high tops, which I was surprised he even owned.

"Lindsay, please go and buy me the largest cup of coffee that Starbucks has."

He kissed her on the cheek instead of giving some cash. She responded with her own kiss that was more like a lick. Dominick waited until she had gone down the street before he spoke again.

"I did some lucid dreaming last night," he said.

"I saw you—"

"You interrupted my dreaming?" he squawked, sounding as juvenile as Cassie or one of her designer-druggie friends.

"For like a second, man. I heard buzzing. I walked in, I walked out."

"It's just that extraneous noises can affect its power."

"Yeah, sorry." I shrugged. "What was the picture that you were holding?"

"So you know Lindsay?" he asked, hearing my question but choosing not to answer.

"Yeah, I know her. How could you tell?"

"I know what's it's like to have a girl pissed off at you. I would've loved to have filmed the tiff the two of you had that explained why."

I imagined Dominick filming us in the room behind that midget door at the party. His camera poring over our bodies while the feather bed spun, I caressed her tattoo, and "Hotel California" blared.

"You do know she is an occasional lover of mine?"

"No...I didn't," I said, but my lie was weak.

"Anyway, now I know why I dreamt of you last night," he said, as if he had just realized this. He put his hand on my shoulder. We were an equal height but he kept pressing down until I became shorter.

"So you're dreaming about me?" I said, trying to keep it light.

"I mean that I was onto something last night, but then you walked in while my absinthe-soaked brain was about to reach its full potential. Now that's lost and gone forever."

"I'm sorry, Dominick. I didn't even know you were in that room."

He shook his head and pressed his hands together in the form of a prayer. His breath smelled rancid as he got in my face, like he didn't even bother with a toothbrush that morning.

"Do you appreciate a fucking thing I've done for you?"

"I...I do. You've been great to me so far," I said, bringing up this flattery from the depths of my toes. "You...you're my mentor."

"I know that." His hands rooted around in the pockets of his sweatshirt. "I just don't like to be messed with."

"I wasn't."

"How am I going to get back my dreams?" he asked, as if I knew all the answers.

"I don't know."

"They're all I have," he whispered softly, a bedtime story to a child. He said it but refused to look in my eyes, as if he was ashamed, a shell of the man I thought I knew. He placed his hand on my shoulder again, looking like he was ready to reveal all the secrets that burned inside of him. How he possibly had no idea where his film was going. How he needed a young brain like mine desperately. He opened his mouth as I waited, waited, waited to hear this beautiful truth, but then Lindsay returned with his giant coffee, and the moment had passed. But it didn't matter to me that I didn't receive verbal verification. Dominick had been exposed, and he was no longer infallible. A dint in his armor had been discovered; the lucid dreams a necessity for a film that was all bits and pieces.

I knew right then that I could have all the great ideas this film needed and eventually take it as my own.

12

LINDSAY WAS HARDLY AN ACTRESS. EVERY WORD AND emotion was overdramatic. She was basically just acting like herself. She fought Dominick's direction, whining at the slips of paper, complaining that she wasn't being guided well enough. Dominick sucked on his pipe and gritted his teeth and tried to save as much face as possible in front of me. The power had shifted between us and would never be the same again.

Her scene called for a breakdown. Dominick had slipped her a red piece of paper as he caressed the small of her back, touching that tattoo of a yellow circle like he was rubbing something into it. Afterwards she appeared different, still a terrible actress, but possessed now, just like Nevie had been back at The Hall. Once she broke away from his touch, she was supposed to walk down the street, and her high heel should give out. This would cause her to collapse, literally and figuratively, a mental breakdown with the broken high heel as the catalyst. In this collapse, she was supposed to see all of her troubles and stand up as a new woman; but all Lindsay the actress could muster was a hot mess of a performance.

"Collapse!" Dominick yelled, calling cut after the tenth take. She had fallen to the sidewalk each time but had not achieved the mental collapse he wanted.

"I don't understand," she said, remaining on the ground, touching the pavement as if held all the answers.

"Collapse! Collapse! Motherfucking collapse!" he thundered, beating his chest in agony.

"But I don't understand my motivation. In college when I was Aggie in *Dancing at Lughnasa*, the director always gave me a motivation—"

"Understand that you were in a fucking college play and this is the real deal. You need to search within to find this collapse."

"But the slip of paper you gave me only says, *You're responsible.* What does that mean?"

He silenced her rather suddenly by clamping his hand over her mouth. "I gave *you* a red slip. That is only for *you* to see."

"But there are no other actors around," she mumbled, through his palm. He finally let go and she looked scared.

"Don't question my direction. The red slips are only for you. That is essential. If I told you the entire plot, I would see false acting. You'd be trying to get into a character, fucking Aggie from *Dancing at Lughnasa*! What I want are Lindsay's real emotions ingested into this character, don't you see?"

He was practically begging at this point, his voice gone soft. He picked up his camera again, his security blanket, and held it in his quivering hands.

"I'm trying, Dominick. I am. I just don't know what you mean."

Dominick looked at me, as if I could explain, but I was just as lost as Lindsay. I thought of past conversations, times when he might not have guarded himself so closely. Days ago when I first met him at The Penny, he had said, "I have at least twenty industry fuckers wanting to take a peek at my new film, but fuck them, they have no soul." At the time, I'd taken a response like that as an admission of Dominick's indie cred, his inability to cater to a Hollywood system, but now I realized that he didn't want those "industry fuckers" to see anything because there was nothing to show.

"Collapse!" I heard him yell again, as he pushed Lindsay to the ground. He stood over her, the camera's lens practically knocking her in the face. "Is it that difficult?"

Lindsay complained about hurting her tailbone, but she started rubbing the tattoo instead, as if it could soothe her, as if it could guide her. She was crying now in a way that made me queasy.

"I'm done with shooting you," Dominick said. "Nevie has a scene coming up, even though she's over an hour late. In fifteen minutes I'm calling it a day."

Lindsay curled into a ball, her face flush against the pavement. Because of her heavy eye makeup, her tears made tiny black puddles. She began rubbing the tattoo harder with a weird masturbatory gaze. When her touch didn't elicit the feelings she craved, she gave up, exhausted, and reached out a hand toward me.

"Don't help her up," Dominick said. "She's done."

He shut off the camera and began to pack it away. As he hunched over, he seemed smaller than usual, defeated.

Lindsay finally got to her feet, pushing past me like an annoying gust of wind.

"I could do Nevie's scene," she said, pulling at Dominick's sleeve. A ball of snot hung from her nose that she sniffed back.

"I don't think you're capable," he said, focusing on putting away the camera.

"Well, I'm here. Where is she?"

She caressed his arm like I imagined she had desperately done before, forever wondering why she'd always be second to Nevie.

"The scene calls for a car crash," he said, robotically. "You get in the car, you crash the car."

He nodded toward a beat-up sedan parked on the corner and then handed her a slip of red paper.

"This is your redemption, Lindsay. If I like what I see, I'll keep it in the final cut. Airbags are all ready to be deployed; you just need to floor it right into that stoplight up the block."

She took the red slip in her hand and wiped away any rogue tears.

"I want you to put everything you have into this take because you will only get one. I want to see the fear in your eyes as you slam on the gas. Do you understand me?"

"Yes," she said, her hand starting to shake as she stared at the red slip.

"Now go mentally prepare while I set up the shot."

"Yes," she said, barely above a peep. She backed away and headed over toward the park's gates, her eyes refusing to look up from the red slip.

"You don't have to hang around for this," Dominick said to me, while he picked up his camera again.

"It's cool."

"She didn't understand what I was trying to accomplish before," he said, slowly regaining a shred of the old Dominick, confident again in his stubbornness. "This will be her last shot."

"It's your vision."

I could've made him feel even worse right then, but there was no need to rub in any salt when it'd be smarter to placate. Sure, maybe I could've gotten a shred of self-fulfillment from seeing a blowhard like him weakened, but then what would I do the next day without his film? It'd be better to join forces for now, make the guy think that we were partners rather than adversaries.

"Listen, Dominick," I said, placing my hand on his shoulder and witnessing a reversal of roles while I stood tall and proud and he became momentarily subservient. "If there are loose ends, if there are parts you still need to figure out, I can help you. I know in your mind that the entire foundation of the film is laid out and it clicks."

"Of course it fucking does."

"Look, tomorrow break down the whole plot for me, piece by piece: the red slips, the green slips, each character's motivations. It may all make sense in your head, but something is getting lost in the translation, and I want to fix that. You haven't even told me the name of the film. Do you know it?"

"It's called *Slow Down*."

"*Slow Down*," I replied, rolling it around my tongue like a sucking candy.

Dominick rose to his feet and patted me on the cheek with a soft, light slap, a splashing of cologne, and then a hard *smack* like we'd been sparring. I staggered in place, my cheek stinging like alcohol on an open sore. With one slap, he erased whatever smug, bullshit grin of fleeting superiority I had, but he didn't relish in my defeat. He hit me and it was done, a simple reminder of who we were to one another. I was still young and immature, and he would never stoop so low as to take advice. He would rather see himself dead.

"What the hell was that for?" I yelled, tasting blood on my lower lip.

"You were lecturing me."

"I was helping you!"

I almost said that I felt sorry for the guy, but wisely didn't go there.

"Helping me?" Dominick asked, to the empty street in a comical fashion.

"Yeah, helping you. That's fucking all, Dominick."

He lunged at me. I stepped back and held up my hands in defense.

"I will tell you what I choose to about *Slow Down*. Don't ever think that you are special and not replaceable."

I was about to yell to the world all the reasons he was a big, smirking fraud who treated everyone like dirt because that was what he actually thought about himself, but I remained silent. I'd let Dominick think he maintained control but not for much longer. The slap made me angry enough to make him bleed.

"Don't feel sorry for me because I had a crummy day with an actress. Maybe I wanted that to happen to further her character, maybe I wanted her to get into the state she's in for this surprise scene she's about to film. Do not ever assume that I don't have the complete upper hand in every single situation related to *Slow Down*. And do not ever give me that smug, fucking grin and think you are better than me because I will eat you alive in the time it takes you to blink."

He was spitting in my face now, sweating and imposing, but broken, and I saw that all too clearly. So I took his abuse and pushed it down into my insides, tucked it around my pancreas where it would stay hidden for a while. I would seek retribution later by bringing out the truth and destroying him when I was ready. I knew that in war it was always better to be stealth and cunning rather than reactive.

I am Jack's smirking revenge, I thought, harkening back to my *Fight Club* idolization. *Oh, yes.*

"Now step aside and prepare to be astounded," he said, pushing past me.

By the time the scene was ready to film, night had descended on Gramercy Park. Dominick had already gotten a city ordinance to block off the street for the car crash. He positioned himself to shoot the car from the back while I was given a smaller camera and had been situated by the stoplight to film Lindsay's expression at the moment of impact. A few onlookers mingled around, but Gramercy Park was the type of neighborhood used to film shoots and most people just walked past as if it was no big deal.

In the car, Lindsay was having difficulty catching her breath. Dominick had berated her even more to get those tears flowing again, and now she looked deranged. Before turning the camera on, he gave her a tiny jar filled with thick yellow liquid. From where I squatted, it seemed as if she was rubbing it into her skin, but I had to squint to make out anything clearly. I turned on the small camera.

"Action!" Dominick yelled, retreating from the car.

Through the lens, I watched Lindsay struggling to light a cigarette before giving up and chucking it out of the window along with a stream of curses. Her foot found the gas pedal, and the car screeched down the street. As it built up speed, I felt a nerve pinch in my neck when I twisted my head. She flew toward me, eyes bulging, a smiling scream bellowing from the sunroof as she plunged into the stoplight, her head snapping against the steering wheel, no airbag deploying.

I zoomed in on her face: eyes still clamped open in shock, a line of blood dripping from her smile. I nearly fumbled the camera but made sure to keep it steady. She sucked in a huff of air, but no breath came out. I shut off the camera and swung open the car door as she tumbled out like a broken doll. The red slip fell from her fist, which I bent down to read.

This is the scene where you will die, it said.

I stuffed the slip in my pocket as Dominick ran over.

"Did you get the shot? Did you get the shot?" I heard, although it sounded like it was being shouted through an intercom. I bent down closer to Lindsay to see if she was still breathing.

"She's hurt," I yelled, but it came out as nothing more than a hoarse gasp.

Dominick finally reached us. He yanked the camera out of my hands.

"Oh shit," he said, tapping Lindsay with his foot. She barely moved. People were starting to crowd around.

"I'll deal with the police," Dominick said, pushing me away.

I didn't budge.

"Noah, go! Go!"

I slithered through the crowd of onlookers, telling myself over and over that Dominick hadn't planned for this to happen all along. I had a crazy image of him cackling while removing the airbags from the sedan.

Before turning up toward Park Avenue, I looked back one last time. Dominick had crouched over her with tears flushing down his cheeks, putting on a show. Lindsay's mouth still slightly smiled, as if pleasing her brilliant director was all that mattered, wholly content that even if she died from the scene today, she'd just given the performance of her life.

13

"HELLO?"

The voice oozed from my cell, luminous and seductive. I heard the sucking sound of a cigarette. Earlier I had reached into my pocket to take out the red slip that eerily foretold Lindsay's fate, but grabbed the number that Isadora had given me instead. Now I pictured her naked on a chair in her bedroom blowing smoke rings out of the window toward the same moon I looked at. The anger I felt toward Dominick was turning into desire for his wife. At this point, there was no use worrying about Lindsay since there wasn't anything I could do to help her. And besides, what kind of moron agrees to drive headfirst into a stoplight?

"Hello?" the voice asked again, this time with less patience.

Act cool, be confident, show maturity. This is a woman, not a girl like you're used to.

"Isadora," I said, the syllables coming from the back of my throat.

"Yes. Hello. Again."

"It's Noah Spaeth."

I sounded like a forty-year old with a wife, two kids, and a stressful job in investment banking. I had to tone it down a bit but keep the collegiate bullshit to a minimum.

"You must have finished your shoot with Dom."

"Yeah. Just ended."

"And then you called me right after? I'm touched."

"CouldIbuyyoudinner?" I spewed, the words jumbled and full of nerves. She laughed instead of answering. "I was just hungry. I thought you'd might like to join me."

"All right, slow down, cowboy. How about Billie's at eight? You know Billie's?"

"Sure, sure."

I'd check it on my cell immediately.

"Great, Noah, I'll see you there. And dress nice."

"Okay, no sneakers?"

I looked down at my Pumas, but she hung up before I could say anymore.

I didn't have time to go home before meeting Isadora. Billie's was on 22nd between Fifth and Sixth Avenue, a few blocks from where we had been shooting. I would've literally had to pass Billie's to get the 1 train to fly uptown, simply just to change from sneakers to shoes. So I stopped at a Kenneth Cole, bought a button-down blue shirt that matched my eyes (something I'd worn on dates in the past, which always seemed to ensure a hook-up), some gray corduroy trousers, and nice black shoes. I tossed out my old wardrobe in the garbage and stopped into a Sephora to bathe in some cologne.

I didn't know exactly what I was expecting with Isadora. From what I'd seen, she was pretty much as bipolar as Dominick, but I found myself wanting her even more than Nevie right now.

Upon entering Billie's, I was greeted by an old school jazz decor that was unfortunately eclipsed by a blaring R & B soundtrack that made it seem like a gay disco. A black hostess swished to the beat and brought me to a table alone. Isadora was late, probably on purpose to make me wait, make me want her more. I looked around at the dim lights and red velvet curtains, the black marbled floors bathed in a golden glow. I thought of Billie Holliday, the restaurant's namesake, shooting up at a table beside me, but a trio of Jersey girls with big hair and loud conversations sat there instead. A waiter came by and I made a request.

"Do you have any jazz?"

"You don't like the music?" the waiter cried, flamboyant as ever with a lavender scarf for a headdress.

"It's not that." I ran my fingers across the table like it was a piano. "The lady I'm entertaining. She likes jazz."

I stopped playing the imaginary piano and slid a twenty from my wallet. The waiter kept bopping his head to the music.

"What kind?" the waiter asked, snatching the twenty and slipping it down his shirt as if he was a showgirl.

"I'll give you another twenty if you have Thelonious Monk."

"Honey, you give me another twenty, I'll go home and get you your Monk," the waiter said. "Give me ten minutes. I live right on the block."

"Thank you."

I didn't know what kind of game I was playing by requesting Dominick's favorite musician. But when I imagined him seducing Isadora to the same beats, I was certain I could do it better.

It took Isadora another twenty minutes before she showed up. I was dipping bread in pesto oil when she walked in with a dark red skirt wrapping around her legs, her toenails matching the color of the skirt. I rose as we met, gently clasping her hand and planting a kiss on each cheek. I tasted her perfume, sweet like the beach, and we fell into our chairs.

"I hope I haven't kept you too long, Noah."

"No, not at all."

The waiter finally returned and replaced the club beats with Monk, the music bouncy and jaunty, like if a saxophone and a piano were having a dream together. We ordered a bottle of wine and let ourselves fall into our own dream-like rhythms.

"Why did you call me when you did?" she asked, plunking a piece of bread into the green aioli. She placed it between her small lips and slowly crunched.

"You left a note in my pocket."

"I know that, but you took a day to call, so what made you decide to do it when you did?"

"I waited till Dominick wasn't around me anymore."

She lowered her eyes.

"Well, I didn't wait. I get what I want."

My neck got hot as she attacked another piece of bread, her small incisors nibbling away. "You look very nice, by the way...." she said.

"Oh you too, definitely, you look amazing. I didn't say it before, but I was blown away when you walked in—"

"Bring it down a notch, Noah, you don't need to try so hard."

The waiter came over and poured glasses of red wine. Once he left, Isadora's eyes glanced up toward the speakers.

"Monk," she said, as the notes glittered.

"Yeah, I think so."

"I love Monk," she said, and stared into my eyes.

"Me too."

"How was the shoot today?"

"I'm going to be honest."

"Please do, and I would know if you weren't."

"It was a mess."

"As opposed to any other day? Did I say that out loud? Tell me what made it a mess."

"I don't know if it's my place to say anything."

"You don't ever need to hesitate with me."

She touched my hand and my neck got hot again. "Whose feelings are you trying to spare, Noah?"

"No one's."

"Well then, be a little more candid in life."

"Fine. I don't think Dominick has any clue what his film is about. I think it's all a façade."

"That's a bold statement."

"He didn't give the actress today any direction. She was lost and therefore the whole day was lost. And then the airbags didn't deploy in the car when she crashed it for a shot. She was taken to the hospital. It was completely irresponsible."

"Dominick thrives on irresponsibility. He thinks it's so *nouveau*, so *avant-garde*."

"She fell out of the car all bloody..."

"Have you seen *Detached*?"

"Yeah. I...wrote the story based on it that I gave to Dominick–"

"Watch it again, it'll tell you everything you need to know about my husband and me."

"What do you mean?"

"He was able to make such a great film that time because the majority of it was inspired by what really happened, and also he had me to—"

"What do you mean? What did you do for *Detached*?"

"I'm not going to spell it out. I've said too much already."

"But—"

"Change the subject. Now. Quickly."

We sipped wine and sat in silence. She seemed sad. Why was everyone always sad around me? She spun the wine glass between her fingers, getting lost in the swirl.

"I hate the quiet," she said.

"I need sirens outside of my window to sleep at night," I joked, trying

121

to lighten the conversation.

"We are the old city, Noah. We knew New York when it wasn't so pretty to look at. When it had a character and mystique. I grew up on Essex Street as a little girl with parents who came from Poland and look at me now."

"Do you miss that New York?"

"I suppose. Isn't that what life is, dealing with the present by missing parts of the past less and less? But I would love to be your age again."

"It wasn't that long ago."

"You'd be surprised how much a decade can change you. I used to laugh every day, at least once, and I'm talking a real laugh, the kind where something pops inside of you. I can barely remember that feeling."

Tears glittered in her eyes, but she wouldn't let them fall. She wouldn't appear helpless. She was more like Dominick than she knew.

"What do you want out of life?" I asked.

"It's so complicated."

The tears were gone, a false smile had erased them and they became part of the past.

"Doesn't have to be."

"What if someone took your dreams and made them their own?"

"I wouldn't let that happen."

"Easier said than done. Before I knew it, it was too late."

We finished our glasses of wine. The song had ended as well. Enough of Monk. That was all forty bucks got me, but the waiter kept some jazz on. It was Coltrane, or at least sounded like Coltrane, more mournful and fitting to our date. Isadora and I would never idly bounce along. The music we'd make would hit like rain on a tin roof: staccato, terse, soul piercing, an affair that threw water in your face and didn't hand you a towel. I could feel our future in my hardening dick.

"What were your dreams?" I asked.

"I was a writer—just like you. I created *Detached*."

"What do you mean?"

She leaned in closer, her mouth furious.

"It was mine, all mine. Parts were from our life, yes, but that movie was my vision, my script."

This was just what I needed to hear. The bitter wife admitting to the sourness of not only her relationship with Dominick, but the truth about him as well: that he was a walking fraud, a lucky son of a bitch who balked at everything unreal in art when, in reality, he was the fakest of them all, an incompetent phony, a spurious schemer.

"That's why it's taken him so long to make another film, right?"

"I refused to write anymore. I gave it up to fuck him over. He has ideas, but they'll never congeal."

The waiter came by and we ordered food, tucking the napkins in our laps and toasting our second glass, toasting this new revelation. I wanted to push aside the table and take her right there. It had probably been eons since she and Dominick actually made love, which was exactly what I decided I would do, delicately like I'd never done before. Isadora would be that girl, that *woman* whom I'd compare all the rest to, even though our days together would never be just memories. She'd be the experience that would change my very core.

My cell rang, loud and obnoxious, destroying my beautiful thoughts of Isadora. Even she frowned at whoever it was. I hoped for anyone on the other line but Dominick.

"Hello."

No answer, just a static buzz. I didn't recognize the number, a 212 area code, which meant it was a landline. It had to be Dominick. After he dealt with whatever happened to Lindsay, he probably figured out that I was trying to seduce his wife. And now he was gonna kill me. I wouldn't be able to sleep tonight, not unless it was with Isadora holding me tight.

"Hello," I said again, as a flood of nausea washed over me. "Who is this?"

But now the static buzz was accompanied by cries from the other end. Sniffles and inaudible moans. A girl. It was definitely a girl.

"Who...?"

"Noah?" the voice said, between heavy breaths.

It was Nevie.

"Fuck!" she screamed, on the other end. I pressed the cell against my ear so Isadora wouldn't hear, even though the sound shot through my eardrums.

"Noah, I'm so messed up right now," she said.

"Why?"

Go away, Nevie. You mess. Clean up yourself.

"Holy shit, I'm ooooooooohhhhh, aaaaaahhhhhhhh. I took so much Fast, and I knew I was taking so much, but I wanted to take so much so

I did."

I held up a finger to Isadora, telling her to wait a moment. She rolled her eyes in disgust.

"Just go to bed," I whispered.

"Dom sent me a text that this other actress got into a car accident because of me, because I never showed up today. I didn't even remember having a call. How is that my fault?"

"I know. I saw it happen."

"My heart is running a marathon," she screeched.

"Just take a cold shower."

"Goddamn you! Come and see me, Noah. I need you."

"I can't."

"What are you doing? You are not doing anything. You need to come to me before it's too late."

"Don't be dramatic."

"I am being realistic. You loved me before, well come and love me now, okay, when everything isn't so picture-perfect."

I was tempted to just hang up.

"I can't right now. I'll call you."

"NO! Because you won't call. Because no one ever calls. I'm tired of broken promises, they're breaking me. Why does everyone want to hurt me?"

"I don't know."

"Noah, it would be so great. I have so much Fast, we could writhe with one another. I know you've always wanted to suck my great tits. I want you, I need you, I love you, and I always have. Please come and show me I'm worth something before I swallow so much Fast I'll choke."

"Go to bed. You will be fine. I have to go."

"So do I," she said, mournful enough to give me the worst chills ever. I hung up on her quick and threw the cell on the table. Then I picked it up and shut it down completely as it gave one last dying buzz.

"I'm sorry, Isadora."

"Messed up friend?"

"You could say that."

Isadora shifted in her seat and gave me a view of her white breasts, not too big but firm and wonderful enough to allow me to forget about Nevie.

"Let's skip dinner," she said, tossing back her glass of wine.

There it was, that devious smile of hers, the only kind of smile she had that rang true.

It was easy not to think about Nevie with Isadora's arm wrapped around my own as the two of us plunged down Fifth Avenue to get a cab at the corner. The night was cool and she had put on a cashmere sweater, buttoned at the top, her fingers frozen against mine, but I felt warm. We spoke like foolish drunks to one another, unfinished sentences and choruses of laughter. I was pleased to just gaze into her eyes like a lovelorn teenager. If she told me to run away with her, I might've just said yes.

"Shit," she hissed.

"What is it?" I asked, nuzzling her mane of hair, glad to get lost inside of it and never have to find my way out again.

"It's that bitch actress Estella. She's up the block."

"What should we—"

She answered by throwing me up against a wall and shoving her tongue in my mouth. I grabbed her by the back of the head and tasted her wine breath as Estella runway-walked past us, not paying any attention to the two lovers finding one another.

I spied the tattoo of a yellow circle on the small of Estella's back. It seemed to ignite an increasing passion inside of me.

"Is she gone?" Isadora asked, breathless, but I didn't answer. I sucked at her neck and fondled her breast. "Good," she said, pushing me away.

I fondled the air for the next few seconds before I realized she was gone, already stomping down the street. I caught up with her.

"Wow," I said, hugging her at the waist.

"Calm down, Noah. I did what I had to do to save both our asses."

I wanted her to save my ass again and again, for it to be her job, ass-saver of America. Maybe it was the wine, *hell yeah* it was definitely the wine, but I was feeling bold; I could still taste her grapey tongue when I asked, "You want to come back home with me? I'll show you my place."

She stiffened in my arms. She arched her chin to the black sky and looked fondly at the moon.

"No. I want to go back to mine."

No planning. No decisions. I loved this new, uninhibited life of instant choices. My characters were gone, too. Goodbye, Nina. It was time to take a break from worrying about my fiction. Sure my brain had turned to mush, but a great mush, a life experience kind of mush, actually living instead of just writing. My brain only plotted now: how to get Isadora into bed, how to usurp Dominick. If I was more aware and less horny, I would've realized that I was about to enter his loft and he could very well be home, but that never occurred to me. All I thought about was the way that Isadora's little skirt tugged on the end of her ass like a fruit wrapped in cellophane.

"No lights," Isadora said, as she put the key in the lock and opened the door. She took my hand and led me into the dark loft. A buzzing noise came from Dominick's lucid dreaming room.

When we reached the bedroom, Isadora quietly closed the door behind her, locked it, and then opened the blinds to let in the moonlight. She took off her high heels and massaged her feet.

"I hate wearing heels. I hate dress up. When I was little it was all I wanted to do. Now I would kill to run barefoot through mud every day."

I sat next to her on the bed and made a gesture to rub her feet, but she didn't respond.

"What the hell am I doing?" she said. "I'm going to have a cigarette, that's what I'm doing." She lit a ladies' cigarette.

I inched closer to her, my lips ready for a kiss, but she pushed me away.

"I'm not done with my cigarette," she said to the moon outside the window, widening her eyes with each forceful suck.

I leaned back against a pillow, took my new shoes off, and threw them across the room. She didn't seem pleased and cringed with each bounce. I said sorry but only in my mind. I said it with my eyes to her.

"He fucks all those girls because he still wants to be fucking her," she said, bored with everything. "Even after all these years since she's been gone."

"Who?"

"He knows I know, but I guess that only makes it worse. Don't answer that, let's pretend it doesn't make it worse, let's pretend it makes it better."

She put out her cigarette and eased into the crease of the bed next to me, her pale arms leaden at her side, her breaths drawn out, and once again, sad.

"Why are you here?" she asked.

"I like you."

"I'm not asking why you're here tonight, Noah. I want to know why you've come into our lives."

"I dunno." I traveled down the curve of her body with my palm. She shivered. "I want what Dominick has."

"And what is that?"

"You."

I scooped up her freezing hand and played with her fingers until our digits danced together. I had distracted her enough to plant a long, smooth kiss on her open mouth. She gave no response, her mouth hanging open like a halfwit as I circled my tongue around her own. Finally, I flipped her over and yanked off that skirt, pushed up her blouse to reveal the small of her back.

But there was no tattoo of a yellow circle.

Just her naked, white skin.

"I thought you'd have a tattoo as well," I whispered, into her ear.

"No," she said, welling up and then wiping away the evidence of her melancholy. "I don't get to be Astrid like all the rest."

Astrid?

The name sounded so familiar, but my soaked brain couldn't locate it from my memory bank.

"I want to go to bed, Noah. Good night."

She turned away from me, hugging the pillow for life support and was snoring in a matter of seconds.

I lay back and stared at the ceiling, murmuring the name Astrid over and over until I finally realized who she was.

14

MY CELL WOKE ME UP. REMNANTS OF MY DREAM, A FUZZY re-creation of Dominick's film *Detached*—check that, Isadora's film *Detached*—lost all shape and contour. I had dreamt of Dominick's Astrid, an amalgam of the redheaded girl from the paintings and my own fantastical goddess. She shared goblets of absinthe while I sucked on her tattoo of a yellow circle, the very one that Dominick had duplicated on his girls, but never the woman he chose to share his life with.

My cell cried out again. It was way into morning. The blinds had been left up and an annoying sun was pouring in as I slid out of Isadora's embrace and leaped over to silence the ringing.

"Hello?" I belched.

"Noah!"

It was Dominick. Certainly not the best way to wake up. The screwed-up-ness of the situation became even clearer: the kiss I stole last night from this man's unhappy wife, his side of the bed that I'd taken as my own.

"Hey, what's up?" I said, and then started talking too much until he cut me off. Any type of cool I tried to maintain was useless at this point.

"Listen, Noah, do you know where Nevie is?"

Nevie? What the hell did anything have to do with Nevie?

"She didn't show up again for her call today, and it's an important one. She's not answering her cell or her landline either."

The conversation I had with her last night slowly came back. It knocked down the wall that the wine had erected in my brain. I pictured her unplugging the phone before all the Fast carried her off into a deep, dead sleep.

"I've got a whole street blocked off for her scene. So listen, you go over to her house and wake her the fuck up. She is hanging by a thread

128

with me, and if she doesn't show up today, I'll fucking replace her. Do this first, go to my loft and grab my camera; I want you to film her. Isadora should be there to let you in. I want it all, whatever state that girl is in, just something that I can edit in with what I'm shooting today. And call me when you've found her."

Click.

I placed the phone down and put on my pants. Goddamn Nevie. I just wanted to lie in bed all day and spoon with Isadora.

"I have to go," I said, to her.

"So go," she murmured, her face buried in the pillow.

"I had a lot of fun last night."

"Hmmm. Was that Dominick?"

She rolled over, her makeup smeared like someone shot her with a paint sprayer. Her hair looked crazy, the outrageous curls reaching out for me as I sat down on the edge of the bed. *Welcome to the morning,* the hair seemed to say. *A thirty-something woman looks a lot different at first light than any of the babies you've been with.*

"I have to go do something for him," I said, inching away.

"Did you tell him about us?"

"*What?*"

"I'm kidding. Hand me a cigarette."

I slid one between her fingers. She lit it and sucked at the morning, smelling like old lipstick and last night's perfume.

"So yeah, it was fun, Noah. Great times. I'll see you when I see you."

The smoke coming out of her mouth reeked with sarcasm.

"I was being serious."

"Well, I was being drunk last night. Go figure. I mean, you're twenty-two, all you know is shit."

"Shit? What the...? I know a lot of *shit*, lady."

I got all fired up with a finger in her face. I would show her that despite our age difference, I could be someone she thought about when life seemed less than stellar: a secret affair, an unexpected tingle.

"You don't have to treat me like a child, Isadora."

She yawned and cupped her hand over her mouth. "Well, when was the last time you were kissed like I kissed you. Huh?"

She touched her tongue to the top of her lip, curled the sheets around her like a toga, and stood. Her breasts bobbed out of the sheets, mad at my accusations. She flicked her lit cigarette at my face. I closed my eyes as the butt tapped against my skin, a second of searing pain before it fell to the floor. I quickly stepped on it. When I looked up, she had already slammed the bathroom door and then turned on the shower at full force. I put on my shoes, grabbed one of Dominick's cameras, and left.

Five minutes later, I found myself incredibly turned on by Isadora's coldness, her indifference. Running to catch a train to shoot me uptown, I thought of her finishing her shower and drying her curly hair in front of the mirror. Maybe she decided to touch herself a little, imagining us together, getting aroused from our recent heated fight. Maybe she acted the way she did because she didn't want to let me see how much I'd affected her. I'd call her later and tell her that she'd been on my mind all day.

And now I had to deal with Nevie. Rescue her from her depression. She always had a personality like the drug Fast: up one minute and down the next. She'd been such a bitch to me on the phone, and it repulsed me to think how much energy I'd invested in her. I pictured her shaking on her bed, pupils spinning and the size of quarters. A week ago if she would've called me, I would have indulged in anything she had to offer. Now it was so past appealing in every way.

Nevie lived in Sutton Place, which meant that when I got off the 6 train at 59th, I still had a long walk until her East River abode, part of an inconvenience that you generally loved as a Suttonite, the distance and isolation from the rest of Manhattan.

Her parents—with some co-op board swing—got her a much-sought-after junior one bedroom by finagling their way with generous donations that would pay for the building's overdue brick pointing. They got her the place to keep her far from trendy downtown and put her in a co-op that would throw her out if she acted too wild. It was their way of maintaining her as much as they could without really having to deal with her, something that made them feel altruistic rather than negligent. Sweep the mess under the rug and no one will know. The room will be clean again.

The doorman presented a problem. He buzzed up to Nevie, but when no one answered there was nothing he could do.

"I am sorry, Mr. Noah, Miss Nevie no pick up," he said.

"She's sleeping and she's a sound sleeper," I began, playing charades by miming sleep and making snoring sounds. "But she has to get up because she's late for work and will get fired."

"Oh no."

"Right, it sucks, *muy mal*. I need to get her up or she will be in trouble."

The doorman finally allowed me to pass, being more embarrassed for not understanding me rather than caring about Nevie's job situation.

Upstairs, I knocked to no avail and could hear the sound of a fan through the door. I figured she had to have a key hidden somewhere. She was too much of a spaz and must've foreseen a night when she'd come home with a hole in her pocketbook and no keys. I felt on top of the door, lifted the doormat, and then spotted a *mezuzah*.

What the hell did she have that for if she wasn't Jewish?

Upon closer inspection, it wasn't really a *mezuzah*, just a small rectangular block of wood with a scribble of an attempted Hebrew letter. I opened it up, and sure enough, there was a key.

I opened the door and shut off the overhead fan, which meant that she was probably home. The bedroom door was closed. I felt sick when I placed my hand on the doorknob, as if something had taken a bite out of my stomach. I doubled back and opened a window to the East River to catch my breath, but my forehead was still baked with sweat. Something was wrong. I turned on the camera like Dominick had demanded and placed my hand again on the doorknob as last night's conversation returned. She had never sounded like that before, and I should've been more concerned.

My sweaty palms fumbled with the doorknob, taking an extra long amount of time to twist it open, afraid to see what was behind that door.

Fuck it. Open it up to whatever the future holds.

The door creaked and then snapped against the wall. I had flung it, too frightened to ease it open. There was Nevie, naked on the bed, crouching on her knees with her white butt in the air and her feet tucked up around her crotch. Her hands contorted behind her back covering the tattoo of a yellow circle, blocking it from the world. Her chin lay against the bed sheets while white snot poured from her nose like spoiled milk, her eyes all red with a stain of blood by her chin. She was moving, but barely, and I had caught it all on film.

"Holy shit," I yelled, almost dropping the camera but keeping it steady. I placed it down on the bed beside her. She was shaking, minimally breathing, but other than that, she was a corpse. I rolled her over and arched her head as red, white, and practically blue colors poured out of her nose and mouth, sticky on my fingers and evil to the touch. I breathed again for the first time since entering the room, rooted in my pocket for my cell, and dialed 911.

She had to be dead. In the cab ride over alongside her beeping ambulance, I imagined her funeral because if she wouldn't die this time, she'd be gone soon enough. I twitched from thinking she deserved it, but I figured I was still dealing with the natural shock. She had no reason to swallow all that Fast. She had an easy life and should be laughing at whatever it was she deemed to be "her troubles." I could make her see that. I could take care of her and love her. Show her what no one else would. Make her love herself if she would let me. I could if she would let me.

Lenox Hill Hospital was not where I imagined I'd be spending my day. I sat in a scoop chair with the camera at my feet and waited for Dominick to show, or for a doctor to come out with news. It had been an hour. How could I have not gone to her house before? She had reached out to me and all I could do was turn off my cell.

I thought of her naked ghost on the bed, fingers draped over that tattoo trying to erase it from her skin, a confused look on her face, mouth wide and veiny eyes poised and waiting for the moment when I'd walk in.

I counted the cracks in the ceiling. Sixty-six. I counted the amount of times the old lady next to me gummed her lip. I lost count. When Dominick finally showed up, I felt old, like I'd been waiting in this hospital for the majority of my life.

"Do you know anything?" he asked, sitting down and shifting in his seat, crossing one leg over the other at the knee. His clothes were neat and he'd been groomed with a new haircut. This was not the Dominick from yesterday. I wondered if he really cared about Nevie at all.

"I haven't heard anything."

"What did she look like when you found her?"

Dominick was scanning the room: the injured, those waiting. He watched them as if he was sizing up a party's attendees.

"I don't remember," I mumbled.

"Jesus. That girl was always teetering. I knew this would happen."

So did I, deep inside. I had been waiting to be her hero. Now that it had come true, I couldn't imagine anything more horrible.

"I met her on Fast." Dominick chuckled.

Who the hell could chuckle at a time like this? I thought.

"Any relationship that begins on Fast is doomed from the start. She'd pop 'em like Pez, addicted to the sex on it. I'm too old for the kind she did, though, cut with a bunch of other stuff. That would just slow me down."

"She called me last night basically saying this would happen," I said.

"Regret is a total waste of time. Gets you nowhere."

"I'm so stupid."

"What did you get on film, Noah?"

"What?"

He pointed at the camera between my feet. *Don't fuck with me,* his eyes seemed to say. *Tell me you got her dying.*

"I got some stuff," I said, my body weirdly icy and hot at the same time.

"Good, tell me exactly what you got."

"Everything. Her OD'ing—"

"My actresses are dropping like flies," Dominick mumbled to the ceiling.

"How is Lindsay doing?" I asked, suddenly caring, my eyes watering.

Dominick stared at his fingernails.

"Coma. She's at Bellevue. Girl was so high that day I'm not surprised it happened; neither were the cops after her stomach got pumped."

"But the airbags never..."

He chewed off a cuticle and spit it in my direction.

"Machinery isn't perfect, Noah. She knew not to go that fast, but the shot I had you get of her as she hit that stoplight..." He kissed his fingers. "Magnificent."

I fumbled in my pockets and felt the red slip between my fingers.

This is the scene where you will die, I remembered it saying.

I wanted to shove that slip in his face and make him accountable for all his negligent actions, but then a doctor wandered out rubbing his hands together. He found us and broke it down quickly. Nevie had overdosed, they pumped her stomach, cooled her down. All the Fast in her system had jacked up her body temperature. The blood was from her biting her tongue. She must've fallen on the bed and clamped down. She would have to stay the night, but she would live.

"She asked to see *him,*" the doctor said, looking at Dominick.

"Of course," he said, shaking the doctor's hand, thanking him for all he had done.

"We'll watch what you filmed later tonight," Dominick said as he walked off with the doctor.

I had a sinking feeling in my stomach. I'd been sure Nevie was dead. I had prepared myself: for the mourning, for the guilt. Now that whirling descent in the pit of my stomach morphed into a ball of *pissed the fuck off*. I had saved her life and she wanted to see *Dominick*? A guy who had called me to deal with her, who made her miserable, who treated her as if she was just a wet pussy to screw whenever he felt like it, and she had asked for *him*? Here she was brought back from straddling the edge of death and Dominick's stupid face was all she wanted to see.

"Fuck you," I said to the old lady still gumming her lip for the zillionth time. I picked up the camera and left.

I lay in bed later that afternoon tossing a tennis ball against the wall, something repetitive and mind numbing. I threw the ball too hard and it knocked my *Fight Club* poster off the wall.

I am Jack's raging bile duct, I thought, feeling like I was going to puke. I didn't even bother to pick up the poster.

I dreaded my cell, wanting nothing less than to hear Dominick's asshole voice. I knew it meant we'd have to watch the film I shot of Nevie dying.

I put on some Neil Young.

You really make my day
With all the little things you say.
All I got for you is a razor love
That cuts clean through.

My cell wailed over the song and I picked it up.

"Get the fuck over here," Dominick said, already drunk or on something. "Don't forget that camera. Don't tell me you have anything else to do. This is what you have to do."

Click.

I threw the cell out of my window, not even thinking that I lived on the penthouse floor and could've killed someone below.

The lights were dim when I got to Dominick's loft. He smoked a pipe over by the window, and the living room smelled of melting plastic. He held out the pipe as I took a mega-hit and shut my brain off. All day I had been eager for something to help me disconnect. I picked up the pipe again and took another hit.

"Is Isadora here?" I asked, thinking about the kiss we shared in public last night. I didn't even care that it might've sounded odd for me to ask.

"No," Dominick said, exhaling another never-ending cloud. "Show me the tape."

So we watched it. Nevie's bedroom door flew open and the camera studied her on the bed: exposed, naked and white, blocking that secret tattoo on the small of her back. I looked at Dominick for a response and saw his eyes light up. He grabbed me by the neck and planted a smoky kiss on my cheek.

"Beautiful."

I fought the urge to deck him.

Dominick touched the screen, the ends of his lips forming a creepy smile. "We've just witnessed genius."

He paused the film. Nevie stared at the camera with her bloodshot eyes, begging to be put out of her misery.

"That's the core of *Slow Down*," he thundered. "She's been going too fast, literally on Fast, and look what it's done to her. Just like in the scene with Lindsay, just like the rest of this rotten city. We're all rushing to get somewhere else but rotting inside. We'll all be corpses by dawn if we keep it up."

Dominick took a final hit from his pipe. The air became even ranker. I held my nose and closed my eyes, wishing I'd never see him again. When I opened my eyes, Nevie still stared back, pleading to be released from all her torments.

"She's going to be a star. Fuck. Oscar, baby. You show me an actress that can convey anything close to what she just did."

He was giddy. He was alive. He was right.

"So cut that sour bullshit look you're giving me."

"I need to use the bathroom," I said, fearing I might puke.

"Use the one down to the hall to the right, *not* the left," Dominick called out, as I booked it down the hallway. A ball of bile crept up my throat. I reached the end of the hallway and heard a strange bubbling noise coming from the bathroom to the left. Even though he told me to use the one to the right, I pushed open the door to the other one.

Inside looked like a mad scientist's lab. A viscous yellow liquid filled the sink. The pipes below had been gutted out, and an array of tubes caught the bubbling liquid. The bathroom smelled of sewage and dead animals, and I couldn't hold back the ball of bile any longer. I spewed into the shower and turned on the water to wash my sick away. As I wiped my mouth with my sleeve, I spied a tattoo gun propped up against the bathtub.

"What the...?" I said, picking up the tattoo gun as my nose detected smoke in the bathroom. I turned around to see Dominick.

"I told you to use the one on the right," he said, blowing a trail of smoke in my face. When it cleared, he had already left the bathroom and was walking down the hallway.

Back in the living room, Nevie still covered her tattoo with her jagged fingernails on the television. Maybe she'd been trying to scratch it off. What kind of power did it have over her, over all of Dom's girls?

"What do the tattoos mean?"

My words hung in the air. It was like when I asked a girl out at thirteen and she took hours to respond, but really, I had only imagined the long wait. She had said yes immediately.

"What do you think the tattoos mean?"

"In the context of the film or in real life?"

Dominick gestured toward a dying Nevie, "What's the difference?"

I wanted to say the name *Astrid* out loud. Had she really died from being decapitated like in the film *Detached*? She'd been real once, the original owner of the yellow tattoo, which had been re-created on the back of troubled girls all over Manhattan. But why?

"I don't know what they mean," I said. If I mentioned Astrid's name, Dominick would know that Isadora had told me about her. So I kept quiet, not because I was afraid of revealing the truth, but because I wanted more nights with Isadora and didn't want anything to interrupt.

"Culture is bankrupt these days," Dominick sneered. "We want immediate explanations, but what about letting an idea, a symbol, marinate for a while? What about having two people in the audience with different takes on what they saw?"

"Very Lynchian," I said.

"Yes, Lynch certainly wraps his films up in layers of mystery, but do they ever encroach on reality? Mine will. My girls will stretch beyond a movie screen and infiltrate this city. They already have. And it is just beginning."

He passed me his pipe again. I took one more hit as the surroundings became beautifully clear: the minimalist paintings, the lines on Dominick's palm, even Nevie's paused dance with death. All of it in high definition once again.

"What's in this?" I asked.

"Fast, of course," Dominick replied, tapping out the rest of the pipe.

"Is that what I saw being made in the bathroom?"

He let out a solitary bark of a laugh. "I created Fast, Noah, with the help of a chemist friend, who unfortunately has passed. But I'm the one that's gotten it out there to the masses. The kind that I learned to cook is completely pure."

"But why—"

"What do you think is in those tattoos?" he laughed again, the color of his face a scary pink. "It's Fast, ground up, dyed, and etched right into someone's back with the tip of a tattoo pen. The yellow circle becomes a reminder so all those girls stay hungry for the juice. Fast eliminates our inhibitions, which will inevitably enhance a performance. Now do you see what I mean when I speak of revolution? You show me a director that is more in tune with what he wants to achieve."

Maybe it was because of the Fast that I had sucked into my lungs, but I couldn't register a shocked response; I felt numb. I stared at Nevie, the little puppet, and wondered if she knew, if she chose this controlled reality because it was still leagues better than what she believed she had before, or if Dominick had deceived all his girls, pushing them hard enough to expire just like he did with Lindsay.

"Fucker," I said, under my breath, and took a swing. I expected to come into contact with Dominick's face, yearning for the guy's blood on my knuckles, for him to truly feel *pain*, but he had already left the room. I didn't know how long I'd been passed out.

I rubbed my eyes as the early hours of the night slunk into the loft, submerging myself in a foul darkness I wasn't sure would ever go away again.

15

NOW THAT DOMINICK HAD CONFESSED ABOUT TATTOOING Fast into the backs of all his girls, I couldn't get that revelation out of my head. The very uniqueness of the act soon superseded what others may have seen as morally wrong. This was the film that Dominick should be making! Where a power-hungry director so desperate for another hit drugged his actresses to achieve authentic performances. Whatever loose-ended plot Dominick had in his mind for *Slow Down* couldn't compare to that truth. So I stayed even closer to him than before. I made up some bullshit excuse about wanting to study his directing style and brought along my own recently purchased camera to the shoots to get some real footage. Since Dominick ate up any kind of praise, he bought what I was selling, and soon I had loads of his insanity on film. In addition, I filmed Estella and Palmer, who I followed around the city even after Dominick's shoots had ended for the night with the guise of lending an ear, but all the while capturing their tirades, their scary withdrawals, and then their enchanted transformations once Palmer took a hit of Fast or Estella injected it into her tattoo. If they wondered why I always carried around a video camera when I saw them, they never asked, for I supplied them with Dom's pure Fast, pumping them with enough to bring them *oh so close* to the edge. I even got Dominick's blessing to do so since the guy was happy enough to not have to deal with either of those "energy drainers" once their shoots ended.

Soon the bad blood between the two of us (from Dominick's eyes at least) became a thing of the past. I was his soundboard now and supported all of the King's directorial decisions. I became confident in steadily manipulating him, which was easy enough to do as long I as called him "a genius" about three times a day. I learned to read his face and anticipate what he'd say so I could agree right away, all the while saving every second of shot film until I'd figure out what to do next with this newfound treasure. Soon I'd decide. But not yet.

Soon came quicker than I expected. Dominick was dumb enough to put me in control of some of his own editing. He set me up in a Chinatown studio where I spent nights over cigarettes and Fast to keep me energized, editing some fluff job from what Dominick shot first and then working on my own film till the sun rose. Fast became my new best friend, something I knew was a bad idea, but all of a sudden I didn't feel accomplished unless I was tweaking by dawn. I mixed dialogue from Dominick's shoots with my own, believing I captured beauty and sorrow, but there were still too many holes. I had an inception of an idea, but nothing else, so I started taking even more Fast to birth some inspiration, telling myself that I'd stop once I figured it all out. *What else should those tattoos symbolize?* I wondered. I pushed that question to the forefront of my brain constantly, but all I seemed to get from asking was headaches.

By dawn, the overwhelming smell of fish would pour into the studio, and I'd spend sunrise with my head in the toilet. Dominick had dictated for me to "get the gold" from what I shot and "lose all the shit," but I felt like I was starting to lose my own shit. My hair had became a non-sculpted mess, my eyes looked like they'd been circled with ink, and an unsightly stress pimple had popped up on my nose. But I didn't care. I was making magic, and pure art meant suffering. Ask Van Gogh. Ask Hemingway. Ask Kurt Cobain or anyone else from the Forever 27 Club. So I ate cigarettes and lost about ten pounds in a matter of days.

On one very rainy night with hail beating against the windows of my studio that stunk like an old wonton, after a horrible day of shooting a simulated sex scene between Palmer and Estella and dealing with those two insecure idiots, I found myself smoking on the edge of a mattress that had been dumped into the corner of the apartment. The sixth Pilsner Urquell of the night was dangling from my lips when I heard a knock at the door. Both the cig and the beer fell to the floor at the exact time, the beer extinguishing the cigarette's cherry and my bare foot stepping in an ashy puddle as I rushed to the repeated knocks pounding on the door.

"Hold on," I said, very drunk, all the more aware how bombed I was once I stood and realized I had little equilibrium. I turned on my camera and set it on the mattress, so used to having it be an extension of me now. The knocks became louder. I looked at my watch and it was late, almost two in the morning. I wondered if it might be Isadora the vixen showing up with a fur coat and nothing under it, but when I opened the door I found Nevie.

"Dom said you might be here," she said.

She stepped inside and shrugged off her coat. If I had lost ten pounds that week, she had lost even more. Her skin had taken on a translucent tone, and her gaunt face caused her eyes to bug. She bent down and picked up the spilled beer, finishing the bottle in one gulp. She looked at the clamor outside of the window and never at me.

"How are you doing?" I asked, sounding cold although I didn't mean to be. This was a trait I began to notice about myself more and more, every word said with a new icy tinge. I shuddered at the thought of how unaffected I'd become.

"You're editing his film?" she questioned, as if she didn't believe that Dominick would ever allow me the honor. Little did she know my real plans for the footage.

On the computer screen, time had paused on Gramercy Park West. It was a dewy morning, and Palmer and Estella began a fight that would soon lead to a fuck.

"Yeah, Dom's been letting me do a lot."

"I didn't try…"

She stopped and then composed herself. I was glad I hadn't left the shot of her overdosing up on the computer. I'd been working on that only the night before.

"I didn't try to kill myself, Noah. I don't want you to think that."

"I'm just glad you're all right," I said, picking at the peeling paint on the wall.

"I didn't."

The pitch in her voice rose, sounding less certain than before.

You're a liar. You would have expired if it weren't for me. Sure Dom had put that Fast in your back, but I know you kept asking for more.

"I just wanted to stop thinking for a moment," she said. "Everything was rushing through my mind so quickly. I felt like if I didn't do something I'd explode so I just started consuming Fast: smoking it, snorting it, rubbing it into my sweat. I guess I exploded anyway, huh?"

She wasn't being cute, and I hated her for making light of what had happened. She was soaked from the rain, and a halo of water had formed around her ass on the bed. The studio took on her damp smell so I opened the window as a chill breeze rushed inside. She shivered and looked at me crossly, but I gave her a look back that said, *Fuck you, you brought in that smell, deal with being cold.*

She needed a hug more than anything, but I remained distant. She probably went to Dominick at first for comfort, but when he wouldn't comply, she went to her next-in-line expecting absolute adoration. Well, not anymore. The power had shifted and I would uphold our new dynamic. She needed to know how it felt to yearn without reciprocation.

"I wanted to talk to you this week," she said, speaking clearly. "I just got the feeling that you didn't want to talk to me, and that's fine, but I needed to say thank you…you saved my life."

She barely got the last words out while black lines streaked down her face from her running mascara. Her palms rubbed at her eyes and made it worse but she didn't seem to care. She reached out and I found myself taking her hand, as we massaged each other's digits. I imagined the camera capturing only our hands, dangling together in the air, miming everything unsaid between us through our years of flip-flop love and abuse.

"I asked for you that day in the hospital, Noah. I didn't say your name to the doctor because I thought you were the only one there, but when I asked for 'him,' I meant you. I still do."

"Lift up your head," Nevie said, and I did through the beer and Fast fighting it out in my bloodstream and liver. Something beat inside of me like a madman on a rampage, but it might just have been the realization that I had been the one she wanted. She looked at me with drippy wide pupils, the only things that weren't bloodshot in her tired sockets. She leaned back against that dirty mattress in the middle of Chinatown and tucked her thin legs around me, drawing me to her.

"I hate Dominick," she said, closing her eyes. She arched her back as I leaned over and stared at her upside-down face. I could taste her lips on my own even though I hadn't made a move yet. Those three little words, "I hate Dominick," hummed from those lips and made my dick harden instantly. It felt right to chuck my brain out of the window into the chilly city and think entirely with my throbbing distraction. Take advantage of her at the moment because I deserved it after all these years.

Our lips touched with curious tongues following soon after. With each new body part I touched, I became awarded with a jolt that sprang from my quivering toes all the way up to my beet red skull. What had been a fantasy for too long was now an awesome reality, and when I was finally ready to have sex with her (after sliding her panties off and spinning them around my finger, the surprise of her Brazilian wax, and no time to even think about putting on a condom), I practically came before I got inside of her. But then I got my shit together and fell into a rhythm. I knew every inch of her body from my imagination and how each part of her might taste, and I was surprised at how close I'd been to the reality: the sweet strawberry warmth of her mouth, the tangy sweat of her armpits, the salty nibble of her nipples. I made love to her, the first time I actually *made love* to anyone, not thinking about anything else but her beneath me. It wasn't a conquest like other girls, and there was no mind-shattering orgasm, the hours just seemed to fill up my heart and make it swell. I fell asleep inside of her, cocooned and deliriously happy.

When I woke up in the middle of the night, she wasn't there. I called her name, but she didn't answer. I wandered into the bathroom and flushed the Fast stash that Dominick had given me down the toilet. I crawled naked over to the camera, still leaning against the wall where I left it. I cradled it in my arms and watched my night with Nevie over and over again on the tiny rectangular screen that held her.

I would always have her now.

Though it had irked me that Nevie ran out without saying anything, I did have an epiphany while watching myself have sex with her that was more important than any hard feelings. Why couldn't I be in *Slow Down?* I could be the soul of the film, the character who penetrates—literally and figuratively—the clique of tattooed girls and tries to help them, especially the film's star (Nevie), but the Fast had hijacked her already and it might be too late. A film like that would be heart wrenching, moving, visually affecting. The only thing keeping my character apart from his love was the drug that had been etched in her back. Together we'd search for who did this to her so we could take the bastard down before he infected anyone else. Then I'd do whatever possible to make her normal again, and even if I couldn't, I'd still stay beside her because she was the only thing that resembled a home. *That would be beautiful...genius,* I thought, echoing some of Dominick's most overused adjectives.

I saw Nevie at the shoot the next day. Dominick was busy dealing with Palmer and Estella down the block—apparently they had a big, emotional scene that required them to *dig deep*, but neither was bringing it. Dominick acted calmer than ever, always a bad sign.

Three other girls surrounded Nevie, all probably with the same signature tattoos; a horde of wafer-thin sticks munching on Dom's required diet of lettuce and sunflower seeds. Nevie sat in the middle stuffing an avocado in her mouth. She saw me but pretended she didn't, until I stood over her and she couldn't pretend any longer.

"Hi."

Her lips were smeared with traces of avocado. She wiped it away with a swish of her napkin.

"Hi."

Why did you leave without saying goodbye? I wanted to ask, but what came out was:

"Avocado good?"

"Yes. Avocado good."

Didn't you feel what I felt last night? I've loved you since the ninth grade when you thought you were punk and had a streak of green in your hair, and you wore T-shirts you bought at Goodwill that were ripped and yellowing even though three generations of your family lived with Central Park views. I've worshipped you since you called me a frog. You always said that I looked like one, just content on my lily pad, eating flies passing by in the breeze. You were always so poetic when you didn't mean to be.

"Does your scene start soon?" I asked instead.

"Yes."

I could love you, Nevie. I could be there for you. I know you want it. Let me help you find the person you used to be. She's not too far gone.

"Red or green slip?"

"What? Red."

If you never wanted me, why did you tease me last night? Did you just need someone between your legs and it could've been me or any other guy? We made love. I held you, and wanted to hold you till the morning sun came. I wanted day to turn right back into night and to do it all over again. Don't tell me I will never feel that again.

"Can I see your red slip?"

"You know Dominick doesn't want his actors showing anyone else their red slips."

"But I have ideas—"

"But *he* is the director, not you."

"*He* doesn't know what he's doing," I whispered.

Don't say you're standing up for him, Nevie. He would rather spit on you than say he loved you. He never will if that's what you're waiting for. I will without a second thought.

"*He* is brilliant and is putting a lot of trust in you."

"*He* has no idea what *Slow Down* is about," I said, getting angry but managing to keep my voice down. "It's all made up the minute he gets to the set. He is a creative cypher. I can make you a star."

"What are you talking about?"

You have Fast in your back, Nevie. It makes you do and say terrible things. It made you love me last night and hate me this morning.

The three lettuce girls were watching our tiff. They all gave me the stink eye for whatever reason. I gave them the same stink back.

"I just want to make you happy, Nevie. That's all. I think I can." I whispered this respectfully, but she wasn't having it. My remark made her bite her lip, and she cut me with her eyes. These beautiful pupils were not the same ones I had wandered into last night; these dripped and dripped with malice.

"Look, Noah, Dominick can't know about what happened between us. I am dead serious. If he does find out, I'm gonna tell him what you just said about him because I love him."

"No."

"No?"

"No, you don't, Nevie. You only love him—"

"Don't begin to psychoanalyze me—"

"Because you know you'll never completely have him. He's someone to chase, and he treats you like garbage and you need that 'cause you're sick."

"You don't know what goes on between us behind closed doors."

I could only imagine, something I wouldn't wish on my worst enemy, something like the way she was abusing me now.

"I don't really care," I said, but I did, more than anything.

"Just keep last night a secret. Okay? Can you do that?"

"Why did you even come over last night?"

My voice cracked, so revealing. She'd gotten inside of me and nothing would ever be the same, just like that time in the agent's loft a year ago when I stole a kiss and her lips never even moved. She had kissed like the dead and left me with memories of her corpse mouth for a year.

"Why?" I yelled, as the lettuce eaters all turned their noses up at me again. "Fuck you," I hissed at them and they scattered away.

Nevie sighed through her nostrils. She looked so delicate, so lovely, but an impossibility. That was all she'd ever be to me from now on.

"I don't know, Noah."

"That's too easy an excuse—"

"Well, maybe it's as simple as that."

If I told her I loved her, it'd be futile, and worst of all I'd be sending that thought out into the world, never to get it back and keep it as my secret. *Let me try to forget her already again. Let those days start now.*

"I was thinking of Dominick the whole time," she said, and instantly I saw her as a ghost, transparent and fading, already gone. I blinked away a tear, as an apparition's hand seemed to graze the back of my neck. I shuddered and swiveled around, coming face-to-face with Dominick.

"What are you kids discussing?" the face asked me, the last thing I wanted to see.

"Nothing," I mumbled.

"Noah was just telling me about the editing he's doing for you, Dominick."

"Yeah, I was curious about what you'd come up with," he said, peering at her breasts spilling out of her baby doll dress. "Although, it's probably nothing I'll wind up using. I'd never leave my work with an amateur if that's all you are. I guess we'll see if you're able to prove otherwise."

I wanted to cry, unable to look at either of them.

"So you'll show me what you got tonight. Get your edits from downtown, meet me at my place, and then we'll go for drinks at No Bar. They sneak in bottles of real absinthe for me. I know the owner very well, and she makes this frozen absinthe smoothie for me that will knock your fucking socks off till tomorrow."

He didn't even wait for an answer and turned to Nevie. "Let's do your scene, girl. You're starting to look moist in the sun."

He took her by the hand and that was fucking that.

16

I SAT ON THE SHADY GRASS BY BETHESDA FOUNTAIN IN
Central Park, watching some children splashing in the murky water.
Beside me, an old man painted a surrealist version of the surroundings:
a jumble of swirls, greens and blues that were supposed to represent trees
and skies. The old man looked like he had been painting it all day.
Slowly, it was starting to resemble something tangible.

When my new cell rang, I almost didn't know what was making that
sound since I had just picked it up at Verizon that morning. I took the
screaming phone out of my pocket and saw it was Isadora. I wanted
peace and wished I had left it at home.

"I'm sorry," I immediately said.

"No. I'm not looking for that."

"I meant to call. Week has been crazy."

"Look, I know you are coming over later tonight to see Dom, so I will
not be there, but I need to see you tomorrow. The Ocean Club. Dinner.
Eight sharp. I will be under the name Barbara Stanwyck. I miss you."

"Really?"

Isadora's words made me feel good, especially after Nevie's earlier
dismissal. I had to admit that I missed her, too.

"Yes, Noah, I miss you. But I have to go, Dominick is here."

I entered Dominick's loft later that day with two edited copies of film:
the piece of shit one I made for him and my other mini-masterpiece. I
hadn't decided whether or not to show it. Right now, I wasn't ready to
reveal my deceitful intentions, but I brought it just in case Dominick gave
me reason enough to change my mind.

Sure enough, he went right for his pipe of pure Fast like always. After exhaling a dense cloud, he offered me a hit. Beads of saliva collected on the back of my tongue, but I had to refuse a drag despite how delicious and numbing it might be. My Fast days were over. As for Isadora, I learned that Dominick had insulted her earlier, causing her to stomp off into the night.

"Good riddance," he said, opening a bottle of Mitjavile's '89 Tertre Roteboeuf.

"This is a decadent masterpiece; it's from a locale named the hill of the belching beef, but it's not a classic. It holds the unfortunate nature of being too ripe."

What a shit-eater, I thought, as he took a sip.

"I have something to show you," he said, turning on the television. "I just DVR'd this."

New York 1 News came up on the screen with the same newscaster that I saw reporting on the girl who overdosed last week.

"Britta Myles here at Bellevue Hospital where Lindsay Nashton, daughter of media mogul Jasper Nashton II, has died. Twenty-four-year-old Lindsay, an aspiring actress in director Dominick Bambach's new hush-hush film, fell into a coma after crashing a car into a stoplight during a stunt gone awry. Doctors had found that the girl had been high on a street drug called Fast when brought into the hospital. Ms. Nashton marks the fifth death this year from Fast along with another actress, Katrina Wixler, and Monday's death of Morris Sydler, a chemistry graduate student at NYU. Other reports of overdoses but not fatalities have come from hospitals, and the mayor is already speaking of this drug as a new citywide youth epidemic. We caught up with director Dominick Bambach this afternoon to shed light on Fast's most recent tragedy."

On the screen, Dominick wiped his eyes while being surrounded by reporters outside of his loft.

"Lindsay was a brilliant actress, but a very troubled soul. She will be impossible to replace. Hopefully she is finally at peace now."

The TV snapped off.

"So I'm already looking for her replacement," Dominick said. "I'll keep the scenes we shot, especially the one of the crash, but Lindsay's role will be more of a supporting one now."

I was still staring at the blank television screen until Dominick snapped his fingers.

"Noah!"

"I can't believe we just stood back and watched her crash," I said, putting my head in my hands. "You don't feel—"

"What? Guilty? She begged me to be in that scene."

"I mean about the Fast."

"At least she went out with a bang. Most people's demises are so boring."

"You can't really mean that."

He looked back at me as if I was the insane one.

"She's immortal now. Don't you see?"

He waved his hands through the air to break up the haze of Fast that surrounded us.

"That chemist the reporter mentioned…was he the guy who helped you create Fast?"

"God, Noah, stop reading too much into everything. I do Fast all the time, and look at me, I'm fine. The world is made up of strong people and weak ones, and if some of those weak people have to go to make more room for the strong, then so be it."

I closed my eyes to picture Lindsay crashing into the stoplight, but instead I saw Nevie in her place. I knew Dominick thought of her as the weakest of them all.

I had to shake away the image of a bloody Nevie spilling out of the crashed car.

"So Nevie looked distressed earlier at the shoot today," Dominick said.

"What about Nevie?"

"I said she looked distressed talking to you."

"I don't know, maybe it was the fact she almost overdosed last week," I said, meaning to be sarcastic but somehow not sounding that way.

"Just take the time to be a little more sensitive to her needs. I know she can be a lot to deal with."

"I'll try," I said, biting my tongue.

"So what do you think about the scenes I've given you to edit?"

Dominick blew another large gust of Fast. When it cleared, I noticed how he had no laugh or frown lines, as if he'd never displayed a human emotion before.

"They've been interesting, I guess," I said, gulping down about five sips' worth of the wine, my mind too jumbled to be more eloquent.

"Interesting? What are you, retarded, Noah? Goddamn, have the balls to give me a less generic response than that."

"For what..." I began, unsure how I wanted to proceed. I knew I needed to shoot a lot more film and therefore still had to kiss Dominick's butt, but I also wondered if I might be able to steal Estella and Palmer away for good. Nevie definitely would be a challenge to sway, but I could hire some other actors to fill in the other roles. That way I could just be honest about what I really thought.

"Sometimes it just doesn't quite feel like a film," I continued.

Now Dominick had an expression. He frowned as if he just realized he'd been pickpocketed.

"How so?"

"Well, it seems like some loosely strung vignettes as opposed to—"

"That's realism!"

"If I never hear that word again," I grumbled, not meaning to let that slip, but this past week of brown nosing had gotten old fast.

"Listen, you little shit, I've told you my philosophy a thousand times," he said. "How can anyone give a truthful performance with eight different cameras and dozens of crew members in their face? I'm not telling my actors how to create emotion, it's coming from inside—"

"Well, it's the Fast."

"You ungrateful pussy, you've got a nerve to question me. I have millions of pages of notes that I was thinking about showing you tonight so you could truly see what *Slow Down* is all about."

I made a gesture with my hand like I was jacking off. If this had been a few weeks ago, I would've cowered from a guy as important as Dominick yelling in my face, but now I felt as if I just didn't care. Maybe it was due to the thick puffs of Fast hanging in the air, or that losing Nevie *again* brought me to a dark place, but I found myself jumping up with the copy of my own edit and shoving it in his hands.

"You need to see this," I said. "I got the talent you need, man." I pictured Dominick's jaw dropping once my mini masterpiece flickered across the computer screen and the jerkoff realized that some punk kid had done more for art in a week than he had done in his entire overrated career.

"What are you waiting for?" I asked, long past acting nice anymore. The true Noah had peeled off the pleasant mask he'd worn for the last month and was ready to rage. I thought of *Fight Club* and how I had wanted Tyler Durden, the more dangerous and intriguing personality, to be the one watching the world explode at the end instead of Ed Norton's mild-mannered Jack.

While hours and hours of disjointed footage didn't add up to much, I had parsed out a semblance of a story for Estella and Palmer's characters. With Estella, her plot dealt with her newly erratic moods. Viewers would assume that Palmer was the reason for her change in behavior, but soon the Fast in her back was revealed as the culprit. The last story would focus on my character and Nevie's. While none of it had been shot yet, our story would be the center of the film and deal with Nevie getting into Fast so she could party all night. If my character was unsuccessful in getting her to "slow down" by the film's end, she might die. As of now, I hadn't decided if I wanted a heroic or tragic ending.

As we got ready to watch what I shot in Dominick's editing room, I became really nervous. To distract myself, I stared at a string of paintings along the wall of Astrid. In the last one, her face had been etched out of the canvas, just a headless body that was painted well despite its morbid obviousness.

"I did those," Dominick said. "All from my dreams." He reached out and touched one, completely detached from the present as he did so.

"When did she die?"

Dominick pulled his hand away from the painting and put his fingers to his lips, as if he had blessed it.

"What does death really mean? She's alive every day in my mind."

He shut off the lights and sat down in his editing chair, shadowed by a pocket of darkness. He turned on his computer as a blue stream cut through the dark. In the blue light, he seemed years older, his face full of lines now. I wondered if I had just imagined it smooth before.

"We'll watch what you filmed and then go to No Bar, nothing spoken between us until we get there. Agreed?"

I nodded as Dominick's face receded back into the shadows. He looked just like the headless body from his painting.

No Bar was located on an unlit street in Tribeca full of factories. It didn't exist to the world from the outside, just like The Penny and probably all of Dominick's haunts. From inside a garage, one entered the bar through the back of an open truck. The truck was just a shell and led to a dim dive bar with a stage in the center and a naked bulb swinging from the ceiling. Dominick hadn't said a word since watching the edits, and I knew he had to be stinging with jealousy.

A few patrons were scattered throughout the booths. A thick, purple-tinted smoke made the whole place feel like a giant potion bottle turned inside out.

Dominick kissed the bartender on the lips when we entered, not passionately but as if he was marking his territory. She had red hair but not as conspicuous as Astrid's. This one had gotten her look from a bottle, and I wondered if Dominick had requested the color. Sure enough when she turned to grab someone else a beer, I spied the tattoo of the yellow circle on the small of her back.

"The usual?" the bartender asked, her luscious lips drawing out each word.

"Make it two."

"Lena is on soon," she said, and then took about five minutes to make the absinthe smoothies. When she finished, she set them frosty on the counter and put a finger to her luscious lips.

On the stage, a woman stepped into the naked light from the swinging bulb. She had red hair as well that stuck up in spears like a wild flame.

"What's up with this place?" I asked, taking a long sip of my absinthe smoothie.

"Shut up," Dominick replied, enraptured with Lena the chanteuse who sang in what sounded like a Scandinavian language. When she finished, Dominick was the only one who clapped, loudly and unapologetically. Lena slinked over afterwards and whispered in his ear to meet her backstage later. He nodded, but he seemed as if he didn't really care now that she had sung.

The bartender came over with two more absinthe smoothies. I was having a hard time keeping up.

"I come here a lot," Dominick said, cradling his drink. "Isadora doesn't know about this place, my home away from home. I think she'd find it unhealthy. She doesn't love me."

"You don't know that," I replied, as the kiss Isadora and I shared looped in my mind. From the way Dominick stared back, it seemed as if he was able to read my thoughts and could see that kiss as well.

"Your edits were shit," he said, flipping a cigarette into his mouth.

"What?" I asked, unsure if I heard him right.

"I said your edits were shit. I have to take a piss."

He got up but I grabbed his arm.

"Hold on, Dominick."

"Noah, I have to fucking piss."

"My edits were not shit."

"Do you want me to lie?"

"I want you to tell the truth."

"Well, I am. Do you want to let go of my arm?"

I let go and he disappeared into the smoke. I lunged for my absinthe smoothie and downed it, then went for Dominick's and downed his as well until I got a brain freeze that felt like someone had stabbed me between my eyes.

The edits were amazing and Dominick is just being petty. That has to be it since no other explanation makes sense.

He returned and frowned at the booth full of empty glasses.

"I see you like those absinthe smoothies."

"Duck you, Dominick."

Uh-oh, I was already wasted. I pressed against my temples in an attempt to maintain.

"Fuck you, Dominick. Not duck you, fuck you."

"Watch it," he yelled, banging on the table. He held his smoking cigarette at me like a weapon.

"You are jealous of me," I said.

"Jealous of what?"

"'Cause I'm young, and inspired, and you are old and over."

Dominick pinched his cigarette. I figured he was probably debating whether or not to flick it at my eye. He took a drag instead.

"Go on, get it all out since you've had some truth serum tonight."

"You're a fraud," I yelled, louder than I expected. Heads turned but I didn't know those heads so I couldn't care less.

"Is that the best you can do?" he asked, so softly that I had to lean in to hear.

"You've got no ideas for *Slow Down*, the film is a joke. You needed me to help connect what little you have."

"Keep going," he said, indulging in one final drag.

"You made *Detached* years ago, and it's debatable if anything from it was actually your ideas and not just…"

"Don't stop, just say it," he hissed.

"We know who was really responsible for making *Detached*."

"Do we?"

"Should I say it out loud?"

He gestured with his palms to continue.

"She told me all about it in bed last week—in your bed."

After I said that final jab, it felt like I'd left my body and watched the rest play out. I wished I had a camera documenting the whole exchange: the telling eyebrow raise I gave Dominick, the arrogant chortle I closed with, the crumbling of a man before my very eyes. We'd reached an inevitable point now and could never return to what we once were to each other. I was never meant to have a mentor. I was meant to be that mentor to someone else, Jesus to a row of disciples.

"Are you done?"

He didn't say it angrily, or he was just good at holding back his anger. Tears lingered at the corners of his eyes. When he finally relented and let them fall, I almost felt bad for being so cruel. The guy I used to be would've never relished in watching someone else's marriage fail, but this new Noah had been energized by my ability to cause this man pain.

"Yeah, I'm done, Dominick."

"Then leave me alone."

He looked right into my eyes, which made me jump out of my seat like a match had been lit under my ass, completely spooked as if I'd seen some awful foreshadowed future. My chair fell to the floor, but I played it all off like I was just amped up from our intense exchange. As I found my footing, I knew I'd been scared because a quiet Dominick was a dangerous Dominick. That lit match might not have been there, but one day, very soon, he would surprise me with it. Just like he had gotten rid of Lindsay to enhance his film, I could very well be next. And then he'd use my death as a minor plot point to justify the killing.

I jetted out the door and through the shell of the truck without looking back. Once I stepped outside into the night air, I realized that the only way to ensure my safety would be to strike at Dominick first.

With that thought, I doubled over and threw up a river of absinthe. After letting it all out, I wiped my mouth, stood tall, and walked off into the night.

17

I DECIDED TO WALK ALONG THE WESTSIDE ALL THE WAY home and wound up on the high line staring at a strip of the Hudson River. Part of me couldn't believe that I'd been honest with Dominick while the other half of me wondered why it had taken so long. I remembered the last person in power that I told off: my horrendous boss, the Queen. The thought made me chuckle. But Dominick had deserved it even more. At least she never pretended to be a genius.

I would've liked to crawl over to Sutton Place and fall asleep in Nevie's lap. My eyes were already hanging low. I wished she could see all of Dominick's faults and realize that I would do anything for her. I thought of us kissing on the mattress in Chinatown, so I lit a cigarette now and had to be content with kissing that. Once I finished the smoke, I trudged down from the High Line and hailed a taxi. When I got home, I climbed into bed and fought my insomnia while choking back a sob.

I will be all right, I said, over and over.

Sleep finally came, which meant I'd talked myself into believing I'd be okay.

I had been to the Ocean Club before since it was a perennial favorite of my father's. A grand old establishment in busy Midtown, unflinching about compromising its dated ways but never appearing out of style. I showed up at five past eight, my stomach rumbling from being neglected all day. I'd just woken up and the last thing I had ingested were the absinthe smoothies at No Bar.

A pretty hostess welcomed me with a smile that didn't seem put-upon. It was the first person I'd spoken to all day, and I was glad for her warmth.

"I'm meeting someone," I said. "Barbara Stanwyck."

Being a huge film buff, I had recognized the name of that actress, known primarily from her villainous turn in the classic movie *Double Indemnity*, where she cons an infatuated salesman into murdering her husband.

The pretty hostess, however, didn't register the name at all.

"The other party hasn't arrived yet, but I'll seat you."

What a surprise, Isadora was late. I'd have to munch on bread till she graced me with her presence.

When Isadora finally showed up a half an hour later, I was shocked to see how far she'd taken the Barbara Stanwyck bit. She had dyed her hair platinum blonde and added heavy bangs in the front with curls along the sides. She sauntered over to the table and didn't apologize for keeping me waiting or for the drastic change in her appearance. She didn't even say hello.

"Goddamn bastard," she said, sitting down.

I fingered my fifth piece of bread, unsure how to react.

"I'm not referring to you, Noah."

"I know."

The oldest living waiter in the world took her order for two neat bourbons and bouillabaisse soups for the table. The waiter winked at her like she was his lady, probably having flashbacks to a time when women looked that way.

"Why did you dye your hair blonde?"

She took out a compact and inspected her lipstick. "Suppose I did." She snapped the compact shut and let out a deep breath. A slight moan escaped from her lips. "Can I tell you something?"

Her eyes darted from side to side, as if someone was watching. She leaned in close and struggled not to cry.

"What did he do?"

I pictured Dominick coming home and taking out his anger on her after the confrontation I had with him last night.

"*Slow Down* is mine."

She said it with such authority that I got goose bumps.

"I don't understand."

She threw up her hands, baffled by my idiocy. "The movie you've

155

been working on was all *my* idea. Just like with *Detached.* Suppose I'm not just going to lie back and take his shit anymore?"

"Why did you give him your ideas?"

Or if I wanted to be honest with my words: *Why were you such a dope twice, Isadora?*

"He steals them, you imbecile. And there's nothing I can do. He's the famous one, and who the hell will believe crazy old me?"

I thought of the story Dominick told me about breaking into Hollywood. The guy had been a thief from the start, stealing his roommate's screenplay because his own work wasn't good enough to get him in the door.

"I believe you," I said. "He's worthless; I even told him that last night."

"I know you did, darling."

"What did he say when you saw him?" I asked, getting cocky, excited to hear about the impact I had.

She got distracted. Something else was on her mind. She fingered her utensils until the waiter came by with our bouillabaisses. The waiter winked at her again and she bobbed a curl in response. That was when I realized her new 'do was a wig.

"There's something important I want to ask you."

"So how pissed off was Dominick?"

"Listen to me—"

"I really ripped him a new one."

Last night I proved I wasn't afraid of anyone, and it had been one of the purest moments of my young life. Nothing looked more pathetic than Dominick's face when I told him he was a fraud.

"Noah, this is difficult for me to say—"

"At first I didn't think I was going to say anything, but I'm a blunt guy and I just couldn't deal with his lies anymore."

She gripped at the tablecloth, squeezing her eyes shut like she was having an aneurysm. A glass of water spilled over. The old waiter came over and asked if the "madam" was all right.

Madam? The waiter probably thought she was my mother.

"I've lost myself," she said, her hands trembling. "You know what it's like to be a writer, Noah, to spend your life creating. And then some talentless fuck with a nice smile comes along and robs everything."

Now she was crying, but she kept it muted.

"If *Slow Down* is yours, why don't you take it back?"

"God, you are naïve."

I gave her the finger.

"Cute, Noah, but I'm serious. I am not the enemy here."

"You were being condescending."

She gripped the tablecloth, as if she was ready to topple the whole thing over. "I'm sorry," she said, releasing the tablecloth from her grasp. "You are wonderful. I hadn't kissed someone in a long time when we kissed."

"What about Dominick?"

"We haven't even made love in months. He only saves that for girls who remind him of the past, either through their tattoos, or their red hair."

"Astrid, right?" I said, ready to hear more about her.

"I want to kill him," she whispered into her bouillabaisse. She picked up her spoon, started slurping, and then motioned for me to do the same.

"What was that?" I asked, slurping as well until we drowned out any surrounding conversations.

"Good, Noah, just keep drinking your soup as if I didn't say anything," she said, very, very slowly.

She didn't seem to be kidding around. People used a word like "kill" in passing. Everyone had a boss they wanted to kill, or an annoying coworker, or the cashier at the supermarket that always puts your eggs at the bottom of the bag to get crushed, but Isadora had said the word with such a conviction that I wondered if she'd already done it.

"I want him fucking dead."

I swiveled around to see if anyone was watching. The Ocean Club had erupted into a din of conflicting sounds: two old cronies cackling at the adjacent table, glasses clanging into one another, the pretty hostess answering the phone, the squeak of silverware against a plate, a phlegmy cough that kept going. All these people existed for the time being, their expiration dates a week, a month, years away. And Dominick existed downtown, too, but it wouldn't be for long. The minute Isadora had said the words that would define the rest of our lives, I had already agreed on the act because it was exactly what I'd dreamed about all day since I left Dominick at No Bar.

"I don't have to ask if you're serious," I said, still keeping a joking tone about the whole thing just in case.

"I'd share *Slow Down* with you. We could make it together."

"What made you want to do this now?"

She scooped up my hand in her own. "Darling, he—"

She turned away, distraught. When she let go of my hand, I felt alone. But she had to let go so she could pull down the neck of her blouse and show me her bruised collarbone, swollen with a purplish sheen.

"He did that?"

I was ready to storm out of the restaurant and kill him. Although I didn't know if by the time I got to SoHo I'd lose my nerve and just rough him up a bit.

"I'm not a weak person," she said. "But I don't know how much longer I can take it. He's always careful to beat me in places I can cover up, never my face."

"I'm so sorry, Isadora."

I went to grab her hand again, to whisper that everything would be all right, but she recoiled away.

"No, not here. We can't draw any attention to ourselves."

"How would we do it?" I asked, going back to my soup and speaking out of the corner of my mouth.

She started slurping again.

"Are you in?"

"I'm listening," I said, but I was all about it. Nothing would sway my decision. My heart started beating fast, so fast, a good fast. I hadn't felt this alive in a long time, maybe ever.

"Everyone knows he's a Fast addict as well as an awful alcoholic. Why do you think he's been so insistent on filming *Slow Down* all by himself? No one in Hollywood wants to deal with him anymore, except of course for his string of whores that use him as their dealer."

I pictured a future where I was a murderer. I thought about a week from now, and then a month, and soon a year. I was certain I could forget it ever happened. I could lock reality in a box and lose the key. And the trade-off would be clearly beneficial. Despite saving this woman from her abusive husband, I'd have full reign over *Slow Down*, and along with Isadora we'd be able to create something amazing. Even Nevie would soon come around once her tears for Dominick dried and I was in control. Oddly enough, this could be the way I might even get her back.

"Tell me what you're thinking," she said, massaging her collarbone, her eyes deliriously wide.

This would be the moment we'd always return to. We'd never be ordinary again, idly bumping along like everyone else. We'd be delving into the kind of life that only existed in a film, and I grinned at that because

I'd always wanted a life that I'd tune into. Finally it was in my grasp.

"Don't worry, Isadora. I'm with you. I'm thinking about the best way to…you know, go about it."

She was relieved; probably unsure of how I'd react, but hoping I'd agree. A lone tear trickled into the only real smile she'd ever given me.

"It has to be Fast," she said, wiping the tear away. "We need to gorge him with it until he overdoses. Fast jacks up your heart rate like nothing else, so it doesn't take much."

"But he won't want to be in the same room with me."

"Just apologize and stroke his ego. The shit will fall for it if you're convincing enough."

"When would we do it?" I asked, looking around the restaurant again and making sure no one was watching us plotting.

"Two nights from now."

"Then what happens with *Slow Down*?"

"I will make a statement that the three of us had been collaborating from the start and he'd want us to finish it. Besides, you said he's barely filmed anything so far so all of the actors will corroborate."

We finished our bouillabaisses. As I put down the spoon, I felt awkward without having something to occupy my hands. I wished the waiter would come back with anything else. Where was the bourbon we ordered? The bouillabaisse in my stomach sloshed around, and my hands were sweating worse than ever.

"Noah, please don't think of me as evil."

"Never."

"I just don't want to be sad anymore."

"You won't be."

She dabbed her lips with a napkin.

"How did you come up with the idea for *Slow Down*?" I asked. The thought just popped out of my mouth.

"Excuse me?"

She spread out the napkin in her lap, rather annoyed.

"I'm just curious. I like to hear about inspiration."

She blew the ridiculous blonde bangs out of her eyes and tapped at the tablecloth with her long nails. Was she stalling for time? Trying to come up with whatever sounded right? I wouldn't let myself believe that. I trusted her wholeheartedly. If I was going to go through with this, I wouldn't question her again.

"I'm sorry," I said, scooping up her hands again, but my fingers were too sweaty and slid right through. "I don't need to know," I said, into her eyes.

"Where's that bourbon?" she asked, looking for the waiter, desperately.

18

I HAD VOMITED BOUILLBAISSE IN THE GUEST BATHROOM ALL over the toilet seat, the sink, and the medicine cabinet. Was this a possible vestige of regret for locking into an agreement to end Dominick's life? I just chalked it up to one too many bourbons. Isadora and I seemed to order more and more throughout the night, as if we might renege on our decision had we remained sober.

Since Cassie's cute friend Maddy was staying over, I didn't want her to hear me retching and went out of my way to graffiti the guest bathroom down the hall with my puke instead. Consuela would have the unfortunate job of having to clean it up. I pictured her scrubbing the bathroom, armed with a toothbrush, her hand covering her nose. Afterwards, I sipped some Pepto and made my way to the living room where Cassie and Maddy were sprawled out on a couch in their bathing suits painting each other's toenails. Maddy had a joint between her lips that smelled suspiciously like Fast. She held out the joint to me while Cassie scowled.

"You look like someone wiped their ass with your face," Cassie said. She and Maddy exchanged a juvenile giggle, but despite her ribbing, Maddy seemed to be turned on by my newfound grunginess and started giving the joint mock head.

I sat down next to her.

"Aren't you girls a little young to be doing something like that?"

"Remember when we used to be so bored with everything, Maddy, and it felt like our feet were just stuck in glue all of the time?" Cassie said. "I never want to go back to living that way."

"Me neither!" Maddy cheered.

"Where did you girls get that Fast?"

"Noah, leave us alone," Cassie whined.

"Ssshhh," I begged, rubbing my temples. "I had a rough night."

Cassie grabbed the joint from Maddy and pulled at it like she'd been smoking Fast her whole life. I searched for the sister who had idolized me not too long ago. As a little kid, she used to latch onto my leg while I pretended to walk around like a giant. When our parents often vanished to some party and never bothered to say when they might return, I'd sneak into her room and tell her ghost stories. I'd crawl in her bed with a flashlight, her eyes growing wider the spookier the stories became. Soon she would forget all about our parents' absence, finding solace in tales of haunted little children worse off than her.

"Your brother is cute," I heard Maddy say.

"Retch! Maddy, he's an old man."

My eye lingered on Maddy and the way her young breasts pressed against her bathing suit.

"You are such a *perv*, Noah."

"Is there anyone you hate?" Maddy asked the room, seemingly out of nowhere.

"I hate Noah," Cassie said.

"I don't hate you," I said, and thought of Dominick instead, a man I needed to hate, and I did, at least I thought so. I certainly felt enraged when I saw Dominick's face, but was that enough? To kill someone, you had to hate every fiber of their being.

"I do hate someone, though," I said. "Enough to want them...."

The two girls now shared in an exaggerated laugh and mumbled about my "lame seriousness." They gave each other a girlish hug with cheeks pressed together. Cassie had twisted her body at an angle that revealed her back, and there it was, my archenemy in my own house, the yellow circle tattoo.

"Where did you get that?" I snapped, shaking her. She hit me back and we began to fight while Maddy watched, attracted to the whole spectacle.

"Where did you get THAT?"

She backed away and traced the outline of the tattoo with a devilish grin. I stepped closer and pushed her toward the couch. Maddy yelped.

"You are out of this house, dick. Mom and Dad will not stand for that."

"Where did you get that, Cassie?" I asked, defeated now.

"He is going to make me famous."

"Both of us," Maddy added, showing her tattoo as well. The girls stood hip-to-hip as their yellow circles taunted. I imagined walking into the living room a month from now and peeling their overdosed and melted bodies off the couch. I never wanted to come back home again; this place had been poisoned now.

"Dom came yesterday while you were asleep, but he was looking for me and any friends I had. He said he really needed to replace this girl who died so I called up Maddy and the three of us snorted a shitload of the best Fast ever. Then he took us to get the tattoos and said we're the stars of his new movie."

"You won't be in his film."

"Fuck that and fuck you."

"I'm serious. He is a monster. He's just recruiting you guys to get back at me."

"The world does not revolve around you."

"Those tattoos are laced with pure Fast!" I said, embarrassed because I was starting to cry.

"Really, Noah, he's treating us well," Maddy said, taking my hand. "This is, like, a great opportunity."

"Maddy, go get me a Corona," Cassie ordered, pointing toward the kitchen and giving her friend a look that said, *take your fucking time to get that beer because we've got some sibling shit to hash out.*

Maddy immediately let go of my hand and sauntered off to fulfill Cassie's demands.

"Don't ruin this for me," Cassie threatened, once Maddy had left. She crossed her leg and bobbed her foot furiously, already a Fast junkie in the making.

"Just tell me he didn't fuck you. Please."

Her foot bobbed even faster. She blew a ring of Fast at the ceiling. She didn't have to say anymore. Dominick had infested this house. He had come in while I was sleeping, primed to infiltrate. He'd been waiting for the moment I would turn on him so he could take over my life just like I had tried to do to him. I never imagined the guy was smart enough.

Maddy entered the living room with the beer but hung in the background like an extra on a film set. I could hear her bare feet pacing back and forth. These girls were so young. They didn't know anything.

"Where is he now, Cassie?"

"I don't know," she said, but she was lying.

She called for Maddy to bring over her beer.

"He's with Dex now," she said. "He said you told him you had a brother, too."

This was the last thing I wanted to hear. Dex could be influenced so easily. Offer him some pot and he'd take a bullet for you. Dominick would promise him the world, and nothing I could say would change his mind. He'd be Dominick's in a matter of minutes, just like I had been not too long ago.

"Where did they go?"

"C'mon, Maddy!" Cassie said, standing up.

She grabbed Maddy's hand. They put on sandals and bounced toward the door, high enough on Fast to just float away. I kept close behind.

"We're headed to a high school party, dick spit. It has nothing to do with Dominick. Just let us go."

She pushed me aside, her and Maddy escaping out of the front door. It stayed open a crack as I watched Cassie drain the Corona and leave the empty bottle in the hallway's floral centerpiece before hugging onto Maddy for support, barely able to stand. If I had any doubts about killing Dominick, this final act of betrayal erased all of them. I had lost Cassie for good now, but I could still save Dex. I just needed to find him in this endlessly large city. But where could he and Dominick be? Where could they both possibly be?

Consuela was in her guest bedroom, a place my parents gave her if it got late enough and she didn't want to go home to Jamaica, Queens. But since my parents had split, she pretty much stayed over all the time. When I walked in, she was watching some dating show on her tiny TV and shoveling a Devil Dog in her mouth. She still had on the apron that my parents insisted she wear at all times, as if she was afraid that they might return at any moment ready to scold.

"What you want, Noie?" she belched. A half-empty bottle of spiced apple rum sat on the bed stand.

"Do you know where Dex went?"

"Consuela do this, Consuela where that? No, how Consuela do, or it is fun to see you, Consuela, good hair today."

"I'm sorry, Consuela, your hair looks very nice."

She removed her wig and let it fall to the floor. Lying on the ground it looked like some furry animal.

"You not the same Noie I raised," she said, pursing her lips.

"What do you mean?"

"You change, and Consuela no like."

She wagged a finger.

"I haven't changed," I said, my voice squeaking and returning to puberty.

"Look, Dex go out! The rose ceremony is coming up on the TV, so…"

She gestured for me to leave.

"I know he's not here, Consuela, but did he say where he went?"

"What, are me and Dex *amigas* now? Give Consuela a break. Check his calendar, the dumbo writes down everything in that."

She threw a Devil Dog at me and brought the spiced rum to her lips, letting out another giant belch.

I backed out of the room, shocked that Consuela thought I had changed so significantly, but I had more important things to do than trying to figure out how I'd fallen in her estimation.

The scrawl on Dex's calendar said he was meeting Dominick at No Bar. I should've known. I headed down in a cab. After entering through the back of the truck, I didn't see Dex or Dominick, so I got a booth hidden partly by the smoky shadows and sipped at a tonic water, unable to even think about consuming anything with alcohol.

When they walked in a half an hour later, Dominick was slapping Dex on the back and ordering some absinthe smoothies. Dex sat in a booth wearing his usual ensemble of glasses without lenses and a mismatched shirt with skinny jeans and beat-up Converse. Dominick sat down eventually and did most of the talking, although I couldn't hear what he was saying. Dex nodded on cue every few seconds and kept flipping his bangs out of his eyes. I knew that meant he was nervous.

After about another half an hour of bullshit, Dominick signaled that he had to go to the bathroom. I jumped at the chance and slid into the booth.

"Noah, what are you doing here?" Dex asked.

"I'm gonna be quick. Don't fuck around with that guy, do you hear me?"

"It's your buddy. You know, the director of *Detached*. He's looking for someone to fill a role in his new film, this lady-killer character he says."

Dex never in his life had a semblance of a clue, and it almost hurt to be honest because he looked so pleased. He believed an asshole like Dominick just like he trusted the whole world. He had to wake up to reality eventually.

"He was lying, dude."

"Why would he do that?"

Dex's face scrunched up like a dog that had been whapped on the butt with a newspaper.

"Listen, Dex, he wants to mess with me. We had a falling out and he wants revenge."

"No, man..."

He gulped the rest of his absinthe smoothie and looked into the empty glass. "You just don't want anyone else to steal your thunder."

"It's not about that."

"It's always about that!"

He knocked over the empty glass. A thin green line of absinthe spilled across the booth. Poor drunk Dex with another notch of disappointment to add to his sorry life. He'd trail behind me until we became old. I wondered if by then I'd no longer have the energy to care.

"Tell him you are not interested..." I began, speaking as if Dex were a child. Waving a finger in his face probably wasn't the best way to convince.

"I am interested!"

"I'll help you. I'm taking over his film. I'll put you in—"

"Why do you give a shit?"

"Dex, I have to go. He's about to come back."

"Fuck you and your mother, too."

"That's also your mother."

"Well, fine, fuck you both. You all suck. The whole family looks at me as if I'm shit. Dominick doesn't."

Dex angled his face to the wall, meaning the conversation was over. I tried to interject, but he had turned even more until he put me out of his sight. I pounded my fist on the table. Dex still wouldn't budge so I got up.

As I went to leave, I spied a girl at the bar watching me. I squinted through the purple smoke and saw it was Nevie. She was half sitting on a stool, one long black boot thrust against the floor like she was guarding the bar while the other leg curled around the stool. I thought of the time at The Penny when I first met Dominick. She had sat at the bar then, smiling her Fast grin. Things had been so uncomplicated in comparison to now. Sure I yearned for her and was dealing with writer's block, but Dominick hadn't infected Dex or Cassie yet, and I didn't have the threat of murder weighing me down. I looked at Nevie now, both of us exhausted. She refused to give me any expression; Dominick had influenced her well. She only moved the slightest when Dominick came up behind her and wrapped his dirty fingers around the exposed flesh of her belly. He whispered into her ear and she pointed through the smoke at me. Dominick's eyes traveled to where she was pointing, and we locked into a staring contest that lasted through eons of tested wills. When he finally broke concentration and made a move to come closer, I walked out through the back of the truck.

If Dominick followed, I didn't know. I just kept on walking without looking back. I went to take a deep exhale, but there was nothing inside of me. When I got to West Broadway, the streets were alive with people, and I still couldn't exhale completely, feeling more lost than ever. I turned down an empty, unlit street where a gust of wind tossed around a plastic bag, but that was the only sign of movement. Maybe I was inviting Dominick to try to attack me and get it over with. I repeated in my mind all of the ways I knew to kill someone instantly. *Go for the throat*, I told myself, pressing my fingers together until they formed the shape of a weapon.

A hand grabbed my shoulder.

"Dominick," I sighed.

"When was the last time you were frightened, Noah?" I heard. "When did you drop your ego for long enough to actually be affected by something?"

Had I imagined those words or was Dominick really there?

"What are you doing here?" the same voice whispered into my ear again. The hand on my shoulder gripped even harder.

"I think you know."

Apologize and kill him tomorrow. Let go of your ego just like he told you to do.

"You're jealous," the voice said.

"I've always been jealous," I admitted, focusing on the cracks in the street to avoid his face.

"That's right," Dominick said, his voice so smooth. He let go of my shoulder. I swiveled around to make sure it hadn't been a ghost that trailed me.

"You said some terrible things to me the other night."

He took a step closer to me again, his hand cast in the shadows. I looked carefully to make sure he didn't have a knife.

"Are you aware of what you said?"

The hand darted out of the shadows as I flinched, but Dominick only held onto his pipe. He stuffed in some Fast and took a puff.

"I had a lot to drink when I said those things."

"True, but alcohol usually brings out our true feelings. Tell me, do you regret it?"

The air dropped in temperature, my surroundings blurred. Puffs of Fast snaked through the empty street. I longed for my imaginary friend, Little Boatie, who I hadn't thought about in years. At the moment, I didn't want to be an adult anymore.

"I came to No Bar to tell you I was sorry," I said, fighting to get those words out.

"You are a spoiled fuck," Dominick said.

"I know, I know." I nodded, my hands shaking as I struggled to set up what would be his demise. "Can I...come by tomorrow night to truly apologize? It's not easy for me to admit that I'm wrong, but I was. You've been...so great."

Lies. Beautiful lies. There was no turning back now, but my hands still shook. The idea of tomorrow, a vision of feeding Dominick enough Fast for him to choke, seemed to be so far away.

"All right, I'll see you tomorrow night," he snickered, and then directed a fist into my gut.

As I slumped to the dirty sidewalk, Dominick's unmerciful laughs filled up the air, the cackles of trolls and those that frequented the underworld. I clutched my stomach, coughed and wheezed, spat up a string of sour saliva. I rolled over and got up on one knee as the cackles became muffled and his shadow disappeared around the corner onto West Broadway.

My hands had stopped shaking.

I was finally ready.

This time tomorrow night, Dominick would no longer exist.

19

TONIGHT'S THE NIGHT, IT'S GONNA BE ALL RIGHT.

Rod Stewart crooned from my iPod alarm as I woke up. My stomach still hurt, either because of Dominick's fist or because the last real meal I had was the bouillabaisse from over a day ago.

I felt a muscle as I rolled over on my side. Rod Stewart kept persuading a young virgin to let her be his tonight. I hit the snooze button. Ten minutes of calm. Ten minutes to get my mind ready for tonight. I lay there for an hour more, smacking the snooze button with a vengeance until Isadora called and said she had all the Fast we needed.

"Time to make this happen," she said, as an order.

"Yes," I replied, and hung up, wondering if I should've said more to prove I was excited.

I was sweating like mad on the B train downtown since the car had no air conditioning. I should've splurged for a cab but needed the extra time the train would take, the suspended anticipation. At Times Square, I fell into the anonymous rush of movement toward the N train and waited until it finally snaked through the tunnel. On the rocking car to Prince Street, I pretended I wasn't about to kill Dominick, that this all existed on some far-fetched soap opera.

Outside of the train, SoHo was mobbed, the air sweltering and soupy for late April. I didn't need to wear my leather jacket, heavy like sandbags on my shoulders and sticking to my skin. I had the desire to fling it off and leave it in a garbage can.

I reached Greene Street and remembered my last week in Chinatown. I played with the change in my pocket as I paced outside the entrance to

Dominick's loft. I was stalling. I ripped into a cigarette and looked up to try to see into their living room. The lights were on and a shadow paced around just like me. Was it an anxious Isadora, or possibly Dominick who sensed something was amiss? I tossed my cigarette and plunged into the lobby's abyss.

Upstairs, Dominick and Isadora sat like cats on the loud red couch, poised and awaiting my entrance for different reasons. True to his nature, Dominick already had a goblet of absinthe in his hand. Droplets splashed on the floor as he stood, which meant that it hadn't been his first goblet of the day.

Isadora sat with her hands in her lap and her fingers laced together. Her knees touched demurely rather than a provocative crossing of the leg. She gave me a nod and a wink, indicating that there would be no turning back.

"Noah, buddy," Dominick said. He tipped back and forth like an uneven seesaw. "What's your poison?"

My legs almost buckled in response to that question. *Poison?* What a word to choose out of all the words in the English language. I gulped and pointed to the goblet of absinthe.

Dominick wagged a finger at me.

"Will you promise not to repeat what happened the other night?"

"Of course, Dominick. I am truly sorry—"

"Little baby is all grown up and can handle his liquor now?"

He shuffled over to the bar, entirely pleased with his dig.

"Yes," I said, sharing a sigh with Isadora as we caught each other's eye.

"It's good to see you again, Noah," she said, playing her role well. She rose to shake my hand and placed a small pill bottle in my fist. I saw it was filled with crushed Fast.

"Nice to see you again, Ms. Bambach," I said, slipping the bottle in my pocket and then realizing that there was no need to pretend to act so formal with her.

Dominick came over and shoved a goblet at me. He waited for me to take a sip.

"Good, right?"

I nodded.

"You can always call me Isadora," she said, batting her eyes at me compassionately. The way she said it made me realize that we'd be together for a long time, locked by our shared secret. During nights in bed, we'd hold each other close when our consciences would become our enemies. Sometimes I'd have to whisper to her that everything will be all right, other times she would be the stronger one. I wanted to hold her right now.

"I will, Isadora," I said, tears flooding my eyes.

"So Isadora will be joining us tonight, Noah. At least until our twaddle bores her senseless."

"I would never be bored with you," she said, biting the words. "But I will eventually head to bed and leave you boys to fight it out to the death."

"She knows we've had our differences lately," Dominick added.

"Water under the bridge, Dominick," I said, raising my goblet.

He responded by downing his absinthe while frowning and wiping away the dribbles with his sleeve. From that gesture, I knew I hadn't been forgiven yet, if ever.

"Dominick and I really enjoyed when you came for dinner, Noah. We'd love to do that again sometime."

She patted him on the elbow to chime in.

"I know it's what I live for," he shouted, as little green balls of spit landed on her face.

"Dominick," she whispered.

"I'm sorry, Noah, that just came out. Sometimes I say things without even thinking, but *you* know how that is."

"We can all be guilty of putting a foot in our mouth," I said, fingering the pill bottle of crushed Fast.

He sat down on the red couch and motioned for me to take the chair across from him.

"I won't embarrass you with the need for a forced apology, Noah. Your presence here solidifies that. See, I can be the bigger man."

"Thank you," I said, finding solace in the glass of absinthe.

Isadora sat next to Dominick on the couch so she was between her men. I looked over to her for guidance. She seemed to be in a wonderful trance with her refilled glass of wine. She was smiling suspiciously, or maybe it just appeared that way because I knew how thrilled she was for tonight's gruesome outcome.

She glanced toward Dominick's goblet, indicating for me to slip in some Fast. The chance came when she asked for him to hand her a Kleenex from the side table. He turned his back to us and I tapped in some Fast.

"How long have you two been married?" I asked, thinking of anything I could to distract him.

"Five years," Dominick said, picking up the goblet again and taking a sip. For a moment, I thought I saw him cringe. This man knew Fast better than practically anyone else and here we were trying to fool him? Suddenly, the plot seemed too absurd, but then Dominick kept drinking away and I felt my heartbeat return to a steady, icky thump.

"I was a June bride, so it will be five years very soon," Isadora said, and she and Dominick gazed at each other for long enough to recall the past but not be bogged down by memories of better times.

"Chin chin," I said, knowing I sounded like a moron, but trying to focus on anything but my wildly tapping foot.

"Most people are not real with me, but Isadora has always been as brutally honest as an unflattering light."

He ran a finger down her face like he was tracing a line of moisture on a fogged window. If I didn't know any better, I would've left the room to let the lovers be alone.

"Make me another drink, Noah," he said, holding out the empty goblet and inviting me to continue his slow killing.

As I tried to remember the steps to make absinthe, I saw him and Isadora kiss. The effect was vomit inducing, slobbering tongues and a passionless embrace. I finished off the drink with more crushed Fast and held it between their devouring faces.

"Thank you," Dominick said, taking a break from smearing the lipstick all over her face to lunge for the absinthe. "So let me ask you, Noah, did you say those terrible things to me the other night purely out of jealousy?"

"Dominick," Isadora chided, looking insane with a smear of lipstick all over her cheek.

"What else would it be?" I replied, fingering the half-empty pill bottle again.

"But why be jealous of me? I've simply worked harder for what I've accomplished and you are still a child. And you may even surpass me one day. Then we can look back on our little squabble and laugh, but for now I will NOT accept defiance by an underling of mine, by someone inferior like you."

"I'm not going to stay here for this," Isadora said, rising to her feet.

"Bed so soon, love?"

"Well, the proverbial pissing contest is about to begin, and I haven't brushed up on my insult-slinging abilities."

"Oh, my dear, you are better than you think."

"I will see you in the morning," she said, tossing daggers at Dominick with her eyes, but her words were said with a hesitant undertone. She would not see him the next morning, and as much as she hated him, I knew she couldn't deny that she'd be affected by his absence.

He waved her off as I stood to bid her goodnight.

"Good luck," she whispered, with her hand on my chest. My insides shivered, and I didn't know if it was a delightful shiver or a regretful one. Once I figured out which one it was, she had already vanished down the hallway.

"She always sours an evening," Dominick said. "Chronically unsatisfied and determined to take it out on everyone around her. She's stolen my soul for too long."

He knocked back the absinthe and held out his goblet.

"Are you sure you want more?" I asked, and then bit my tongue so I could stay ruthless.

"I feel really hot now. Is it hot in here?"

I nodded and refilled the drink, adding another spoonful of the crushed Fast.

"I want music," Dominick said, snapping. He sat down and stood up again restlessly.

"How about some Monk?"

"Yeah, yeah, yeah."

He dashed over to the stereo system and cranked up the volume until Monk poured into the room and surrounded us in a piano chorus.

"Did I ever tell you how I came up with the idea for *Slow Down?*" he yelled over the tinkling keys.

I handed him the fresh drink and nodded toward the painting above the couch: a solitary yellow circle on a blank canvas.

"No, no, that was done after," he said, hugging himself like he was wearing a straitjacket. "I had just lost my one true love, my heavenly Astrid. I drove down some avenue in the middle of the night catching green at every stoplight. Finally one stoplight turned yellow, the color burning into my mind, and I wanted to resist it, to speed up and just let God decide what would happen, as I'd run through a series of reds. I wanted that head-on collision, I wanted to feel something again because

I'd never been so numb before. I tasted the anticipation of glass shards on my tongue, as I'd soar through the front window, but then I found myself seeing the yellow light in the distance, a beacon of hope, a promise of a new tomorrow, and like magic, I eased up on that gas instead and came to a stop. By the time the light turned green again, I had mapped out the entire plot."

My shivers returned because I didn't want to believe Dominick's story; it had beat Isadora's nonresponse. But I couldn't let that thought consume me now. I had taken the murder too far already.

Dominick knocked back the goblet again and let green streaks dribble down his chin.

"Do you want more?" I asked, my voice cracking. Part of me wanted him to refuse so I could run out of the loft and make believe this night never happened. But the goblet was tossed to me and I had no choice.

Dominick began to lose control of his facial tics. His muscles started to spasm, and he looked at his wiggling arm as if it were an alien appendage.

"Are you in love, Noah?" he asked.

"Yes," I said, dumping out almost the entire bottle of Fast, desperate to end this torture already.

"I killed her," he said, crying what looked like green tears, but it was really just a mix of some spittle on his face.

"She's okay now," I said, meaning Nevie, but he shook his head.

"She had betrayed me with him, with my fucking father. A man so emotionally bankrupt, so...beastly in his vengeful cruelty."

"Nevie?" I asked, but I knew that Dominick was speaking about Astrid.

"Pass me the absinthe, Noah, and stop holding it like a little BITCH."

He grabbed the drink before I even added the absinthe. The goblet was filled with pure Fast, but he was too far gone to realize. He chomped down on the poison and let it filter through the gaps in his teeth.

"And this purgatory I've been in since is all because *she* found out," he hissed, his eyes darting toward the shadows spilling from the hallway.

He draped himself on the red couch, humped it lightly, and then licked up a bit of Fast powder that had spilled.

"Are you all right, Dominick?" I asked, shaky.

"Everything is so fast and awful, isn't it, Noah?"

"The world has become like that."

I sat down next to him. I could hear this man's heart, beating like it was trying to burst through his chest. A thin white line of pus dangled from his nose.

"I made that painting," he said, glancing up at the yellow circle. "After that revolutionary ride where I almost died."

"It's very good."

We both stood and stared at the painting. We tipped our heads to the side to look at it from a different angle.

"It has so much *genius* behind it."

"Who were you talking about before, Dominick?"

"Hmmm?"

The music cut off suddenly, and he collapsed back onto the couch.

"You said you've been living in a purgatory ever since 'she' found out. Who were you referring to?"

Dominick stood up and fell into my arms, slurring. He stammered to his feet and rested his hands on my shoulders, his nose touching mine as he looked directly in my eyes.

"She'll destroy you as well," he simply said, and then let go to shuffle over to the bar for more absinthe.

"I think you've had enough."

I was crying now, choking up tears from deep within.

"Please, Dominick."

I looked at my reflection in the glass coffee table and was shocked to see how pale and unrecognizable I'd become.

"What's this?" Dominick asked, scooping up more of the crushed Fast he'd spilled.

"Shit," I said.

"Should I eat it?" he asked, sprinkling it onto his green tongue.

"No!" I yelled, and knocked the rest out of his palm. We watched it disintegrate into the air until he shrugged his shoulders and sucked at the remnants on his tongue.

I heard a buzzing sound throughout the loft, now that the music had ended. It reminded me of the feeling you get when some electronic appliance is on in the house, but you can't figure out what. The buzz came from down the darkening hallway. The buzz was watching me closely.

Dominick went into the kitchen and turned on the sink faucet. He stuck his head into a stream of cold water. He then waddled over, drenched.

"You hate *Slow Down*," he said, taking off his shirt and throwing it to the floor.

"No, I don't, Dominick."

"Bullshit, you do. You think I'm nothing."

He got in my face and pushed me. I slid back due to the wet floor but caught myself on the kitchen counter.

"I apologized to you!"

"You patronized me!"

"You did the same. I worked hard on the editing I gave you. I didn't want it to come to this."

"What do you mean you didn't want it to come to this?" he slurred.

"I wanted to learn from you, I…"

But I had to stop, knowing it was all lies. From the moment I met Dominick I'd been plotting.

"*Slow Down* is my *Citizen Kane*, my fucking *Godfather*, the one they'll study till the end of time. Every piece of it will fit beautifully; it has to. I've seen that in my lucid dreams, how it transcends…and…and…"

He slapped his head.

"My fucking brain is not WORKING LIKE IT SHOULD, NOAH!"

He smacked his forehead repeatedly until he drew blood. I coolly got out a pack of cigarettes from my leather jacket, lit one, and observed this man's demise. I blew a train of smoke, as he whimpered in response.

"You can lie to yourself in these last moments, Dominick, but lying is all you do. Isadora is the one with the talent and not the monster you make her out to be. You stole *Detached* from her, you stole *Slow Down*, and you'll just keep on thieving unless someone stops you."

"That's right," he managed to laugh. "She told you all of these truths in her fucking serpent arms. You're a fool."

I picked up the goblet and made a final glass of absinthe for Dominick with the rest of the crushed Fast. I held it to his lips and forced one last, deadly sip. He recoiled by spitting it out, his eyes aware now.

"Welcome to my purgatory then." Dominick sniffed as his pupils spun and then rolled up into his brain until only a zombie stared back. The zombie shuffled over to his painting of a yellow circle and touched it, soothingly.

"Home, it's where I want to be. I want to go home to her," he murmured, pointing toward the yellow circle as if it could lead him to where he desired, but his head had become a heavy medicine ball and pulled his body down into the glass table. In that slow-motion instant of descent, I watched him spread out his arms with a smile before he crashed right through the table in a beautiful crescendo, the glass sounding like tinkles from a piano as its shavings glittered across the floor and sliced through his face and body. One trapezoid shard hung from his neck, and a noise escaped from the open wound like a deflating tire. His body rose and fell, rose and fell, and then moved no more.

My stomach bubbled as I clenched my bowels. I cupped my hand over my mouth, threw up a bit, and then swallowed it back, telling myself that I deserved to keep the foulness inside. Dominick lay at my feet. Dominick was dead. The music from the stereo picked up again, as if on cue, its terse, jaunty rhythms saving me from the silence. I lowered my head and slouched out of the room toward the darkness of the hallway and the bedroom where my forever partner in crime waited.

Upon entering, the red light of a video camera pointed toward a naked Isadora on the bed with the sheets covering her privates. She said hello to me with her foot fondling my crotch.

"Come here."

I fell into her with a sob and she rubbed my back. A kiss tickled my earlobe. She pulled off my shirt and tossed it to the floor. I looked at my chest with disdain, my stomach expanding and contracting from my deep breaths. I imagined those breaths stopping completely. She circled my nipple with her tongue, made it hard, and then kissed me coldly on the neck. My belt was unbuckled as my pants slid down to my ankles and my boxers soon followed. I stood quietly, subdued, but harder than ever before. I started fingering her like my fingers were knives as she beat the sheets with her fists.

"Is he dead?"

She moaned as I spread her legs and whispered inside of her that I had killed him.

She screamed when I started fucking her, but I wouldn't relent. I fucked her and she screamed until morning came with different screams from outside the bedroom. I'd been dreaming of a world where yesterday didn't exist, but as a dour sun streamed through the blinds and brought me back to reality, Isadora's arms felt like a vise that might never let go.

"I think someone found Dominick," she said casually, as if waking up to deafening screams was just like every other morning.

20

THE SCREAMS COMING FROM OUTSIDE ISADORA'S BEDROOM wouldn't end. I shot out of bed and found my boxers while Isadora yawned at the ceiling. I headed down the hallway with her trailing behind and wearing my collared shirt. When we reached the living room, the screams became replaced with sobs.

Nevie sat crouched over Dominick's body, her chest heaving as she gulped for a breath, her face blemished with tears. But I was more concerned that the body was no longer by the broken glass table but had moved fifteen feet during the night to its final resting place under the painting of the yellow circle. A bloody handprint streaked down the painting that had not been there last night.

"Fuck," I said, as Nevie looked up from Dominick's body.

"I had a key," she said, apologizing.

She held up a bloodied key and then let out a screeching howl that I would never forget.

After we got a hysterical Nevie on her way, I figured I shouldn't be there when the cops arrived. I'd walk the city, clear my head, get myself to stop shaking.

"Wish me luck, lover," Isadora said, pulling me close for a kiss. After a cold peck, I slid out of her embrace and escaped to the front door with a halfhearted "luck" under my breath. She turned toward a mirror in the foyer and told herself to "cry, cry, cry," while slapping herself across the face. When I looked back from the doorframe, her face was already flushed with exuberant tears and a satisfied smile.

Stepping into the elevator, I gazed at my own reflection in the mirrored doors, the double who I'd face from now on.

"Murderer," I said, and then waited to see my reaction.

The elevator beeped loudly as it descended away from the reality of what had occurred upstairs.

My reflection seemed like it was begging not to be judged. I clasped my hands together to stop them from trembling. As I stared into my eyes, a demon lurched from out of my reflection: horns and fangs, a red tail like a knife held between its sharp fingernails, a bloody smile and a cackle to boot. I jumped back, but then—*poof*—the demon dissolved.

The elevator beeped one last time as I reached the bottom floor.

In the lobby, a piercing silence rang in my eardrums. I pushed through the front door and found myself craving crowds, glad for once to be in SoHo with a pack of shoppers down Broadway. The morning was cool and my jacket was thin, but I breathed in the cold air until I stopped crying.

I passed a mother laughing with her two kids, the three of them arm-in-arm creating a blockade across the street that I had to weave around. None of them even noticed me, caught up in their own jubilation, and I wondered if I'd ever laugh like that again, or if each laugh from now on would always die down.

I swung onto Mercer Street as faces zoomed by, indistinguishable, but I tried to take in each one and see if I could tell what they were thinking. Had any of them ever killed someone before? Were they able to hide it well? I had to learn to do just that, tucking the guilt deep down until I'd release it back into the world on my death bed, a final absolution that all my bedside loved ones would chalk up to dementia. I had a scary thought that I might long for this day, when I'd finally be free.

My feet moved separate from my mind, and before I knew it, I was at the Hudson River. I watched a chilling dew steam from the waters, the Statue of Liberty standing with her torch to the sky, a docking Circle Line cruise, and then an overweight runner coming toward me with his face mashed from the wind, tired and out of breath, slowing down until it looked like he was running underwater, until he was barely moving at all, until he stopped in his tracks and stared at me, panting, both of our hearts racing.

"I'm sorry," I said, my voice sounding like it had never been used before. The man scrunched up his face in confusion. "I'm sorry."

And then I took off as fast as I could. When I finally turned back to look, the runner was just a dot along the Hudson. Once he had finally disappeared into the morning dew, I couldn't hold back my tears any longer and gripped the side railing as the demon wailed from inside.

It was late at night when I returned to the loft, ample enough time for the cops, fire department, and coroner to leave. I had texted Isadora to make sure she was alone and she had replied with a *see u soon, stud* and a winking smiley face. In the elevator going up, I faced the wall instead of the mirrored doors. When they opened, she waited in the doorframe, ready to pounce in her negligée.

"They bought it completely," she said, yanking me inside.

The living room had been cleaned and seemed empty without the glass coffee table. The painting with Dominick's bloody handprint still hung, the cops probably assuming that it was simply art and not evidence.

Isadora grabbed my crotch as I wiggled out of her grasp.

"What's wrong?"

"I don't know," I said, pacing. "I walked the entire city today, I feel—"

"Sssshhh."

She slinked over and touched her fingers to my lips, kept them shut. "We're all right," she said, into my eyes. "There's no suspicion of foul play. They saw his Fast lab in the bathroom; they found his stashes everywhere. I showed them the bruise on my collarbone and said I was afraid to say anything about his illegal activities. I have to go for questioning tomorrow, but I'll make sure to sell it good."

She fondled my crotch again. "We did it."

"I'm not worried about getting caught."

"Then what?"

She kissed my neck, left lipstick on my chin, found my mouth and devoured me whole. I became lost in her embrace, momentarily detaching myself from all my worries until I saw the bloody handprint on the painting again. I de-suctioned myself from her, shivering.

"Noah, stop. Baby..."

I shook my head until I was shaking it so fast I began to get a headache. "I don't like myself very much anymore."

She grabbed me by the shoulders. "No, you listen to me. This needed to happen."

I shook my head furiously. She slapped me across the face.

"You get a grip. I've always believed that we are in charge of our destinies. Mine was not to be an abused victim while that son of a bitch got all the glory."

"You hit me."

"Do you see this?" she said, pointing to her bruise. "There are a lot of people in this world and now there is just one less asshole. No one will miss him in the end, I promise."

I ran my fingers over her bruise and then kissed it.

"You are a hero," she said. "Do not ever forget that. Don't let this break you."

"I'm afraid."

"You control your destiny. We have a movie to finish. Look toward your future and only see success. Never look backwards. Do you understand me?"

I nodded, but that wasn't enough for her. She clasped my head in her hands and said it again.

"Say that you're a hero, Noah."

"I'm a hero."

"Good. Now meet me in the bedroom and get ready to fuck me senseless."

In the darkness of the bedroom, Isadora helped purge what had burned inside of me. While planting her against the headboard and doing her from behind, she made me say over and over that I "killed him, killed your husband, killed Dominick, left him dead." After what seemed like hours of shouting my confessions, she ran her tongue across every inch of me, every last bit of my guilty sweat. After a year of normal, pleasant sex with a girl like Margaret, I transformed that night: I had Isadora on the floor, up on the bureau, upside-down, twisted and contorted like a circus freak. I gagged her with the pillowcase; I spanked her hard when she demanded it; she choked me and I choked her back until the two of us were asphyxiated, gasping for breath, coming together. The sheets had been soaked and stained after our marathon as the early morning light pierced through the shutters. I rose on shaky legs, a smear of blood across my fingertips that I rubbed into my eyes, my body entirely spent and excavated, as if she'd taken my soul and left me blissfully hollow, nothing at all rattling inside anymore, the demon fleeing down the fire escape and vanishing into the night for good.

As I felt my way toward the bathroom, the red light of a camera followed me. I could hear the camera's whir, storing what had transpired between us, the depravity of what it witnessed. Lying on the bed, I could have sworn I saw Isadora give it a wink. Her gleaming smile dripped blood as she played with herself for show.

I turned away and locked myself in the bathroom until morning finally arrived.

I left the loft as early as possible to avoid Isadora, no direction in mind, but then I found myself hours later in front of Nevie's apartment. Luckily the doorman recognized me and let me go up even when Nevie didn't respond on the intercom. I knocked but when no one answered I found the same key inside her makeshift *mezuzah* and opened the door.

A gust of Fast welcomed me upon entering, the air thick with its soupy haze. My heart thumped as I imagined she overdosed again. I ran toward her bedroom, knowing I couldn't handle it if I was responsible for another OD. I swung open the door, coughing from the smoke, waving it from my eyes as I made out a lumped figure under the covers.

"Fuck. No, Nevie."

Her bedside table held the evidence of how she spent the past day: Fast cut up and snorted, a smoking pipe with it stuffed inside, and a tumbler of a viscous liquid like the kind I had found in Dominick's sink. I covered my mouth and bit into my palm, tears blurring my vision. I bent down to move the sheet away and deal with her corpse.

Her foot stuck out, porcelain white, the nail polish chipped like a little girl's, this perfect foot. I latched onto a big toe and hoped it'd be warm.

"Nevie?"

The toe twitched. I jumped back as the lump under the covers shifted with a moan.

"Thank God," I said, wiping my eyes and taking a deep breath. I removed the sheets.

"Who's there?" she asked, removing her eye mask. She shrugged when she saw me, her eyes bloodshot and raw.

"I just wanted to check up on you," I said, backing away.

"I'm fine."

She inched toward her bedside table and picked up the tumbler. She stirred the liquid with her finger and then rubbed some onto the small of her back.

"Nevie, maybe you should eat something."

When she finished rubbing the Fast, she placed her fingers in her mouth licking up every last bit and wincing at its foulness.

"Stop," I said, pulling her hands away from her mouth, but she fought me. "Stop!"

She growled at me to go away and I almost hit her. I held out my hand ready to snap, but then I saw the Fast had already kicked in; she was floating now.

"Noah," she said, and held out her hand.

"I thought you were d..."

I stopped myself because I couldn't say it, but she knew what I meant. She shook her head.

"I can't believe *he's* dead," she said.

"I'm just glad you aren't."

I sat down next to her and she leaned against my shoulder. I petted her long black hair, all I needed in this stinking world to feel okay. Her eyes fluttered and rolled back into her head and she was already snoring.

"Nevie, wake up."

I patted her cheek until she opened her eyes again, momentarily seeming like she didn't recognize me at all.

"It's me."

She reached over me for the pipe.

"No, you've had enough."

She pushed me aside and grasped it in her fist.

"You do not own me," she said, placing her lips around the pipe.

I love you, I wanted to say.

"I need a lighter."

"Nevie, you've had enough."

"I need a lighter," she wailed, but I grabbed the pipe from her lips and threw it to the floor. She watched it shatter to pieces.

"Why did you do that, Noah?"

She beat the sheets and dove for the bedside table, her nose trying to sniff up a fresh line.

"No," I said, holding her back. She fought in my arms, but it was useless. I shoved her back on the bed, picked up a garbage bin, and dumped all of her Fast inside.

"What are you doing? No. I need...I need...that's all of my stuff!"

"This is for your own good. You want to hide under the covers, fine, but you're gonna do so sober."

"Noah, please."

She licked her fingers, trying to get every last bit, and then collapsed under the sheets sobbing uncontrollably.

"Just leave me be...just leave me be...just leave me be...just leave me be..."

I held the garbage bin to my chest and headed for the door. Her perfect foot had slid out of the sheets and dangled over the edge of the bed. I stared at its porcelain doll-like beauty and couldn't imagine a world where I'd never see it again.

"I love you," I said, my heart swelling madly, and then I closed the door.

Back at home I napped through the afternoon, my dreams twisted and dark, splattered with blood. I woke up to hearing my name. In my dream, I knew that someone was calling me, but I chose not to respond.

My eyes shot open as a bead of sweat dripped down my nose. Dex stood in the doorframe.

"You left your phone in the living room; someone's been texting you nonstop."

He threw the cell on my bed.

I wondered what would happen if I confided in Dex. Sad to say, but my brother was the closest person in my life. He'd understand, he had to. You stand behind family no matter what. *Ha!* My family would cut me off like a cancerous limb. If I ever got caught, they'd pay off my bail, get me a hotshot lawyer, and once I'd been convicted, they'd pretend I never existed. But not Dex. He'd be on the other end of a glass partition baking me pot brownies once a week and trying to make me laugh with some dumb impression, his clothes still as mismatched as ever.

"Snap out of it, dude," Dex said. "You were, like, just staring at me."

I had treated Dex like shit when Dominick tried to cast him in *Slow Down*. He had every right to be pissed off at me. I wanted to tell him sorry for treating him like shit too often. I wanted to be a better big brother. He stood there, my baby bro, scratching his uncombed hair, still in his boxers and a wifebeater by late afternoon, a bag of salt-and-vinegar chips tucked under his arm.

You know I'm an ass, Dex, but you know how much I care about you. When I was five I'd pretend to be your dad, and you even used to call me that cause it pissed off our parents so, especially Janet. Remember the time you made yourself fart all through dinner because the 'rents had snooty guests over and the wife with the big hat kept making faces at us because we were laughing so hard that milk came out of our noses? Or when I was fourteen and put you in the first film I made about a dorky kid who eats a magical cereal that makes him cool? We thought we'd get into festivals from our ten-minute work of art and spent a whole day doing mock interviews for David Letterman. We had some good times, baby bro, and there's no reason why they have to end.

But I said nothing.

"All right, weirdo," Dex said, leaving the room after I didn't respond.

"Fuck," I said, throwing my arm over my face, and then looked to see who had been texting me.

Isadora—twenty-two times.

Meet me on the bureau
Meet me on the bureau
Meet me on the bureau....

In the bedroom, Isadora waited on the bureau, the lights off, a strip of moonlight like a bolt across her face. The red light of the video camera watched me enter. I took off my clothes and fell into her.

"The funeral's tomorrow, Noah. Let me see your sad face."

I didn't change my expression.

"Looks good to me."

She wrapped her legs around me and squeezed.

"Hi, hero."

She groped my dick and made me hard, pushed me inside of her. She arched her back and bucked in rhythm with my thrusts, her nails digging into my back and creating fresh scars. She bared her teeth as she moved in for a vampire kiss, but I closed my eyes and tried to calm my thoughts. Clouds. Oceans. Seagulls along a beach. And then Nevie's foot spilling from the sheets, dangling like heaven on a string. I took that foot in my hands and planted a sweet kiss. The sheet fell away and there she was, her face lively like it used to be before the Fast. When we were young, and she smelled like sunflowers perfume after her punk phase ended, smoking a blunt at her country house in Southampton after a round of golf at her parents' club, both of us dancing around a bonfire on the beach. She had picked up a giant seashell and placed it to her ear, her eyes growing wide.

"What do you hear?" I asked.

The blunt she had handed me hung from my lips.

Tears fell from her eyes.

"It sounds so beautiful," she said, and made me listen. I heard nothing, just a soft whisper, but I knew right then, as she continued her dance around the fire, that I loved her more than I even loved myself, and I always would.

I came inside of Isadora with a ball of tears lodged in my throat.

21

AS DOMINICK'S COFFIN DESCENDED INTO THE GROUND, I made a decision. The Noah that I'd known my entire life didn't exist anymore. The minute I slipped the Fast in Dominick's drink, I had become someone else. I'd also have to cut off everyone from my old life since they were all liabilities, connections to what I had done, except of course for those involved in *Slow Down*. Those people had to stay to complete my film; otherwise what would've been the point of losing my soul?

After the funeral, Isadora invited guests to the loft who treated the event as if it were a party. Dominick didn't have friends, he had associates, moochers. No one even shed a tear. They raided his liquor cabinet, did Fast in rooms, told stories of his indulgences, his wild times, not as a way of commemorating, but simply to bolster their own status. They had partied and drugged with the newly dead and lived to tell the tale.

Nevie was the only one who cared. I passed her a cup of coffee because she seemed frozen: blankly staring at everyone, no recognition of time or place. She accepted the coffee but placed it down on the side table without a response.

Isadora played her role well, angling for that Best Actress trophy. She dabbed away tears and reminisced about stories of Dominick, which seemed made up. She chatted with Palmer and Estella in the corner. I wondered if she was already working to keep them interested in *Slow Down*. Palmer had grown a teenage mustache that looked dusted with cocaine while Estella fought to remain the thinnest woman on Earth.

Soon Isadora needed to mingle with other attendees, and Palmer and Estella decided to bother me instead. This annoyed me, since Nevie had finally risen from her chair of gloom and was eating crudités like it was the sole reason for her existence. I would have to wait till I could talk with her.

Estella was wearing a very un-funeral green dress that loosely hung from her body. Palmer had on sunglasses, the only black he wore. As I looked around the room, I realized that Nevie and I were the only ones who bothered to dress appropriately.

"Terrible," Estella said, playing with her blonde hair like it was a puppy and retaining a murmur of her poorly constructed Eastern European accent.

"It's horrible to say this, but I saw it coming," Palmer said, and posed for a pretend picture when someone glanced their way.

"I know. I did, as well."

"And after all the work we did," Palmer said, as he poured some colorful punch into a martini glass. "I hate to sound inconsiderate, but this was supposed to be my big break."

I put my arms around them both and channeled Dominick.

"I don't know what Isadora said to you both, but we are not about to scrap *Slow Down*. Dominick and I discussed every detail of this, and if I'm being honest, the script was never complete. Dom had ideas but they were muddled; I have a complete concept for this film and Isadora's permission to see it come to life."

Palmer and Estella walked with me. Sobriety was a distant memory in their minds, and they had become excited again. I kissed them both on the cheeks and shook their phony hands. I had no idea how I'd figure out a complete plot of the film, but at least I had sold them and they seemed more than game. Nevie would be the most difficult to convince.

I took a deep breath and proceeded over to where she stood by the crudités. She was methodically chomping on baby carrots, eating each one in three quick bites. I grabbed a carrot as well and chomped in sync.

"Hi," I said, with as much genuine sympathy as I could convey. She responded by finishing two more carrots and then taking me by the hand and leading me out of the living room. We reconvened in Dominick's lucid dreaming room. I fiddled with the gadgets while she burned her tongue with the coffee she brought along. She looked so sad, so pathetic. She'd never understand that I had to kill Dominick.

"I loved him," she said.

"Did you?"

Frail. Sunken. Her face white as cotton. Two days had passed and she spent them under the covers.

"I love him even more now."

She smiled at his gadgets, his hopeful way of achieving better ideas. *Let her believe he was amazing. At least that will give her something.*

"I'm glad that he and I patched things up before…"

"I don't want to talk about death," she said.

"I'm going to finish *Slow Down.*"

She didn't seem to care.

"With Isadora's blessing of course. Dom's blessing too. He actually told me that if anything happened to him I should continue—"

"I don't want to *talk* about it. That could have been me."

I understood what she meant. She saw a reflection of herself the morning she found Dominick: overdosed from Fast, sped up and going nowhere. I went to hug her, but Isadora peered into the room.

"Noah, can you help me with something?" Isadora said.

"Uh, yeah, sure."

I caught Nevie's eye to make sure she'd be all right by herself, but she had already picked up one of Dominick's gadgets and became absorbed with it.

"Come," Isadora said, pulling me into her bedroom. Once inside, she slammed the door and pressed herself into me, knocking my head against the wall. I went to rub it but she grabbed my hands and forced me to grope her ass as she bit my lip.

"This party is so boring," she said between bites.

"We just came from a funeral."

"Oh, you won't see me going out like that."

She nibbled my lip like a carrot, which made him think of Nevie. I wondered if Nevie had gone back to the table full of crudités or if she was waiting in the lucid room for me to come and dream with her.

Isadora broke my fantasy by jamming her tongue in my mouth. It tasted like perfume. She had sprayed on too much, rather old lady-like, and I could only picture an elderly Elizabeth Taylor licking my chin instead.

"Isadora," I said, pushing her away. "Not now."

"Why not?"

"You have to look sad for all those people out there."

"So fuck me right here, nothing will make me look more distraught than that."

She licked my chin again and stifled a giggle.

"Cute."

"Tell me what you did to him," she said, as if she didn't know, as if she had just discovered her husband's body on the floor and wanted answers.

"Do you want to know *everything*?"

She nodded and hopped up on the bureau. Next to her sat the video camera. She always said the voyeuristic quality turned her on unlike anything else, the beauty of tapping into the far recesses of my brain.

"I killed him," I yawned, unable to stop thinking about Nevie eating those carrots, the way she was careful and diligent with each bite, as if she knew she was living on borrowed time and wanted to make the most of each taste. She could be pathetic, but she could be my pathetic, and Isadora could be dismissed once I finished filming *Slow Down*. I still needed her permission and financial backing so I jabbed my middle and index finger inside of her as her legs kicked up in the air with her silver panties tying them together. The bureau knocked into the wall and she covered her mouth so no one would hear her orgasmic yelps. The promise of watching our lovemaking later always thrilled her, but we never did, the hours of logged film seeming to just disappear.

Now she came and shimmied up her panties, then patted me on the cheek before leaving the room.

I smelled my fingers, sighed, and followed her out.

Isadora loved pasta, but more than that she loved to watch me cook pasta. She tracked me with the video camera as I added olive oil and sundried tomatoes to a bowl of farfalle. The guests had all departed from the loft, and she had demanded pasta. I'd tried to find Nevie after I screwed Isadora, but she wasn't by the crudités or anywhere else.

"Why are you filming this?" I asked.

"Just stir," she snapped, and zoomed in. "We can watch it later. I think it's sexy."

She had wiped the fake tears away and couldn't look more pleased with the state of her life.

"Today was fun," she said.

"A blast."

"Sarcasm. Wow, Noah, that's so original coming from you."

She loved her remark and became enamored with herself. She stepped back from the kitchen and was now filming the entire living room. She zoomed in on Dominick's painting of the yellow circle.

"There's blood on the painting. His blood."

I still couldn't fathom how Dominick had moved fifteen feet after crashing through the glass table. We both stared at the ominous handprint until the red light of the video camera started blinking.

"Fuck, the battery is low," Isadora wailed. "Just come and fuck me instead."

She stormed off. I stopped stirring the pasta and lumbered toward her gray bedroom. She had already hopped up on the bureau. I watched myself in the oval mirror behind her as I began thrusting. I was deep inside of her, but in the gray-tinted light that eked into her bedroom, I couldn't see my once blue and wondrous eyes. They looked like the eyes of the old and spent.

I slept next to her that night, shivering because of the open window. She snored as if she was annoyed with her dreams and kept at a leg's distance from me. In the morning, I quietly gathered my clothes and tiptoed out of the room, my throat sore and burning for medicine as I waddled into the day's first light.

Back at home, I lay in bed, not wanting to move. I shifted in and out of horrible dreams, my mind trying its best to recall pleasant times, but I wondered if I'd ever had any truly happy moments. I thought of summers long past at a home my parents rented in Sagaponack. I'd be napping in a giant beanbag chair as the sun trickled against the glass patio door before setting into the waves on our private beach, the plastic hot and sticky against my skin but comforting like nothing else. Dex would be crawling beside me, gurgling at every new image before his eyes. I would pick him up to tell him stories. Our parents would set down their drinks momentarily to smile at their eldest boy who spoke so profoundly. I would tell Dex about how big the world was and how we were just tiny dots to God in the sky. I'd tell him about right and wrong, about listening to teachers at school, about being good to Mommy and Daddy, and to always play, to always have fun, and to never stop being happy.

When it finally became dark, my parents would bid me goodnight with their gin breath and tuck me in with slobbery kisses, but the sheets were never tucked in tight enough. I'd call them back to tuck me in tighter, and would call them again and again, but they never bothered to return. So I'd try to do it myself, but once one side became tucked good enough, the other would unravel unless I stayed perfectly still, so that was what I did, arms pinned at my sides like I was dead, thinking about anything that wouldn't make me cry because I hated that this bed was not in my home, and even my real one on Central Park West felt like an alien's chambers.

So I'd cry and cry, just like I was doing right now, many years later.

The sound of my cell ringing woke up me up later that afternoon, my face flush with sweat and tears. The ringing stopped when I didn't answer, but then just started ringing again. I knew it was Isadora because Dominick used to behave in exactly the same way. Persistence ran in their family.

But this time I wouldn't answer.

I picked up the phone and hit ignore.

22

I PUT ON A BATHROBE AND MEANDERED INTO THE KITCHEN, searching for Consuela to make me a hearty breakfast. When I couldn't find her, I fixed myself a bowl of Frosted Flakes and had a cup of black coffee, the two mixing like a nightmare in my mouth. Nevertheless, I munched and crunched, the caffeine and sugar desperately working to disengage me from sleep.

After finishing, I went out on the terrace and stared at Central Park. The tiny trees. The scattered people smiling, frowning, discovering, killing. I was a killer now too. *No! That was someone else, the other Noah.* I'd show the world that nothing could break me. I smiled now at the tiny trees and the people the size of bugs. Fame and fortune were closer than they'd ever been, and I needed to love myself completely, just as much as I used to before my life changed.

So I gave myself a strangling hug and headed inside.

I went into the den where Cassie was texting on the sofa in her pajamas. Her hair was in pigtails and she looked like a little girl. She punched angrily at the keys on her cell. Whoever she was texting was responding just as fast as she could send out the texts until they were texting over each other, not even paying attention to what the other was typing. Finally, she threw the cell to the floor out of exhaustion.

"Is Dex home?" I asked.

"Conservatory. Idiot."

Her upper lip trembled, and I could see she was fighting back tears.

"You know he's dead," I said, after debating whether or not to ask if her boyfriend Steve had been the reason for her angry texts. The two of them always seemed to be fighting like adults with real problems.

"Yeah, I heard he's dead, overdose or something. He was an asshole and a perv anyway."

"Do you like yourself, Cassie?"

I was surprised at myself for asking her this, but I wanted to know, I had to know.

"What the fuck do you mean?"

"Day in and day out. You've become this awful sub-human. You're so angry, but you have everything. You can do anything you want."

"Uh, you're just as terrible a person as I am, Noah. You don't give a shit about anyone but yourself."

"I have morals."

"You have morals like I have a dick."

"Do you know that I'm directing *Slow Down* now?"

"Bullshit."

She chewed on a fingernail, nervous that I might be telling the truth.

"Dominick and his wife were financing the film on their own since no studio wanted to deal with him anymore, and she wants me to complete it."

"So what are you saying, I don't have a part in your movie anymore because I'm mean to you? I'm still your goddamn little sister, and…I can tell Mom and Dad about all the shit you've been pulling this last month: stealing my car, losing your job, hanging out with a druggie lowlife like Dominick. They will make sure you're out of this house—"

"Fuck this place, this isn't a home."

"Yeah, well, where's your home then?"

I thought about this for a minute and imagined myself as an itinerant, roaming around and never settling down, but then I pictured Nevie lying on her bed and spreading her arms wide as I nestled in her wings.

"Goodbye," I said, and turned to leave.

"Wait, so am I really not going to be in your film anymore?"

She had jumped up, her hands clasped together in prayer.

"You're not going to be in my *life* anymore. None of you."

I walked out without seeing her response, but I knew her usual sour face too well. She'd brush off what I said and forget about it until I didn't return home the next day, or the day after, or for weeks and months down the road, and then she'd remember. She had taken our relationship for granted, and now I'd be gone. She'd recall all those times as a kid when she'd grab onto my leg and pretend I was a giant. Sometimes this would make her laugh, but other times it would hurt too much to remember, so she would learn to forget about me. Eventually she'd learn to forget about our parents as well since they never returned from their travels and their postcards petered out more and more over the years. She'd go to college and really begin to abuse Fast until she'd drop out and then teeter for the rest of her life, never settling down with a job or a husband, never having a family besides those she partied with until they died off, or faded away, or grew up. Sometimes she would touch the tattoo of the yellow circle on her back, now warped from skin that had begun to sag, and she'd reminisce about a time in her life when the horizon was limitless because she had more money than she knew what to do with. Now she had none, and even though her rich and famous brother had so much to spare, she'd never contact me and allow herself to feel inferior. She'd go to her semi-early grave, stubborn as ever, but believing she was golden, as the Fast ate out her insides after decades of indulgence and caused her to implode one dark December day near mid-century.

I stood at the front door of the conservatory with a mangled plum in my mouth, the juice sticky down my chin. I watched Dex playing a symphony on the grand piano, and I wished I were intelligent enough to recognize the composer. Through all of Dex's lackluster traits, my brother really did possess a hunger to be rounded, and not just for appearances. He read Kafka when no one was looking and attended Fellini films without a mention of doing so. I did all of those things as well, but I had to make it known that I did. Otherwise, why do it?

I interrupted Dex's symphony since I was jealous of his talent. We had attended lessons together, but Dex possessed a grace on the piano that lingered long after I quit the 3rd Street Music School because I hated the Suzuki method that they insisted on instilling.

I chucked the plum into the garbage and picked up a glass of orange juice on the piano to take a sip.

"What is this?"

"Mimosa," Dex said, motioning for me to give it back.

"Are we square?" I said.

"You're pretty square," Dex smirked. "But yeah, I can't stay angry at you; I'm eternally chill."

"Uh, I meant that I'm okay with letting go of my anger toward you."

"You should try being eternally chill sometime."

"Eternally stoned is more like how you are," I said, picking back up the mimosa and gulping it down.

"Dude, now I have to go back into the kitchen to make another."

He swiped back the mimosa that had almost been drained.

"I wasn't apologizing before, Dex. I was just making sure we were cool."

"Noah, it's too early for your bullshit."

He got up to go past me, but I held him back.

"Bullshit? You're the one who's bullshit. What are you doing with your life today, tomorrow, the next day, huh? It's a weekday morning, who the hell fucking plays the piano and drinks mimosas?"

"What are you doing that's so amazing besides telling everyone else what they should be doing?"

"I'm directing *Slow Down* now," I said, getting in Dex's face. "That's what's up, bitch."

Dex sipped the last remnants of the mimosa, trying his best to ignore me.

"Did you hear me?"

He shrugged and kept sipping, smug as ever. I fumed because he should've been kissing my ring, begging for me to make him into a somebody.

"Dominick is dead," I yelled, grabbing him by the collar.

"Yeah, I know, fucker. I know."

We tussled with each other until I pushed him away.

"I'm the boss of this film, Dex, so show me some respect."

"That's rich," he said, taking one final drink of the mimosa.

"Wipe that smug grin off of your fucking face."

Dex grinned even wider, his teeth full of orange pulp.

I knocked the glass out of his hands, causing it to shatter against the wall. At the moment of impact, I had a flashback of Dominick crashing through the table and the sound of his death. Now I watched bits of orange pulp cascade down the wall as if it had been Dominick's blood.

"What the hell is wrong with you, Noah?"

"Shut up!"

My tears returned, the sensation akin to a breakdown. My thoughts became scattered. Dex eyed me like I was from a different species.

"Screw you, Dex. I came in here because I was ready to get an apology from you."

"You are on crack. Why should I apologize?"

"I went out of my way to give you advice about Dominick–"

"Get bent—"

"And I was gonna give you a part in *Slow Down*, make you famous, make your life finally worthy…"

"Are you loaded?"

"I'm more lucid than I've ever been. Now, am I getting that apology anytime soon?"

"Hell no."

"Dex, do not throw away this opportunity because of your pride. You're just being vengeful and pointless."

"I learned that from watching you."

I wanted to punch him, my fist begged for a connection.

"You really wouldn't put me in *Slow Down* because I won't cater to your oversized ego."

"You're the one with the ego."

"There's more of Mom and Dad in you than you realize. You exist in this self-absorbed bubble just like them—"

"So, I'm selfish?"

"Completely, dude. You make it your mission to treat me like shit to cover up your own insecurities. I know I'm not as smart as you, but I do more than just look at titty magazines and dress ironically. You labeled me a long time ago, but you don't really know me, and you do that with everyone, you highlight one aspect of a person until they become a caricature."

"Let it all out, fucker. Say whatever you've been whispering behind my back."

"People are just characters to you; they're not living and breathing. You use, abuse, and discard. And fine, maybe you'll achieve fame and fortune one day—"

"I will."

"So great, you will. Bravo. But you are rotten inside." He put his hand on my heart and pushed. "There is nothing there."

For a moment, I thought that Dex had figured out about the murder, but there was no way. He was simply retaliating, and I knew my brother's victory here would be meaningless. Once *Slow Down* got released to a slew of accolades, he would be lining up to be treated like dirt again. Then I would get that delicious apology I'd been waiting for.

Dex knocked into my shoulder as he pushed past me to leave the room, the last time we'd ever speak in person again. I didn't want to have it end this way, but I couldn't help it, this was who I was now. Ruthless, just like how I always boasted I could be.

I left the room, threw some of my shit in a suitcase, and ran out of the apartment with a fury boiling inside of me, storming all the way to the East Side to see Nevie. She was the only human contact right now that I could stand.

If I knocked on her door and she refused to answer, I knew I'd just disintegrate while she watched through the peephole. I hoped she'd find it in her heart to open up the door and let me inside because I was afraid of what I might do to myself if she turned away and allowed herself to forget about me entirely.

When I got to Nevie's place, she didn't answer again when the doorman buzzed, but the guy let me up anyway saying he believed that she was home. I knocked on her door to no avail, envisioning my imminent dis- integration, but then I tried the doorknob and sure enough the door opened wide.

She was sitting on the floor Indian style on her chic rug that looked like cowhide. She fed cigarettes into an ashtray, evidence of how she'd spent the night. I wheeled in the suitcase with everything I felt like I truly needed from my parents' place, not a clue what I was planning on doing.

"I've been painting," she said to an easel in the corner of the room. The colors were splattered with disarray, not very well done, but at least she wasn't in a Fast coma.

"I'm glad you're doing something, Nevie."

"Dominick always said painting was a good release, but I'm not in mourning anymore. I feel an intermittent sadness, but that's all."

"Do you want a hug?" I sighed with my entire body.

"No."

"Can you give me one?"

She rose on unbalanced legs and placed her arms around me, quietly and carefully, one had cupping the back of my head and the other resting on my hip. She always gave great hugs, and I didn't want to let go.

"How are you doing?" she asked, letting go too suddenly. When she realized how it upset me, she allowed my fingers to remain grazing her hipbone so the two of us would still be connected.

"I've been better."

She smiled warmly, so fulfilling and all encompassing. Everything became that smile, and I let myself truly look at her. I pictured her at different stages in her life: as an innocent child with freckles on her nose, as a mother wringing her hands on a cinched apron and slipping loose strands of gray hair around her ears. I longed to see her as she was and be there to watch her become my future, as she'd tuck those gray strands of hair around her ears after a long day with our kids. I'd open the door and she'd smile foolishly after a long day apart. This amazing Nevie I wished for was tucked deep inside the whittled down girl who stood before me and begged to be sculpted into someone great, someone decent, someone I could call home.

"Do you want some tea?" she asked, nibbling at a hangnail. "I made a lot of black currant iced tea."

"Sure."

She made her way to the kitchen, leading with her head down and her shoulders slumped. She poured two glasses and we stood beside each other, the fluorescent light bathing us in its sickly glow. She turned the lights off.

"It's too dark in here," I said.

"I don't care."

I let the iced tea swim in my mouth, cold and dull tasting. *Don't try to kiss her. Keep that iced tea in your mouth and your mind elsewhere.*

"Are you excited about directing *Slow Down*?" she asked.

"I'm scared. I have no ideas."

I couldn't believe I had admitted that out loud, but it felt good to be honest about something for once.

She scrunched up her nose and tried to touch her tongue to the tip. She was leaning against the counter. My whole world could be in that kitchen. I leaned closer to her.

"Stuff will come to you, Noah. I'm sure you'll do great."

"I know. I plan on making you a star."

I was almost pressing against her. Our shirts flapped together from a stray breeze coming in from the living room. She backed up and sat on the counter, swinging her feet, allowing herself to be touched by my promises.

"A big star," she said.

I drummed my palms against her knees, not sexually but playfully, calming down her swinging legs.

"My frog," she hummed, planting a kiss on my lips like a precocious child would. The kiss felt distant, as if I didn't need to be present for it, as if a wall would've sufficed for her. "You just need to find a muse."

And into her eyes, I said: "I already have."

"Yeah, Isadora," she responded, moving my hands off of her. They rested by my sides, still buzzing from her touch.

"No."

"It's fine, Noah."

"But it's not how you think…"

"It is, and it's fine."

"I just need to be with her right now because of *Slow Down*, that's all. She's business to me."

I went to touch her knees again, wanting to tell her that I loved her and then rewinding time if she dismissed my adoration so I could convince her better the next time. Nevie always had so much power. Even now, she could still cause my heart to shatter with a flip of her panther-black hair. She ran her pale fingers through her smooth bangs now, assured once again of the power she yielded. This girl was not meant to overdose on Fast; she was not weak. She was meant to turn heads, to be whispered about in awe, not as misfortunate gossip.

Put your hands on her knees again and tell her how you truly feel. She will accept you; she has to. She needs you as much as you need her, and you'll balance each other out forever.

"I'd never want someone to think of me as just business," she said, angry that the word was even used, slinking away from me down the counter.

"I'd never say that about you."

"That's how Dom thought of me."

"No, he didn't."

"Yes. He did," she said, seemingly all right with this analysis. "Well, he was business to me, too."

Dex had called me out before by saying I was a user and abuser, but Nevie was no different. That was why I loved her. We both shared an unwavering drive for personal acceleration. I placed my nervous hands on her knees again, and she didn't refuse this time, so I went even further by tucking my head into her wings like I had imagined.

"Someday I'll tell you to meet me on my lily pad," I whispered into her chest. "I'll just say 'lily pad,' and you'll come, no matter what's going on in your life or mine. And we'll go so far away from here, once we're ready, once we've bled New York dry. Because in the end we're meant to be together and we won't survive any other way."

The knobby bones in her knees speared my palms as I rubbed them soothingly. I thought of our one night together in Chinatown and how I couldn't wait to wake up to a never-ending tomorrow in her arms.

We were not evil. We were opportunists in our own ways. We were where we needed to be, in that kitchen, with each other. She had put in her time with Dominick and now I would do the same with Isadora to solidify a great life for the both of us, to have fame and money follow along for the rest of our lives.

I did not need to say that I loved her again because it was moot; we both loved the wild future and the fact we'd reach it together, eventually. I kissed her in the middle of her chest.

"One of us just needs to say 'lily pad' and we'll know, we'll know that it's time," I whispered to her, as my head rose up and down from her weighted breaths.

"Yes, my frog."

I closed my watering eyes, finally at peace.

I could still smell a hint of Nevie's perfume when I entered Isadora's loft with the key she had given me. Nevie and I would be together in time, but business had to be taken care of first. I would never tell her what I did to Dominick. Even if she was able to forgive me, I couldn't marry her, have children, and wonder if she might change her mind once she realized that she could never be with someone as soulless as me.

I stared at the paintings on the wall that exuded a kind of sadness I never noticed before. They held the knowledge of what had happened in this room. They had an allegiance to their creator and were not about to concede to the one who had taken him away.

"I can't look at it anymore," I said to the painting of the yellow circle with the bloody handprint. I took it off the wall, ready to trash it to pieces, but a tiny door had been hidden in the wall behind the frame. Curiosity burned and I opened the tiny door to find a bound screenplay for *Slow Down* written by Dominick Bambach along with reels of film.

"What the fuck?" I said, everything falling from my hands. Part of me wanted to hide what I just found and pretend it never existed, but then I wondered if I might be throwing away any good ideas. Since I had no new ones, I picked up the screenplay and turned to the first page.

For the next two hours, I sat down on the red leather couch, absorbed with Dominick's creation. The entire film was all there, beautifully written. The plot focused on Estella and Nevie, along with Lindsay and a recast actress as well, who had all fallen in with a cult leader named Tom (who was obviously Dominick), a man who had etched a drug called "Quick" into the yellow circle tattoos on their backs so he could manipulate them like marionettes. What he wanted were as many girls as possible to fall under his spell until an entire city was at his whim, a way of making him feel important again after so many years of numbness. Years ago, he had lost the love of his life, a woman named Ashley (obviously Astrid) who pioneered the idea of injecting Quick inside the first yellow circle tattoo he had ever seen. But Quick made Ashley wild and crazy and caused her to break up with Tom and begin an affair with his father, which became too much for him to handle. So one day he broke into her apartment and killed her. A moment of restless, brutal passion. He had always regretted this hasty act, and now he was only able to feel at peace by re-creating her in the guise of other women. For Estella, Quick spoiled her relationship with Palmer and kept her severely thin. For Lindsay, she got hooked easily and started flunking out of school and influencing her friends to do dangerous things. After she died in a car crash due to Quick, another girl in her clique took up her reins and the whole downward cycle started up again. The main character, Nevie, just wanted to party on Quick every night till dawn and ultimately died from being unable to slow down. Dominick also created the character of Nevie's boyfriend named Nolan (obviously based on me) who tried to help her get over her addiction to Quick, but his love was not enough to fix her in time. Blazing with anger, Nolan confronted Tom and killed him to save all the yellow circle girls stuck under his thumb and then became the true hero of *Slow Down*.

Just like I had used Dominick to worm my way into the film, he had used me all along to create a character. If the pages in my lap and the truth they conveyed hadn't completely stunned me, I would've been absolutely impressed.

After reading the last page, I let the screenplay spill from my hands to the floor. I had killed Dominick because I thought he was a fraud, which couldn't be further from the truth. This man had always been brilliant, his greatest act of genius being his art of manipulation.

As I processed all this new information, the lock to the front door clicked open and Isadora shuffled inside with a bag of groceries held to her chest. Even though I didn't know how to feel about what I'd just discovered, it was clear that she was a liar. She glanced at the screenplay on the floor and then at me.

"Noah," she said, and sunk to the floor. She took off her high heels and crawled over to me until she was sitting between the yellow circle painting and Dominick's screenplay. She placed her hands on my knees just like I had done to Nevie. The shock I felt before now turned to rage.

"You used me to get rid of him," I said, wanting to snap her neck.

"No, we wanted the same thing. This doesn't have to change anything."

She made sure to look deep into my eyes as if she were trying to hypnotize me.

"I never wanted him dead," I said.

"Of course you did."

"You were gonna make me think these were your ideas?"

I picked up the screenplay and shoved it at her. Immediately she took offense and let go of my knees.

"Those are not all of Dominick's ideas; he and I collaborated together."

The screenplay unraveled from its binding as it fell to the floor again. She began to pick up the scattered pages.

"Did he even ever beat you?"

She kept picking up more pages and pretending not to hear.

"You're psychotic, Isadora."

"Noah, don't act foolish. Not after all we've been through."

"I killed an innocent man."

She laughed at that. "Fine, so he was talented, he had ideas. But innocent? That man killed his former girlfriend, and I've had to live with that secret."

"No, you blackmailed him with it. Dom was so right about you."

She went over to the bag of groceries and refilled any contents that had spilled out. She palmed a can of Starkist tuna with her back to me.

"Blackmail is a harsh word, Noah," she said.

"I brought my suitcase to stay here, but I haven't unpacked it yet, and I never will. Not after this."

She stood and slinked toward me, clearly in command of the situation. She had probably known it would come to this one day.

"You don't have the kind of money to make *Slow Down* without me. So why don't you just drop this whole morally superior act and put away these groceries?"

She held out the can of tuna.

"I never loved you," I said. "That's all I'm guilty of."

"That and murder."

"You're guilty of all of that, too."

"Of course, I didn't love you either. We were never going to run off into the sunset like we were in some goddamn movie. You're just a fucking child."

"Don't call me a child."

"Fine, I'll call you a moron since I'm not the guilty one. I filmed you the night Dominick died, and I've filmed you confessing many times since. So I guess I am a talented moviemaker, you fuck. Just watch those videos make the rounds from police station to police station across the city. You'll be the most infamous star on the planet."

"All you know how to do is blackmail."

"That's right. And I had to get rid of Dominick since he was ready to leave me because he didn't care anymore if I exposed him about Astrid. I lost all my power, but I have a feeling that you'll comply. You'll make *Slow Down* a success and keep me in the kind of lifestyle I've gotten used to."

"You're insane."

"And you've just hit the jackpot, Noah. *Slow Down* is all written for you, most of it has even been filmed, and your biggest competition is six feet under, so it's about time you get over this *boo hoo me* act."

"But it's not my film," I said, swallowing hard, the pit of my stomach feeling like a thousand worms were crawling around from organ to organ.

"Not so fast," she said, winking. "*Slow Down* is yours since no one else knows the truth and never will. Sometimes we only get one golden opportunity in life and this is yours. If you don't take it, get ready for twenty years in the state pen while I'll just find someone else who's young and dumb enough to come and take your place."

"But—"

"But nothing. Stop being a fucking baby and meet me on the bureau."

She threw the can of Starkist at me, connecting with my forehead and then turned around and headed to the bedroom with a long blown kiss my way that hurt even more.

I watched her disappear into the shadows of the hallway like I had seen her do many times before. I would be stuck here for the rest of my indentured life.

My body split in two as a shred of me turned toward the front door to dash back down to Sutton Place and sweep Nevie far, far away despite whatever troubles would follow us; but my other half overpowered the capricious side, and I headed toward Isadora's bedroom instead.

Epilogue

"IS THAT THE END OF YOUR NOVEL?" KRISTY FROM APEX Studios asked, because Noah hadn't spoken in over a minute.

He was staring at his cell phone with his sunglasses still on, refusing to answer her. The silence stretched out. He could tell it made her fidgety. She was looking around at everything in the apartment that proved whether what he had told her was true. The wedding photo of him and Isadora on the side table where he looked miserable and Isadora looked triumphant. The red couch that she was sitting on which had once belonged to Dominick Bambach. And worst of all, the painting of a yellow circle on a blank white canvas with a bloody handprint at the bottom. *Dominick's bloody handprint!*

"So what do you think?" he asked, crushing a pack of cigarettes in his palm that he wound up devouring.

She still gave him that full wattage smile.

"I think some people will want to celebrate you and others will be repulsed. But copies of the book will fly off the shelves and droves will flock to the theaters. We'll make a killing."

She tapped her fingers against the glass coffee table that sat between them.

"But...?"

On the table was an old newspaper clipping from the *New York Times* with the headline, *Fast on the Decline Due to Director's Demise: The End of an Epidemic*. He saw her eyes flicker across it as he felt beads of saliva pooling at the back of his tongue.

"I just found the ending rather abrupt."

"Isn't life sometimes that way?"

"It left me a little unfulfilled after the ride you took me on, if I'm being honest. It'll need more of a happy ending."

"What if there is no happy ending?" he said, and glanced at his cell phone again.

"Okay, but you have to know that Barry will want a more upbeat ending, especially once it's adapted into a film. Since Noah's the hero, albeit the flawed hero of the story, the audience will want him to be with Nevie at the end rather than Isadora."

He caught her glancing at his wedding photo again.

"Where's your wife now?" she asked, angling her chin at the photo.

"You're thinking too much about my real life."

"Isn't that the point?"

He didn't like the way she kept smiling, like she had pulled a fast one on him. *What's the point of all of this? What's the point of anything if Nevie never calls?*

And with that thought, his cell rang, just as if Nevie had timed it. He answered it before he could see who was calling.

"Hello," he said, desperately.

"Noah, my boy! Barry Bronfeld here." The man sounded like he was in a jet stream due to the noise in the background. "I believe the sun has already set in New York so I trust that you and Kristy accomplished what you needed to today?"

Noah let out a half-hearted, "Yeah, just finished."

"Tell me we've got a fucking masterpiece here, kid."

Noah took a deep breath. "We've got a fucking masterpiece here, kid."

"Noah, you are one hys-ter-ic-al bastard. Hope I've invested wisely, superstar. Oh Christfuck, I got Russell Crowe nagging me on the other line. *Ciao.*"

Noah started to get up slowly as if the air had turned to soup, but then his cell started ringing again.

"Yes?" he said, answering it by the first ring.

"I'm flying down Broadway in a taxi," the voice screeched. "L.A. was horrendous, I was hounded the whole time about when your next project is going to happen."

Isadora. He squeezed the cell in his hand, as if it was her neck. He'd dreamed of doing that many times. Sometimes he even woke up thinking that he had done it.

"Noah, you better have been behaving all weekend. You were so shifty right before I left, like you were plotting something against me. Sometimes I think you despise me."

"I do."

"You should be bowing down and kissing my feet every day for what I've done for you. I've kept you out of j-a-i-l. I'm trying to get your career going again, but you won't show me this *project* you've been working on. I don't like secrets."

"You are venom and one day I'll just vanish."

"What was that? The reception is breaking up. Now run me a bath for when I get home, tepid like I like it, a spritz of lavender perfume, and a bowl of cherries on the side. Repeat that back to me."

"Go fuck yourself."

"I love you too, darling. And tonight you better get me to come. You're going to eat me out from A-to-Z, and no stopping midway and complaining that your tongue is tired."

"I'll make sure to chew on some glass before."

"Ouch, baby's getting kinky. Now repeat what I asked you."

Another call started to come through. Isadora was still yammering away, but he clicked over to the other caller instead.

"Hello?"

"Hi," a voice replied, barely above a peep...Nevie.

Noah whipped off his sunglasses.

"Hey!"

A rush of adrenaline coursed through his body, unlike any drug he'd ever done before. But he warned himself not to be too hopeful. She could be calling to tell him goodbye forever.

"Is this a bad time, Noah?"

"No, not at all."

"I got your note. I mean...I don't understand what it means."

"I've always wanted to tell you," he said, digging his fingernails into the worry lines on his forehead. "You deserve to know what really happened. I am so sorry."

"The note said that you're responsible for Dominick dying? How is that possible?"

"It's more complicated than that. Let me explain it to you."

"Is *she* there?"

"I haven't seen you in so long," he said, his voice getting shaky. "I miss you."

"I don't want to talk anymore if she's there."

"Isadora means nothing to me, don't you understand? She's been blackmailing me, but it's all gonna be out there anyway. It doesn't matter anymore."

He looked over at the digital recorder on the coffee table.

"You're not making any sense, Noah."

"She's had me in chains, fucking chains for too long. I refuse to let it go on anymore. That's why I agreed to do what I'm doing right now, to tell the real story and fuck all the consequences."

"But giving me that note today? I mean all of that happened years ago. Those were bad years, really bad years for me."

"Sometimes I imagine just running away with you. Leaving behind all the fame because it's empty, meaningless—"

"Noah, you're the only thing left in my life from then. And you're married."

"But I'm ready to end it with her."

"Sometimes, I think of how I need to get out of this city before it eats me alive," she said, after a pause. "The other day my agent said I was getting a little bottom heavy. I weigh ninety-nine pounds. I eat cigarettes for breakfast."

"But you're not using Fast anymore, right?"

"I want to. But then I wonder about having a family, how that could ground me for good, save my life."

"That's want I want, too."

"But that's all just a fantasy. You know I'll be dead by the time I'm forty. It's in my blood. If it's not Fast it'll be something else. Look, I gotta go."

"No, no wait!"

"I love you, Noah, I do, but hearing from you like this today. I've been strong and I've done it without Fast for a long time, over a year. I mean, I think about it constantly, how it tastes, how it felt rushing through my body."

"That's why you need me to take care of you."

She didn't answer, the static hiss of the phone like a knife in his chest.

"Nevie, remember when I told you that if I said a certain word, it'll mean it's time for us to take off. No matter what else is happening in our lives."

"We were so young then. So stupid."

"Who's to say we still can't be? I can't sleep, I can't breathe, everything is just a blur speeding by. But it doesn't have to be like that for us. There's a whole world out there, there are places we could get lost in and never return from, there are places I can show you that we are all each other needs."

"Noah," she hushed. He could tell she was crying.

"But I need to come clean to you about everything I've done. I need for you to know who I really am."

His eyes darted over to the painting of the yellow circle with the bloody handprint and then he saw Kristy from Apex Studios. He had forgotten that someone else was in the room all along. Kristy had her eye on the digital recorder, ready to exploit the tragedy of their lives into big bucks. But his story didn't have to end that way. He could walk away from stardom by pocketing the recorder and going after Nevie. He could let Isadora reveal his dark secrets and hope that they'd be far enough out of reach from the law. He could take out all the money from his bank accounts, cut up his credit cards, and make a break to a place like Mexico with her by his side. Live in some one-stoplight *puebla* with chickens skirting across the roads while the two them became tan enough to be unrecognizable to anyone they once knew. Had had once heard of a town called Zapotlanejo. Loosely translated, it meant "the place of abundant frogs" from the Nahuatl word *tzapotlán*, as if it were named solely for Nevie and him. He could grow a beard, they could dye their hair and live modestly but abashedly, live for each other. Pop out some kids and raise them with morals, teach them a trade where they used their hands, where they worked hard on a farm and contributed to the development of their little town, their little heaven. Grow old together and watch the sun set every day while listening to the susurrus of frogs croaking symphonies from the lily pads in their backyard pond. No more photographers, no more cult of fans, no more press junkets and phony interviews, no more drive for him to chase fame and create make-believe, just the desire to be good to her.

And he could finish this novel, maybe even begin it with Kristy placing her purse down on that red couch. And it would only be written for Nevie. He knew she'd be shocked at first, but then he hoped she would let him rest his head against her shoulder so he could cry until he'd been exorcized. Let the universe still think he was a murderer, or let them think he was a vanished genius. She was the only opinion that mattered to him anymore.

"I'm coming over to you now," he said into the phone. No sound emitted from Nevie's end, just silence. He fought with that silence, begged for it to break, waited for a beautiful response. "I'll take a cab to you and we'll go, we'll just fucking go. Disappear from everything. You won't be dead by forty. I'll take you away from this cesspool of a city and make you happier than you've ever been."

"Noah, please don't," she said, after what felt like forever. "Just...let me go."

"Nevie, listen, listen to me."

"What...?"

"Lily pad," he said, his mouth tight and determined. He pressed the phone against his ear, pleading for a reply. When she didn't make a sound, he felt a shift in his insides, his organs jumbling around in a free-for-all. They say your life flashes before your eyes when you're about to die, but he was experiencing that now. It was all Nevie: the punk wannabe from ninth grade with a streak of green in her hair, the deliriously high girl on a Hamptons beach before they graduated college, the curve of her body beneath his own on that mattress in Chinatown, and finally, when he brought his suitcase to her house out of desperation but then told her to wait for him, that their time would come.

Eons passed before she finally took a breath that sounded like, "My frog".

"Is that a yes?"

"But disappear...just like that? Noah, that's crazy—"

"Yes. Cause I'll be dead before I'm forty too. Cause you'll be saving me as well. The media will do what they want with it. They'll blame the fact that we're gone on drugs, moan about talent that's being wasted, the same tired celebrity story. Who the fuck cares?"

Another endless lull, the sound of her breathing a painful crackle in his ear.

"Let me come to you, Nevie. You can make a decision then, face-to-face. Just let me come to you."

"I don't know..."

"I'm getting a cab right now. Just allow me to do that. This is what I need, okay? What we need. So don't say no. Not without me being able to see you again. I'm hanging up."

"Noah—"

He ended the call before she could answer.

As he stood up, dazed but exhilarated, he saw Kristy reaching for the digital recorder. She almost grabbed it, but he was quicker.

"No," Kristy hissed, her perma-smile long gone. She was clenching her fists so hard that her knuckles had turned white. "This is Apex's property now. Barry will...he'll fire me if I don't deliver this. He'll leave me too, I know it. This is my life."

"This is *my* life," he yelled back.

"Our lawyers will bleed you."

"You wanted Nevie and I to be together. That's what can happen, don't you see?"

"I wanted you to be together at the end of the book and the film, I don't care about your real life."

"It's not right to make money off of what happened. It's sick."

"Mr. Bronfeld is not someone to be fucked with. He'll demolish you."

"He'll never find me."

Kristy lunged for the recorder, her foot catching a lump in the carpet as she lost her balance. When she hit the glass table, he had a flash of déjà vu. But she didn't crash through like Dominick had; she bounced off and landed on the floor.

"Please," she said, clasping her hands together, her face all puffy from the onslaught of tears. "I've worked so hard to get where I'm at. I've been going, going, going so fast since I got to L.A. over a decade ago. Just to make it. Just to be *someone* there. And what will I have left to show? I'll have nothing. I'll be back in my hometown before I know it with no chance of ever getting out again."

"Maybe that'll be the best thing that ever happened to you."

He ran out to the hallway before he could see her response and took the elevator down to the street below. When he emerged from his building, a swarm of paparazzi waited to pounce with their flashbulbs. From his apartment window, he saw Kristy poke her head out, wailing at the night sky. He inched toward the curb and put two fingers in the air as a cab stopped at his feet.

When he opened the door, the horde of paparazzi snapped their pictures. He covered his face as he stepped inside and the cab sped away through a yellow stoplight about to turn red.

In the zooming taxi, he imagined a future where those were the last shots the paparazzi would ever take of him. In this fantasy, no one would ever know for certain if he ever made it to Mexico with Nevie by his side. If she forgave him for what he did to Dominick. But the public never saw her again either. She never made another movie, or even got her picture taken again at some hot new club. Manhunts were sent out to find them but to no avail. The police would soon lose interest as new stories trumped the two missing starlets. Apex Studios would move on. Barry Bronfeld would boast about a new investment. Kristy would get a pink slip. Isadora would find a new sap to leech off of. Their parents would spend the first year employing private detectives to track them down and then give up as well. In this fast-paced, wildly connected world it's difficult to vanish without a trace anymore, but Noah and Nevie would succeed in doing the impossible. They'd become legends for a while, ghosts that people thought they saw on the street, until they were eventually pronounced dead and forgotten, just like they wanted to be.

Afterword

It's exciting that *Slow Down* is being reissued by its new publisher All Due Respect for its five-year anniversary. Seems like a lifetime ago, and I'm thankful that a new audience will get a chance to read my debut novel. The book is about horrible people doing horrible things to another, but there's an underlying pulse of sweetness that exists at its core. It's a takedown of a society that is moving at way too fast a pace, but also a love story between Noah and Nevie. They are cruel to each other throughout, but truly love another and know that the only way they can survive is to leave everything and run away together. The question is whether they make it. I like to leave that up to interpretation. I go back and forth myself deciding about their end. Both of them certainly want to escape their lives, but whether they have the guts to do so is for the reader to decide.

The first draft of this book was written when I was twenty-two in 2001. I'd just graduated college and worked an awful job similar to Noah where we were honestly abused. I had a chair thrown at me at an office Christmas party at P. Diddy's restaurant by a drunk superior. I was fired pretty much in the same way as Noah and used that as fuel. Job prospects were grim due to a dot.com burst and 9/11 on the horizon, but I was lucky enough to still be living at home and would write in Gramercy Park every day. I remember how happy it made me to be able to create and feel like I had a chance at getting published. I was listening to Coldplay's "Yellow" and I thought of the line, "We were all yellow." I imagined a Manhattan where people had the same tattoo of a yellow circle on the small of their backs and the book developed from there.

While I tried the publishing route, it just didn't happen. So I stuck the book in a desk for ten years and then pulled it out after getting an agent. We tried the big houses but they found the book "too mean." Noah was unsympathetic, and editors didn't see a wide audience. We sent it to Jon Bassoff, an amazing writer who ran New Pulp Press at the time, and he bought the book for precisely that reason. He loved that it was about horrible people doing horrible things to one another. And this kicked off my career.

Looking back, I'll always be proud that *Slow Down* was my debut. And even though a lot of the characters are tough to like, they are human. There are times when Noah is vulnerable, and even sympathetic, you just have to look closely.

In terms of the mantra Slow Down, it couldn't be more applicable today. Writing this, the world is in the midst of a pandemic, and my hometown New York City has been hit harder than most places. We have been moving for years at such a fast pace, not allowing ourselves to take a breath between twenty-four seven news cycles, and social media, etc. I hope we come out of this slowing down just a little, realizing what is important, not letting life just zoom by. So, be like Noah, I guess. Well, be like part of Noah. The Noah that finally wakes up. And thanks for reading!

—Lee Matthew Goldberg, April 21, 2020

LEE MATTHEW GOLDBERG is the author of the novels *The Desire Card*, *The Mentor*, and *Slow Down*. He has been published in multiple languages and nominated for the 2018 Prix du Polar. The second book in the Desire Card series, *Prey No More*, is forthcoming, along with his other novels, *Eating the Sun* and *Orange City*. He is the editor-in-chief and co-founder of Fringe, dedicated to publishing fiction that's outside-of-the-box. His pilots and screenplays have been finalists in Script Pipeline, Book Pipeline, Stage 32, We Screenplay, the New York Screenplay, Screencraft, and the Hollywood Screenplay contests. After graduating with an MFA from the New School, his writing has also appeared in the anthology *Dirty Boulevard*, *The Millions*, *Cagibi*, *The Montreal Review*, *The Adirondack Review*, *The New Plains Review*, *Underwood Press* and others. He is the co-curator of The Guerrilla Lit Reading Series and lives in New York City. Follow him at LeeMatthewGoldberg.com.

On the following pages are a few
more great titles from the
Down & Out Books publishing family.

For a complete list of books and to
sign up for our newsletter,
go to DownAndOutBooks.com.

Some Awful Cunning
Joe Ricker

Down & Out Books
April 2020
978-1-64396-086-9

Ryan Carpenter is an underground relocation specialist who helps people escape the danger and traumas of their life and start over. After agreeing to help the young wife of a Texas oil baron relocate her stepson to escape criminal prosecution, Ryan learns more than he wants to about the oil baron, his wife, and the stepson.

Haunted by his own forced relocation, Ryan betrays his client and is forced to scramble for his life, which only puts him face to face with the childhood past he's been trying to escape his entire life.

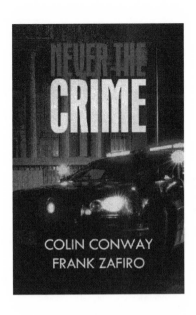

Never the Crime
The Charlie-316 Series
Colin Conway and Frank Zafiro

Down & Out Books
June 2020
978-1-64396-108-8

The greatest danger that Officer Tyler Garrett faces might not be Detective Wardell Clint, who is doggedly trying to prove he's dirty. Instead, the swirling maelstrom of city and department politics threatens to destroy his plans to rebuild after a controversial shooting almost two years ago.

From the mayor to the chief to the officer on the street, everyone seems to have an agenda.

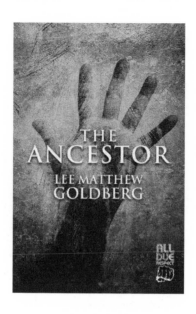

The Ancestor
Lee Matthew Goldberg

All Due Respect, an imprint of
Down & Out Books
August 2020
978-1-64396-114-9

A man wakes up in the Alaskan wilderness with no memory of who he is, except for the belief that he's was a prospector from the Gold Rush and has been frozen in ice for over a hundred years.

A meditation on love lost and unfulfilled dreams, *The Ancestor* is a thrilling page-turner in present day Alaska and a historical adventure about the perilous Gold Rush expeditions where prospectors left behind their lives for the promise of hope and a better future.

Shotgun Honey Presents Volume 4: RECOIL
Ron Earl Phillips, editor

Shotgun Honey, an imprint of
Down & Out Books
May 2020
978-1-64396-138-5

With new and established authors from around the world, Shotgun Honey Presents Volume 4: RECOIL delivers stories that explore a darker side of remorse, revenge, circumstance, and humanity.

Contributors: Rusty Barnes, Susan Benson, Sarah M. Chen, Kristy Claxton, Jen Conley, Brandon Daily, Barbara DeMarco-Barrett, Hector Duarte Jr., Danny Gardner, Tia Ja'nae, Carmen Jaramillo, Nick Kolakowski, JJ Landry, Bethany Maines, Tess Makovesky, Alexander Nachaj, David Nemeth, Cindy O'Quinn, Brandon Sears, Johnny Shaw, Kieran Shea, Gigi Vernon, Patrick Whitehurst.

Made in the USA
Middletown, DE
21 June 2020